EX LIBRIS

_____

# The Museum of
# Mary Child

**Cassandra Golds**

**Kane Miller**
A DIVISION OF EDC PUBLISHING

First American Edition 2009
by Kane Miller, A Division of EDC Publishing
Tulsa, Oklahoma

First published by Penguin Group (Australia) 2009
Text copyright © Cassandra Golds, 2009

Jacket design: Kat Godard, DraDog, LLC.

For information contact:
Kane Miller, A Division of EDC Publishing
P.O. Box 470663
Tulsa, OK 74147-0663
**www.kanemiller.com**
**www.edcpub.com**

Library of Congress Control Number: 2009922719
Printed and bound in the United States of America
1 2 3 4 5 6 7 8 9 10
ISBN: 978-1-935279-13-6

FOR LULU

# Prologue

A shaft of moonlight. A barred window. A bed of straw, and a young man, little more than a boy, chained to a wall. The chains prevent him from lying down and so he sleeps, exhausted, slumped against it.

The cell is damp and, somewhere, a steady echoing *drip … drip … drip …* of water falls from the distant ceiling into a puddle on the stone floor. The young man's hair is very dark and his face pale – unshaven, smeared with dirt, and weary. But this cannot hide the gentleness and innocence of his expression, which is child-like, despite the long limbs that, if he were standing, would make him very tall. Indeed, even if there was no moonlight, his face would almost glow with its own light.

The young man sleeps.

Meanwhile, the night sky above the prison stirs with a strange breeze, or a hundred tiny breezes.

The small barred window is ten feet above the boy's head. Even if his eyes were open he would see little through it. Nevertheless, the courtyard is filling with birds. One here, two there, three over there, in quick succession, they drop out of the sky and land on the icy cobbles. Chirruping busily, hopping, fluttering, they cross the courtyard and gather at the window, peering down through the bars.

They are not wild birds. In fact, they are the kind that usually live their lives in cages – canaries, finches, budgerigars and the like, with the odd parrot or cockatoo amongst them. They have flown across the great Park, past the palace and the Houses of Parliament and the great Cathedral, over the grand mansions of the rich, and the tumbledown houses of the poor, over theatres and churches and market squares, over the consulting rooms of physicians and the evil smelling larders of apothecaries, over dark, stuffy workshops where seamstresses and cobblers and milliners and wigmakers ply their trade, over public houses and newspaper offices, to get to this window.

At a signal from their leader, an aged white canary, they flutter into the cell, following the shaft of moonlight like tiny angels descending on a ladder of light. Once inside, they perch on and around the young man, while above them, the larger birds keep watch.

And there, in the moonlight, the little birds begin to sing.
The song fills the cell like the voices of a choir in a cathedral.
The echoes bouncing from the stone walls make a chorale of,
not hundreds, but thousands of song birds, as if all the birds
of the earth are singing to comfort and to heal.

As they sing the young man's eyelids flicker and open.
He blinks; he pushes himself up with the heels of his hands,
winces automatically with pain, and yet seems not to notice.
His eyes travel from the birds on his knees, to the birds in
the straw, to the birds struggling to get a purchase amongst
the stones of the wall, and fluttering as they change position.
There must be hundreds.

There is barely an unoccupied space. A pair of canaries is
perched on his head; he can feel their wiry feet in his hair.

For a moment his face fills with yearning. Tentatively, he
holds out his hand as far as the chains allow. Sure enough,
a finch and a white canary fly over to perch on it. Then the
yearning passes into sadness, and he looks at them with a
complicated expression on his face – half tender, half ironic.

"You think you are dreaming," says the white canary,
looking at him with her bright black eyes.

The young man is not surprised. He smiles faintly. If
the canary had not spoken he might have allowed himself to
hope. Now he knows he is asleep. His eyes are rueful, as if he
thinks the joke is on him.

"So I am not to be freed by magical birds," he murmurs.

The canary looks at him steadily.

"No," she says. "We are birds, but we have no magic. And yet we can help you. Tell me your grief, my son."

The young man's eyes are very dark, so dark that in the dim light they seem cavernous. He is looking not at the bird but inside himself.

"My grief …" he says, and the old canary knows he does not really believe that he is talking to anyone. He pauses, then closes his eyes and lowers his head, as if he has experienced a sudden, sickening pain. "I could say that my grief is that I have failed utterly. I could say that I grieve because I have lost everything. I have helped no one, and I myself am doomed. But," he says, "in the end, there is only one grief – and that is that I have failed *her*."

"Do you believe that there is truth in dreams?" asks the canary.

The young man is startled. "I have never been asked that in a dream before," he says, after a moment.

"Remember us tomorrow," says the canary, with great seriousness, "and remember what I tell you now. Do not despair. Tell stories. Will you remember?"

"Tell stories," whispers the young man. "But what stories? Why? And to whom?"

"Be consoled, O thou without wings. Know that you are prayed for, with every note of song, by The Society of the Caged Birds of the City. All will yet be well."

With that he feels her push against his finger as she flies off. The other birds follow her immediately. But before each of them departs, they fly towards him in a soft, swinging arc and brush the tips of their wings against his ear or cheek. They are still singing as they leave, one by one, through the bars.

As the young man – who still believes he is dreaming – gazes towards the window, his face is again filled with yearning, and the tears glisten in his eyes. But the cell is silent except for the steady *drip … drip … drip …* of water falling from the ceiling to the floor.

In that city, there is another place of imprisonment: the Madhouse.

The Madhouse is a simple building, as simple and faceless as a child's first drawing of a house, except that such a drawing would not have so many windows. From the outside, whether by day or night, it seems empty. But it is not empty. It is crowded. Not with mad people, but with secrets.

Within its walls are secrets that no one dares tell, and that no one would believe. They are packed inside it as stuffing is packed into a rag doll. And sometimes, when a rag doll is ripped open, a little jumble spills out.

The Caged Birds of the City swoop out of the prison courtyard, along the deserted street, and down onto the footpath outside the main entrance: for in that City, the Prison and the Madhouse stand side by side. In the shelter of the doorway into the Madhouse lies a very young woman.

She is curled up, like a stray cat, and she shivers from the cold as she sleeps. Her honey-colored hair, as curly as wool, springs around her like a crazy halo. Her face is tortured with woe. She is dressed oddly, in a shapeless smock and hessian slippers, and holds a bundle against her chest.

Descending gently in twos and threes, the birds perch around and over her, folding their feet beneath them like nesting mothers. Huddling together, they make the softest, warmest of coverlets.

When the girl stops shivering, the birds begin to sing softly, not with the abandon of the song in the prison cell, but in a soothing manner, as if they were settling a nest of hatchlings to sleep.

But the girl stirs unhappily.

"Damned," she murmurs feverishly.

"Not so!" says the white canary in her ear. "You are loved, and you are free, if only you choose to be so. Do not despair, my child," she urges. "Seize what has been given you!"

But the girl takes no comfort. Her sad face is as full of yearning as that of the boy in the dungeon, although there is a great difference between them. He longs to be free. She longs to be imprisoned. She begins to brush away the birds, as if they are insects, and to huddle closer to the door. Driven away, the birds rise into the air, their faces grave. They are reluctant to leave. They look to their leader for guidance. They had intended to stay with her through the coldest part of the night.

The white canary looks into the girl's face.

"We can do no good here," she pronounces with a sigh. "The poor creature cannot hear us. She will not let herself. Do not fear. The mice will follow her. The mice will send us news. We must wait for other opportunities. Come, fellow birds."

So the Caged Birds of the City flit wearily across the City, over public houses and newspaper offices, over dark, stuffy workshops and the suites of lawyers, over theatres and churches and market squares, over houses both grand and derelict, past the Palace and the Parliament and the Cathedral, and across the silent park.

As they fly, one or another leaves the group to return to its place of residence. One gets back in through a chimney. Another through a secret hole in the roof. Yet another through an open window. There they secrete themselves into their cages: for, although their owners do not know it, each bird is capable of using his or her clever beak to get in and out of his or her cage. There they gratefully tuck their heads under their wings and snatch what hours of sleep remain.

When the grey morning light creeps into their rooms, their human gaolers arise and remove the night-covers from the cages, never knowing that their fragile pets are members of a secret network formed to do good: the Society of the Caged Birds of the City.

As dawn breaks over the City, the girl with the honey-colored hair awakes also.

"What, still here?" cries the charwoman, as she opens the door of the Madhouse. She dumps her bucket on the threshold and brandishes her mop. "Go on! Git!" she says. "There ain't room for you here no more. Didn't you hear what the magistrate said?"

The girl scrambles to her feet and retreats. Then she darts downwards and kisses the hem of the woman's skirt. She is shaking with cold and desperation.

"P-please, m-mistress. P-please let me in," she begs through chattering teeth. "I have n-nowhere to g-go! I have n-no h-home but this one!"

"Well, you ain't averse to sleeping on doorstops, dearie. I would've thought accommodation'd be no great problem to the likes of you. Watch out!" and she throws her bucket of soapy water over the steps.

The girl just manages to avoid it. Like a cat, she springs out of the way, lingers for a moment, then gradually creeps back.

"I'm not letting you in," says the woman, not bothering to look up. She is scrubbing the steps on her hands and knees.

The girl hovers.

"I told you to git. Go on, hop it!" The woman seizes her mop, dives down the stairs and goes after the girl, raining blows on her thin back until she is forced to take to her heels.

Her purpose fulfilled, the charwoman goes back to finish the stairs.

But the girl has not run far. She has slipped into a dark alleyway, a little way down the street and opposite the Madhouse. From this vantage point, she gazes fixedly at the building in which she has lately been confined.

It begins to snow, but the girl barely notices.

She is trying to think of an answer to her unusual problem. She is by no means without cleverness, and desperation would ordinarily sharpen it. But she is dizzy with hunger … aching with cold … and the sky is distracting her. She finds it terrible, like a gigantic eye staring at her from above. It is many years since she has experienced the sky without a window, or a high-walled garden, to contain it.

Unconsciously, she has been drawing closer and closer to the wall. Bit by bit, she sinks to the ground. Still gazing at the door of the Madhouse, she huddles into as small a space as possible. She is a tall girl, but she can make herself surprisingly unnoticeable. Already, she has become all but invisible to passers by.

She will stay there for three days, trying and trying to get back in. Then, defeated, she will set out on a long, cold journey.

In his cell, the young man is also shaking with cold.

Yesterday, as the gaoler chained his wrists for the first time, he asked for something, anything, to make or do. A vista of bleakness opened in his mind, a vision of day upon day with nothing to do, with not even the remotest possibility of usefulness. This was a greater terror than the cell itself.

But the gaoler had laughed, and then, with a sniff, limped out. There was a bunch of keys at his hip. As he limped, they jangled, and the jangling, like everything else, echoed. When he shut the door, the process of locking it seemed to go on for fully five minutes.

The young man's mouth is dry with terror. He simply does not know how he will bear the life that now stretches before him.

He stares at the ceiling.

It is like a night sky without moon or stars.

"I will never see the sky again," he thinks.

Then he remembers the birds.

For a moment, the cell is filled with moonlight and hundreds of tiny singing creatures. Then they are gone, and the cell is dark once more.

"How strange," he thinks, "that although dreamers can be imprisoned, their dreams cannot."

And then –

All at once –

Stories, he thinks. Tell stories.

For a moment he searches his memory. Pictures flash out of the darkness – witches, maidens, wise dolls, magical birds. Then, with the air of one beginning a long and difficult journey, he whispers to himself:

"Once upon a time …"

# PART ONE

## Heloise's Story

# The Caretaker's Cottage

Long ago and far away, in a time and a place that never was, there lived a girl called Heloise. For as long as she could remember, Heloise had lived with her godmother in a caretaker's cottage adjoining a larger building in which she was not allowed to set foot.

She knew that this building was a museum. Though what a museum was she was not entirely certain. She also knew that taking care of it was her godmother's (and her own) livelihood. Her godmother worked hard, keeping two houses with the assistance of a grim, old serving woman by the name of Mrs. Moth.

Almost every day, visitors came calling at the cottage for someone to take them through the museum. Some of these people were quite poor – an affable, rough-spoken man, say, with a plump, pink-cheeked woman and three or four gaping children. Others were rich, for the museum was well-known and attracted all sorts. Oddly enough, Heloise's godmother had no set ticket price, but ran the museum by voluntary contribution. So while the poor people pressed their hard-earned pennies into her hand, the rich tipped carelessly. Thus she made a decent, though by no means extravagant, living. Of course, being a lady, she never spoke of money.

The visitors Heloise liked best were the pleasure parties of well-dressed young men and women. She would stare out the upstairs window of her bare little room as they climbed out of their carriages at the front gate – the young gentlemen handing down the young ladies – and walked gaily up the path to the front door of the cottage. The gentlemen always offered the ladies an arm to lean on. If there were more ladies than gentlemen, then one or more of the gentlemen would have a lady on each arm. And how the ladies dressed! In their high-waisted muslin gowns, matching gloves and straw bonnets, trimmed with ribbons and roses, they seemed to Heloise elegance itself. Heloise leaned on the window sill drinking in every detail. She had definite opinions about sartorial matters. Sometimes the young men were handsome, too, and elegant in a manly way, although she was not so interested in what they wore. Then one of them would pull the little bell rope at the door and Heloise would hear Mrs. Moth clomp along the bare boards of the hall, wiping her hands on her apron.

"May I help you, sir?" she would ask in a profoundly depressed tone of voice upon opening the door.

If the party was excitable and a little foolish there would inevitably be a titter from one of the young ladies, which might even develop into a full-fledged giggling fit.

"Are we right in thinking that this is The Museum of Mary Child?" the young gentleman would say, trying to sound dignified.

"It is indeed, sir. Would you be wishing to be taken through it?"

And now, with two or three of his companions giggling, it would be difficult for the young man to maintain his equilibrium.

"Y-yes. P-please. M-my g-good w-woman."

"Come in, sir. I'll fetch the mistress," Mrs. Moth would say, with as much severity as she could muster. When she had shown them into the drawing room and left them to regain their composure, she would hurry upstairs to alert Heloise's godmother. But Mrs. Moth's hurrying was not so much quicker as heavier: a deliberate *clomp, clomp, clomp* up the narrow, wooden stairs. At least you could always tell when she was coming.

At this point Heloise would return quickly to her work. For Heloise was always working, from the time she got up to the time she went to bed – except for the hour's brisk walk that she took at two o'clock every afternoon with her godmother, if she was unoccupied, or with Mrs. Moth, if there was a party being taken through the museum.

Heloise looked forward to the walk. They lived in the countryside, and she loved everything that grew, or galloped, or grazed, or growled. She loved the sky, whether it was blue or grey or speckled with clouds, and especially when it was bruised and purple and split with electricity; she loved the soil, whether it was muddy or dusty, and especially when it was just ploughed and squirming with worms; she loved the grey donkey with the sooty cross on his back in the field next door, the horses who never stopped eating, the cows with their beautiful eyes and eyelashes and, most of all, the sleek farm cats who slinked out to say hello (her favorite was a white one with one green eye and one blue). But whether she was with her godmother, who talked to her of improving subjects, or Mrs. Moth, who had an inexhaustible fund of true stories that ended sadly, she was never allowed to dawdle – not to stroke the cats, not to pick a flower, not to give a carrot top to the donkey. For that would have been A Waste Of Time.

Heloise's godmother was a beautiful woman. She was tall, slim, graceful, and young. Younger than Heloise realized. She had a luminously pale complexion with a slightly hectic flush, and unusual eyes, green as emeralds, with heavy black lashes and brows. They tipped downward and seemed to speak of suffering on her own part, and compassion for the suffering of others.

Heloise's first memory was of her godmother's face. It seemed to her that she remembered the very occasion on which she had opened her eyes and seen it for the first time.

Her second memory was of her heart clenching with love.

Her third memory was of reaching out to touch that lovely face.

Her fourth memory was of her godmother's hand brushing her fingers away.

And her fifth memory was pain.

When these memories flashed upon her, they were always followed by another that seemed to have nothing to do with them. Near the end of the backyard there was a natural clay deposit. Normally it was smooth and not to be walked over, lest one slipped. But Heloise remembered a time when there had been a cavity in it, as if a great deal of clay had been scraped out. She did not know when this had happened or why. It seemed too long ago.

Godmother's hair, which was the color of honey, was wildly curly, but she arranged it with such severity that even someone living in the same house would have been unaware that it was not straight. Her voice was low-pitched and very quiet, although Heloise knew instinctively that this was because she had a large voice, which she continually suppressed. She dressed with an austerity that reminded one of a nun, and rendered her something of an oddity in the community in which they lived.

Her main object in life, or so it seemed to Heloise, was

Being Good, but her ideas about what Being Good meant were unusually narrow. The three of them, Heloise, her godmother, and Mrs. Moth, were the only people in the parish who did not go to church, an omission which was almost unheard of. But it was not because they were libertines, or unbelievers. Indeed, Heloise was taught to read on the Ten Commandments.

The truth was that Godmother's religion was peculiar to herself, and much stricter than the one practiced at the parish church. For that matter, it was a good deal stricter than the Bible.

Heloise's godmother had Ten Commandments of her own, and Heloise amused herself by listing them:

1 Thou shalt not waste time.
2 Thou shalt not wear pretty clothes.
3 Thou shalt not think about pretty clothes or look at them on other people.
4 Thou shalt not play.
5 Thou shalt not imagine, for to imagine is to invent untruths.
6 Thou shalt not laugh, for behold, nothing is funny.
7 Thou shalt work all day for the good of others, whether they like it or not.
8 Thou shalt not ask questions.
9 Thou shalt eschew the word "love" and the phenomenon to which it refers.
10 Thou shalt not have a doll.

Heloise sighed. She did so long for a doll.

Every morning, except Sunday, Heloise sat down at nine o'clock sharp to begin her three hours of daily lessons. She added, subtracted, divided and multiplied, and practiced reading and writing. Anything beyond that her godmother regarded as A Waste of Time. She believed Heloise should be taught only what was necessary in order for her to lead a sober and useful life. So History, Literature, Languages, Geography, Botany, Music, Drawing, Art Appreciation and any other study that might broaden the mind were not for Heloise. Heloise had no idea that there was even such a thing as Current Events.

The wars and revolutions of recent times had passed her by, never having been mentioned in her hearing. She did not even know the main story of the day, though it was gossiped about in every market square and church hall in the land. The Crown Prince, a promising young man, it was generally thought, had gone missing in dramatic circumstances. The newspapers had been full of it for months. But Heloise's godmother did not buy newspapers.

Heloise loved the Bible. It was, after all, a book full of stories – although her godmother did not see it in quite that light. However, the Bible in the caretaker's cottage was a curious piece of work. Someone had meddled with it. Many pages were stuck together with glue. Other pages had passages scored out with black ink. To someone more worldly than Heloise, this may have seemed sinister. But this vandalized

Bible was the only book Heloise had ever seen. Had she thought about it, she would have assumed all books were like that.

Heloise did not waste time broadening her mind. Instead, every afternoon, after she had eaten every jot and tittle of her plain though wholesome lunch (Waste Not, Want Not), and returned from her brisk walk, she worked.

This usually meant sewing. There was an orphanage in the neighboring town – Saint Suffering's Institute for Waifs and Strays at Bell Toll – and both Heloise and her godmother made clothes for the orphans. Heloise's godmother chose the materials, cut the pieces, and did the parts that required skilled sewing, while Heloise learned to sew by being set tasks, like hemming a petticoat. They also knitted stockings and baby clothes. Girls were usually taught embroidery, and worked on pretty "samplers" that were often framed and hung in their bedrooms. But Heloise's godmother did not approve of embroidery or adornment, and the orphans' clothes were very plain. Even plainer, if possible, than Heloise's own.

This made Heloise sad. She knew orphans were thought to be unfortunate creatures, and she felt as if every stitch she sewed was destined to make them just a little bit unhappier.

"Might not the orphans feel better if they were wearing nicer clothes, Godmother?" she ventured once.

"What nonsense you talk, child!" replied her godmother, as she skillfully turned the collar of a shirt. "As if such a worldly thing could make a difference one way or another, except to a worldly mind! In any case," she added, "as you ought to know by now, happiness is A Waste of Time. Let me hear no more about it. And lower your voice when you speak. It is too loud."

"Yes, Godmother," murmured Heloise. Her besetting sin was a carrying voice. She tried to straighten her back. Sewing always made her shoulders ache.

Heloise had two dresses for winter and two for summer. The summer dresses were made of cotton, the winter dresses of wool. Her weekday dresses, summer and winter, were dirt brown. The dresses she wore on Sundays and for special occasions were black. Even dirt brown can be nice in the right material, with the right trim – and black can be beautiful. But Heloise's godmother only bought plain, serviceable fabrics. Neither she nor Heloise owned jewelry or ribbons or lace or kerchiefs with which to trim their gowns. Heloise's outfit was completed by a white, starched calico apron that was worn over her dress when at home, and a white mob-cap that covered the top of her head. There was a summer bonnet and a winter bonnet, to wear on her walks, and a summer pelisse and a winter pelisse, to wear over her dress when necessary. In addition, she owned a brown, woolen shawl and two nightdresses, which were white. Her camisoles, pantalettes and stockings were white too. Her indoor shoes – which were kid slippers – were also white. Her outdoor shoes – which were lace-up boots – were black.

All in all, her clothes were not much different from the

ones she made for the orphans. Heloise wondered if she was an orphan too.

"Am I an orphan, Godmother?" she had asked once.

"Lower your voice. And do not ask questions," her godmother had replied.

Of course, Heloise did not understand what an orphan was. If asked, she might have hazarded that it was a child who wore particularly dreary clothes. But she knew she was different because, although she did not go to school (the village school was "not for the likes of us"), she saw other children on her walks.

Some of these children were the sons and daughters of farm workers. There was a pretty, flaxen-haired girl of about twelve, whom Heloise held in special regard. The girl looked after a herd of white geese. Heloise sometimes saw her, walking barefoot along the road, guiding the large, noisy birds with her crook. On such occasions Heloise and her godmother, or Mrs. Moth, stood aside to let them pass. The goose-girl curtsied a little roughly and bid them good afternoon.

Heloise wanted to be just like her and have a flock of friendly geese to sleep with. Though she longed even more for a doll.

Then there were the Vicar's children. Heloise knew them by sight, although she had never set foot inside their father's church. There were five of them, two boys and three girls, and Heloise was fascinated by them. All five were very alike, with haunting, deep-set brown eyes – their mother's, the Vicar said – but they were merry and played noisy games among the tombstones behind the Vicarage, scandalizing the parish, although the Vicar did not seem to mind. Their mother was dead, but the Vicar's older sister lived with him and saw to the children – when she wasn't lying down in a darkened room, moaning softly, with little muslin bags full of cold, drained tea leaves on her temples.

"Is my mother dead?" Heloise asked her godmother once, as quietly as she could.

"Don't ask questions," her godmother replied.

There was also Lady Blantosh's daughter, Prudence. She was thirteen and rather plain, but she wore the loveliest, daintiest fur-lined muffs and boots and fur-trimmed pelisses and bonnets in winter, and the lightest, gayest silks and poplins and organdies in summer – precisely the clothes it was most wicked for Heloise to think about.

But none of the children Heloise saw, whether rich or poor, wore clothes as plain or as odd as hers.

And there was another difference.

There was a very great deal that Heloise did not know about herself.

She did not know how old she was.

She did not know how she had come to live at the caretaker's cottage. She could not remember having arrived there, and assumed it must have been when she was a baby. But who had brought her there, and why?

Heloise did not even know what she looked like, for there were no mirrors in the cottage. At night, she could see her reflection in the bedroom window against the dark outside, but that reflection was dim and gave only a rough impression of her appearance.

If she had known what she really looked like, she would have been shocked.

The truth was that Heloise was an odd-looking child. She had porcelain skin without the ghost of a blush, and black hair that was thick and wavy. Although it was quite long, it fanned out from her head, as if she had been struck by lightning. She was small-made and terribly neat and unruffled, rather like a doll on a shelf. Her eyes slanted upwards and looked like nothing so much as twin green fires. But it was not just her coloring or her features that made her odd-looking. There was something remarkable about her that was not easy to define – something eerie. Anyone seeing her for the first time would have been frightened, although they would not have known why.

She had no reason to believe that she was related to her godmother by blood. Apart from the fact that they both had green eyes, they certainly did not resemble one another. And yet, stern as her godmother was, sometimes Heloise caught the young woman looking at her with a strange expression. It was somehow hungry and … what?

Proud?

One Sunday, when she was out walking with her godmother and Mrs. Moth, Heloise heard a strange thing.

On Sundays it was their custom to walk late in the day; thus, on the country road, they often saw people on their way home from Evensong.

On this particular evening, they passed a farm worker family – father, mother and several children, including a young boy sitting on his father's shoulders and a tiny girl in her mother's arms. Just as the father tipped his cap to Heloise's godmother, the youngest child, oblivious to the presence of strangers, joyfully and rather loudly said:

"*Beau'ful* Ma, I do so love you, that I do!"

There was a burst of kindly laughter among the family. But embarrassment too, for in that time and place it was not considered proper to express one's feelings in public.

"Hush, my little kitten," the child's mother said softly. But she did not sound angry. "I love you too, my precious," she murmured. As they passed by, Heloise heard a kiss from the mother, and a little chuckle from the child.

Heloise wasn't allowed to turn her head. She glanced sideways at her godmother from under her eyelashes. Heloise's godmother's eyes were downcast, but her face was uneasy.

"Godmother? What does that word mean – 'love?'"

"Lower your voice," said her godmother immediately,

glancing at Mrs. Moth, who was clomping stolidly beside her. Then she said, "And don't ever let me hear you using that word again. There is no such thing as 'love.' There is only 'charity.'"

"What is 'charity,' Godmother?"

"I said lower your voice, child!" said Heloise's godmother; her own voice was even quieter than usual. "Your second utterance was louder than the first." She sighed and murmured, "'Charity' is doing good to others, whether they – or you – like it or not."

"But what is the difference," whispered Heloise, "between charity and love?" She was afraid that her godmother would terminate the conversation by telling her not to ask questions. Curiously, she did not.

"'Love,'" said Heloise's godmother, "is *wanting* to do good for another, because it would give you both joy." She paused and in that instant Heloise thought she saw a fugitive shadow behind her eyes. However, she continued resolutely: "We are all of us evil. And to love something evil is wicked. Therefore we should shun love and do works of charity instead.

"Love is the greatest of all Wastes of Time."

That night, as she lay in bed, Heloise found herself thinking of the child's utterance. She could hear it in her mind, the pure, musical voice, and the mother's reply. She could see it in her imagination – the child leaning against her mother and tilting her head to look up at her face, while the mother looked into the face of her child. Heloise understood that, to the child, her mother's face was the most beautiful thing in the world, and that the mother felt the same way about her child.

She fell asleep holding her pillow tightly against her, sometimes dreaming that she was the mother and sometimes the child.

"Godmother," Heloise asked one day, "might I please have a doll to play with? Oh, please, Godmother. The Vicar's daughters all have one," she added in a rush.

Her godmother had turned pale. She swallowed before she answered. "Certainly not. Playing with dolls is ... A Waste of Time."

# Moses in the Bulrushes
# and Making Adam

Heloise was not allowed to play. It was one of her godmother's eccentric Ten Commandments. The Fourth, in fact. Heloise had two adults to supervise her, but she was not watched all the time. And when she was not watched, she played.

Many of Heloise's games were undetectable to an observer. Sometimes she went all day, pretending she was wearing the most exquisite gown – a dress of emerald green velvet, trimmed with white lace at the throat and wrists and tied at the waist with a black satin sash, for example. And of course neither her godmother nor Mrs. Moth had any idea that she was doing this – although they might notice how exceptionally careful she was not to spill anything, or rub against a dirty surface, throughout the day. With games like this it hardly mattered whether she was being watched or not.

But there were times when she was set a task – twenty sums, for example, or the hemming of a petticoat – and left to complete it while her godmother took someone through the museum, or Mrs. Moth attended to the bread-making. At those times Heloise made haste to complete the task as quickly as possible so that she could squeeze in some time for make-believe before either of them got back. Fortunately, her hearing was good, and she was nimble and clever. She always made sure to disrupt the room as little as possible, so that it could be put to rights, and she could be back in her chair almost as soon as she heard a foot on the first stair.

Now if Heloise had had a doll, her games would naturally have revolved around it. But she did not have a doll, so she improvised. One of her favorite games was Moses in the Bulrushes. She started playing it almost as soon as she first read it in the Bible.

This game was deeply satisfying and needed little in the way of props. Heloise's pillow made an extremely good Baby Moses. Pretending to be Moses' mother, Heloise sang Moses to sleep, walking up and down the room and jigging her pillow in her arms, as she had seen mothers do when they visited the museum or when she passed them on a walk. When baby-pillow-Moses had dropped off, she lay him carefully on the bed and then sat nearby while she worked at his invisible basket of rushes, lining it with daub and pitch, although she wasn't completely sure what daub and pitch were. When she was finished, Heloise gently picked Moses up and, without waking him, put him in the basket. Then she called her little daughter Miriam. Together they stole down to the (invisible) Nile river (which flowed parallel with her bed), and there Heloise knelt on the muddy bank, and floated Baby Moses in the water. Then she told Miriam to hide behind the chair to see what happened, and hurried home, weeping with agitation.

That was when Heloise became Pharaoh's daughter. (She scarcely knew which role she liked best.) Listening carefully to make sure that neither her godmother nor Mrs. Moth was on her way back, Heloise stood at the doorway of her room, or preferably a few steps down the hall, so that she could make something of an entrance. In a stately manner, surrounded by her ladies in waiting, she made her way to the river and pretended to get ready to bathe, handing layer after splendid layer of (invisible) clothing to one (invisible) lady-in-waiting or another. But then she spied the basket and found Moses in it, crying.

"Behold!" she said under her breath, with a nervous glance at the door. "It must be one of the Hebrews' children." And her proud Egyptian heart melted. "Poor little babe!" she muttered, picking up the baby-pillow-Moses and rocking him in her arms. "My father hath commanded that all their male newborns be drowned, but …

"I shall adopt him. What ho! You over there, hiding behind that chair – I mean rock! Are you not a Hebrew maiden? Find me a nurse from amongst your people, and I shall pay her wages!"

And so it came to pass that Moses' mother, who had given him away to save his life, raised him after all, by pretending to be his nurse.

Heloise rarely managed to get all the way through this game before she was forced to abandon it for fear of being caught. But it was very real to her, and she found that she was never able to treat her pillow with anything less than affectionate respect. She never threw it, or dropped it on purpose, and always cuddled and whispered tenderly to it at night.

She was attached to her pillow, it must be said. But she still longed for a doll.

Then there was her other favorite game, the Making Adam game.

Heloise loved the bit in the Bible where God made Adam out of the dust, and breathed the breath of life into his nostrils. Ever since she had first read it, it had made her feel like trying it herself.

Sometimes she pretended she was alone in a world so new that the Garden of Eden hadn't even been planted yet. She found a nice patch of primeval dust beside her bed and pretended to form a man out of it. It was absorbing work, so absorbing that she sometimes forgot to listen for a foot on the stair. She particularly liked doing the fingers. And the breathing at the end.

But although she somehow felt she knew exactly what she was doing, the game made her feel faintly guilty. So, satisfying as it was, she did not play it often.

Time passed. Heloise was older, although she still did not know how old she was. Little had changed in the small house adjoining the museum. Heloise was taller, her hair a little darker, her eyes a little greener. She could read the Bible for herself, and could sew better than many a grown woman. But little, as I said, had changed. And yet Heloise had grown sad.

The truth was that she was lonely, although she did not know what lonely was, and so did not recognize it. All she knew was that her days were long and there was a weight, an ache, in her heart that never lifted.

She had always been a solemn child. Now she was a melancholy one. The happiest time of her day was bedtime, for as she lay in bed waiting for sleep, she cradled her pillow and felt she was comforting it. And comforting it comforted her.

It was not long before she had invented an odd game, a kind of prayer. As she lay in bed, she imagined talking to the doll she did not have – for she had begun to believe that this doll she so desired already existed.

And so she prayed to it to come soon.

Heloise had ceased to wish for any old doll. She knew that what she wanted was one doll in particular, the doll that was destined for her alone. She did not know how it would come to her, she did not know how to overcome her godmother and Mrs. Moth, but she found it impossible to believe that this could not somehow be achieved. She had no choice but to believe it. For if she had not, she would have despaired.

The world was a harsher place now that she was older. Once, she had not troubled herself about the museum. To this day she had never seen inside it. But now she knew that The Museum of Mary Child was dedicated to preserving the memory of something bad, something regrettable, something unfortunate, although she did not know what it was.

Heloise had learned much from observing the visitors who came to look over the museum.

When they arrived they were thrilled, exhilarated, like people who had agreed to a dare. When they left, however, it was different.

In their various ways, they seemed subdued, chastened, even uneasy – although the men often joked loudly, as if trying to show that they had not been affected.

"I wish we had never come," more than one young woman said on her way out.

If there were children, sometimes a little one cried.

Heloise was not like the young maidens in fairy tales who are forbidden to enter some place, yet find themselves compelled to enter it nonetheless. Never in her life had she looked closely at the museum on her way past, much less tried to peek in the windows.

And yet, the idea of it haunted her. Sometimes, on nights when she could not sleep, no matter how hard she clung to her pillow, she feared that something from the museum would escape, find its way into the cottage, drag itself up the steps, and come for her.

She was sure it knew where she lived.

# Beneath Behind Below

One glorious afternoon in autumn, when the air was crisp as an apple and the world smelled of damp soil and ripe, fallen fruit, and bonfires burning dry leaves, Heloise stood gazing out her window.

Idleness was not tolerated and such a thing would never have been allowed if she had not chanced to be alone and unobserved. Indeed, Heloise was supposed to be working on an orphan's flannel petticoat. But she had sewed yesterday, and the day before, and the day before that. She felt with all her heart that even one minute's more sewing would be insupportable.

Heloise rested her forehead against the windowpane and shut her eyes. Sometimes she was subject to a strange feeling, a feeling that there was something living inside her. It was as if there were two Heloises. The Heloise on the outside, who was small and calm and obedient. And the Heloise on the inside, who was big and powerful and rebellious. It was torture for the inside Heloise to be confined within the outside Heloise; she was in chains.

Small Heloise felt sorry for the big Heloise. But she did not know whether she was good or bad, whether her imprisonment was just, or unjust. As for big Heloise, she was angry. Small Heloise knew it, and sometimes it frightened her.

Heloise sighed and opened her eyes. She fell to thinking about the children at the Vicarage – about how they played together like a litter of puppies. Only the day before she had seen them joyfully occupied with a strange, jumping game. It had attracted her notice because it seemed more disciplined than the games they usually played. It seemed to have rules, and they took turns, and the eldest – Bede – was keeping score. They had chalked a pathway of numbered squares along a slate walkway in the graveyard behind the church, and were hopping back and forwards along it one at a time. As Heloise passed, the youngest daughter, Lucy, had waved.

"Disgraceful!" her godmother had said. She had never approved of the Vicar's children. "Playing! In public! For all to see!"

The game was hopscotch, but Heloise did not know the names of any games.

It occurred to her that a tamer version of the game might be adaptable to her room. Chalk was out of the question, but the wooden floorboards had lines built in. She would have to decide how many made a square, and perhaps use bits and pieces to mark the outer borders. It was a little daring – it might be hard to pick everything up again before her godmother or Mrs. Moth appeared in the doorway – but as long as she started clearing the floor the very second she heard the first step on the stairway she should be all right. They had never caught her yet.

Heloise glanced around. The bareness of the room was something of an advantage in this case. The most suitable place was the vacant strip of floor that ran parallel with the right side of her bed. Heloise went quickly to her work table and collected a ruler, a pair of scissors, her slate and slate-pencil, and a few scraps of material.

"Three floorboards equal one square," she murmured, trying to remember how big the Vicarage children's squares had been. Then she placed her odds and ends to mark each square's vertical borders. It took a little imagination to see a hopscotch grid there, but Heloise had no shortage of that. Now to the hopping.

Heloise hesitated, wondering if this might be audible downstairs. The floor of her room lay directly over the ceiling of the drawing room; fortunately, as her godmother was in the museum and Mrs. Moth in the kitchen, this would be empty. Anyway, one can hop quietly.

Cautiously, she set off up the grid.

She was surprised how much fun it was. She did not

really understand the game or how it was scored, but hopping from square to square made her want to laugh. It also made her breathe heavily, and she had to keep reminding herself to listen for that first step on the stairs. She had hopped up and down the grid three times before she began to notice something.

One of the floorboards was different from the others.

It was the third one in the second of her makeshift squares. It felt peculiar, less stable, when she hopped on it. And although she was making as little noise as possible, she noticed that it sounded a different note when tapped by her slippers.

Heloise thought about it as she hopped.

Then she stopped hopping. She had an idea.

What if it was mice? What if there was a nest underneath the board? A family of baby mice living under her room!

Not everybody likes mice, but Heloise did. Already, with a quickening heart, she saw herself feeding them and keeping them as secret pets.

Heloise did not know that the house was full of mice who watched everything that went on. She did not know that certain mice were watching her now.

She knelt on the floor next to the board. Then she put her ear close to it. She could hear nothing. Perhaps they were asleep. It was daytime after all, and she knew that mice were nocturnal creatures.

Heloise wondered if she might be able to lift the floorboard. She could always put it back again, or at least she hoped so. First she collected everything off the floor. Then she got the big iron shears from her workbasket. She was thinking that she might be able to pry the floorboard open by fitting the sharp end of the scissors between the strange board and its neighbor, and then levering upwards. If the board had been an ordinary one, this would not have been possible. But the board was not an ordinary one. Although nail heads were visible on the surface, nails were not holding it down. Instead, nail heads, without any nails attached to them, had been pushed into the holes and the board had been stuck down with mere glue.

So it came up easily, bringing with it strands of clinging, rubbery adhesive.

Heloise's heart was thumping. This had already gone farther than she had expected. Might she indeed see a nest of pink baby mice?

What she actually saw almost killed her with shock.

"Heloise!" came her godmother's voice as she started up the stairs.

Heloise slammed the board into place, flew back to her work table and seized the flannel petticoat.

The room was spinning.

For it had seemed to Heloise that, lying face upwards in the hollow beneath the floor, she had seen a doll.

And when the doll had looked up into the sudden light and seen Heloise's astonished face, it had smiled.

# Heloise Waits

That afternoon felt as if it was the longest in Heloise's life.

She did not know if what she had seen was real; indeed, if she had known what madness was she might have suspected herself of succumbing to it. Could she have made herself ill with longing, ill enough to see things that were not there?

The thought frightened her, and yet, as the afternoon wore on, she found it less and less convincing.

She must have seen it. It must be true.

It was the miracle she had been waiting for.

A more worldly child may have been preoccupied with why the doll was hidden there, with who had put it there and when. But Heloise was not. It was all so simple, as miracles always were, or so Heloise believed. There had been obstacles; they had been overcome. Indeed, the doll had not even had to get past her godmother and Mrs. Moth, for it was there already. It had been beneath the floorboards all along.

Now it was merely a matter of waiting.

For, of course, she would not be able to play with it in the open. Like everything else that was really important, it would have to be a secret. And so it would have to wait until she could be sure of being unobserved.

The waiting was tedious. Never had she listened more skittishly to her godmother's improving subjects; never had her daily walk seemed to pass so slowly. All the time there was the necessity of seeming meek and collected when what she wanted most was to run and jump and laugh and skip to shake out her impatience! Then there was yet more sewing, and then the achingly quiet ritual of supper, and her godmother's stern reading from the Scriptures before bedtime.

And yet it was also true that these hours were lit up with zest and joy. It was almost as if she had found a reason to live. It was almost as if a long ordeal, one she had not even been aware of, was over at last.

When finally it was time for bed, Heloise could hardly contain her excitement. When she lit her candle from the fire in the drawing room, her hand was trembling, but did either of the women notice? As she bade them goodnight, she was careful to lower her eyes lest they read in them her secret. And she tried to climb the stairs, not with a joyous spring in her step, but as slowly and gravely as possible.

But she need not have worried. Mrs. Moth at her knitting, and her godmother frowning over the month's accounts, suspected nothing.

Heloise entered her room, her candle held carefully before her. She placed it on her work table, undressed, then blew out the light.

Instead of climbing into bed, she stood in the center of the room, listening.

All was quiet.

Heloise crept over the floorboards and knelt beside the bed. She ran her hands over the wood and quickly located the loose board. Then, with her nails and the tips of her fingers, she pulled it up once more.

At that moment, she almost lost faith. It was so different, coming back in the cold darkness to what she had first seen in a shaft of early afternoon sunlight. Perhaps, after all, it was not true.

She could see almost nothing in the inky dark, no matter how she peered. But in her mind's eye she recalled how the doll had filled the cavity beneath the false board, where her head had been, where the hem of her skirt had been, and the smile that perhaps Heloise had only imagined.

With trembling hands, she reached in and scooped her out.

And, yes, yes, it was true.

Heloise's eyes filled with tears.

It was the very first time she had touched a doll.

Her arms told her that the doll was as tall as the distance from her fingertips to her bent elbow, and her fingers told her that she was carved out of the smoothest, softest wood. She had a high forehead, a long, delicate nose, lips so finely molded they might have been porcelain, a softly pointed chin and a long neck. Her hair was so finely carved that Heloise could feel every strand. It was parted in the center, rolled up modestly over her ears, and tucked into a chignon on the nape of her neck.

Her body was wooden, but it ended at the waist. Rather than a lower body and limbs, the doll sat on a kind of bell-shaped, cage-like base, which was concealed by – wonder of wonders! – a stiff, silk skirt.

Heloise sat cross-legged on the floor, cradling the doll. Her scent was intoxicating – a blend of wood and silk and rosewater and something Heloise could not name. Perhaps it was simply the musty scent of long imprisonment. After a moment, by way of a greeting, Heloise kissed the doll gently on the forehead.

The night was bleak and windy. Clouds blew in dapples across the moon. Heloise listened carefully for any noise on the stair, but she could not even hear the click of Mrs. Moth's knitting needles. So, with the doll resting in the crook of her arm, Heloise slipped to the window seat.

A tree grew close to Heloise's window; the wind was making its foliage brush like fingers against the panes. As the clouds skidded across the sky, the moon appeared, disappeared, appeared, disappeared; Heloise held the doll in what light there was. It was in this dappled way that she got her first lasting impression of what the doll looked like.

Her hair was chestnut brown and her face was not exactly pretty, but kind and wise; her expression carved with miraculous softness out of the wood. She had been painted very delicately: she had cheeks tinged with the faintest blush, a palely rosebud mouth and the finest arched eyebrows. Her eyes were cast modestly down, and her head was inclined. The bodice of her dress, which was simple, with long plain sleeves, was painted delicately on her upper body. The doll's gown, Heloise noted with some surprise, had an unfashionably low waist. In addition to her skirt she wore three petticoats, which made her gown billow outward somewhat. Her finely molded arms curved close to her chest, one a little above the other, as if she were holding something. The color of her gown was in fact sky-blue, but in the moonlight Heloise could not make it out, any more than she could see the roses in her cheeks or the chestnuts in her hair. To Heloise's eye she seemed to be painted in the most delicate of all palettes, every possible shade of grey.

Heloise wiped the tears from her cheeks with the back of her hand. They had been falling from her eyes without her really noticing. Then she breathed a long, trembling sigh, a sigh that was part rapture, and part relief.

She did not want to sleep. She wanted to sit up all night, until dawn streaked the sky. She wanted to be awake and ready when the light began to change, to watch the new morning painting the daytime colors on her beloved, brush stroke by brush stroke, like a great artist. But her eyelids were drooping, and she was beginning to tremble with the cold. She carried the doll to bed and settled her comfortably beneath the covers. The doll was cold, and a little hard for cuddling, but Heloise solved that by wrapping her in a section of the coverlet.

Heloise had never been so happy. She rubbed her cheek against the doll's carved hair.

"My name is Heloise," she whispered into her smooth wooden ear. "What is yours?"

And, just as she began to drift into sleep, it seemed to her that she heard a voice. It was as clear and as joyous as a church-bell on a wedding day, and it said, "*You may call me Maria.*"

# Heloise and Maria

Now began a happy time for Heloise. She had not realized how life could be transformed by a friend.

How could anything be dull or lonely when, if it was not done with Maria, it was told to her later?

It was surprising that Heloise managed to spend time with Maria when she was so busy, and was so often observed.

The truth was that, owing to her cleverness, almost all of her time was spent with Maria. She could not take her on her walks, or to meals, but then these times of separation only served to supply the two of them with interesting topics of conversation afterwards. And Heloise had no need to say anything aloud. She had only to glance at Maria, or think of her, to be convinced that the doll knew what was in her heart.

It helped that it was Heloise's responsibility to keep her

room clean and tidy. It was she who made her own bed, she who dusted and swept, and she who washed the windows once a week. As she spent most of her time in her room and as it was she who arranged it, Heloise found it a simple matter to keep Maria nearby, if not exactly in plain sight.

When she slept, Maria slept with her, low down in the bed and wrapped carefully in a corner of the bedclothes. In the morning while Heloise made her bed, Maria observed her from an open bedside drawer, which could be shut discreetly if necessary. When Heloise had to leave her room, Maria retired to her secret cavity beneath the floorboard – in case someone should come in and see fit to disturb Heloise's things. And while Heloise worked, Maria sat close by, peeking out from between the wall behind her desk and the large work basket that sat on it.

Heloise was supervised, it was true. But her guardians were not observant women, or not keenly observant, anyway. They were both, in their own ways, too unhappy and too self-absorbed to notice much outside their own spheres and their own dark worries. However, even they could not help notice how happy Heloise was. As the days passed, her face, which had once been pale, had grown rosy, and her eyes bright. She had stopped asking questions, having come to accept the fact that they were never answered, but she no longer sighed as if burdened by an invisible weight. Instead she went about with a secret smile, not unlike the modest, serene little smile on the wooden face of her doll.

"Child's all lit up like fairy lights," remarked Mrs. Moth mournfully, as she watched Heloise climbing two stairs at a time up to bed.

"Take care of the candle, Heloise," her godmother called after her sharply.

"Yes, Godmother," Heloise called back, without turning around.

"No good will come of it," sighed Mrs. Moth, as she took up her knitting. "Mark my words. No good ever came of 'appiness."

"Indeed no," said Heloise's godmother, shocked at the very thought. And she stared into the fire, her handsome brow furrowed.

And so Heloise's life had become a happy one, in its own way. But along with happiness had come something else.

Fear.

At night, Heloise sometimes lay in bed worrying about ways she could lose Maria. The thing that frightened her most was fire. Heloise knew that houses burned down, and with them everything a family owned. She knew that the most important thing was to rescue the people. But she worried about how, if ever trapped in her room by fire, she would get Maria out. She comforted herself by thinking up plans.

"I will tie you to my chest using one of my nightgowns as a harness," she murmured into Maria's hair. "Then we will climb out the window and down the tree."

But what if the fire consumed everything they had to live on – the museum as well as the cottage – and they fell into poverty, and had to go to the Workhouse, where perhaps no dolls would be allowed, and there was no place to hide them?

"Well, then, I will hide you under my dresses," said Heloise resourcefully. "I will have to let them out, but I daresay I could conceal you quite easily, with waistlines as high as they are these days."

Then Heloise drifted from worrying about fire to worrying about something more ordinary. What if her godmother or Mrs. Moth were somehow to discover Maria and take her away?

"Well, then, my dear, I will steal you back, and we will run away together. For I could not go on living without you."

And then she fell asleep.

As autumn advanced and the days grew cooler, Heloise began to feel that Maria needed a winter wardrobe. After all, silk, though beautiful, did not keep one warm, and the sky-blue color of Maria's gown, lovely as it was, spoke of spring or summer rather than the approaching winter.

Heloise had not yet learned to knit. One day, watching her godmother working at a black stocking for an orphan, she gathered up courage and asked:

"Godmother, will you teach me to do that?"

Her godmother stopped knitting and looked up. Heloise could see that she was pleased, and yet she hesitated.

"I would like to be able to knit stockings for the orphans, too," added Heloise. "And my needlework is very good, now."

"I hope you are not proud of your needlework," said her godmother promptly. "Pride comes before a fall; however, learning a new accomplishment may help you to grow in humility. You will, after all, be a beginner again. Go to Mrs. Moth and ask if you may borrow some knitting needles."

It was not long before Heloise was knitting stockings with her godmother, although her godmother had to turn the heels for her. But when her godmother was at the museum and Mrs. Moth in the kitchen, Heloise worked on a woolen cloak and muff for Maria.

She had not been taught how to do such a thing. But Heloise was nothing if not resourceful, and invented her own method. She simply knitted a square about as wide and as long as Maria's height from her shoulders to the ground. When it was big enough, she finished off and threaded a scrap of narrow ribbon along one side, in and out of the stitching, about an inch from the end. She then tied this around Maria's neck, and voila! Maria had a warm black cloak with a gathered, Elizabethan-style neckline and a bow at her throat. The muff was even easier – just a small oblong that Heloise sewed into a cylinder.

Heloise was very pleased. The only thing she regretted was the color. It was so heavy against the sky-blue of the gown beneath. But the only wool she had been able to come by was the wool her godmother used for the orphans' stockings, and they were always black. True, it set off Maria's creamy complexion, but to Heloise's eye it looked as if she were in mourning.

"What if I were to add a little trim?" she thought.

Heloise, unlike most girls in her day, had never been taught embroidery. Her godmother disapproved of it – indeed it violated at least four of her personal Ten Commandments. But Heloise began to study any embroidery that came her way, with an eye to copying it. The best opportunity she had for this was on her Sunday walk.

The people coming out of Evensong were always dressed in their Sunday best, and often embroidery was shockingly in evidence. The dresses of babies and young children were frequently embellished with it, and many of the female parishioners had embroidery on their gowns. The most beautiful embroidery was often to be seen on the waistcoats of the men, the elaborateness of which put their ladies' gowns to shame.

All that beauty made Heloise wistful. The thread they had in the cottage came in only four colors: black, brown, white and red. Black was useless, brown not much better, and white seemed like an odd color to embroider in. That left red. "Well," thought Heloise, "red against black is at least dramatic," although she had never seen anyone wearing such a color scheme, perhaps because it seemed somehow unladylike.

The thing would be to keep it delicate.

But the thread was not heavy enough. How might this be overcome? And then Heloise had an idea.

Rosebuds! Red rosebuds. Nothing could be more ladylike. Heloise's favorite flowers of all were violets, but there was no possibility of coming by any purple thread. And if the thin red thread was doubled, tripled, knotted even …

As well as finishing her first pair of stockings, Heloise was working on a red flannel petticoat, the first she had made entirely by herself, from the cutting out of the pieces to the final hemming. She began to collect scraps of red thread.

"Have you much to do on that petticoat, child?" asked her godmother one morning at breakfast. "If the weather holds I would like to send a batch of clothes to Bell Toll at the end of the week. The Vicar has charitably offered to take them in his trap."

"It's almost finished, Godmother," said Heloise. "And so are the stockings."

In fact they *were* finished, but Heloise was keeping them by her as camouflage for the work she was doing on Maria's cloak. Through patient experimentation she had discovered that a rosebud of sorts could be constructed by collecting a number of short pieces of red thread together, tying them into a knot, then using the ends to secure them to the cloak, poking them through with a needle and tying them around the back of the knitting. Heloise had decided that she wanted twenty-one rosebuds – three rows of seven – studded around the cloak. It was coming along nicely.

"How elegant you will look, my dear!" she whispered to Maria. "And you will be warm, too."

Soon afterwards, as Heloise was working on the cloak, she was surprised to hear the sound of carriage wheels and horses' hooves coming up the driveway. It was late autumn and visitors were becoming rare, however, she was pleased. "What luck!" she thought. "A visitor to the museum. That should keep my godmother occupied – well, for half an hour at the very least."

She was working happily on the last row of rosebuds.

"Not long now, Maria," she murmured.

Maria was, as usual, silent.

It was a shame that Maria could not answer her. On their very first night, it had seemed to Heloise that Maria had spoken her name. But she had not said anything since. Perhaps Heloise had been dreaming.

Heloise was so passionately grateful to have Maria at all that she was reluctant to admit even the slightest imperfection in their relationship. So it was only in the lightest way that she mused aloud:

"I wonder what you would say to me, Maria dear, if you could talk?"

She glanced casually at Maria's serene little face. Then a strange thing happened. There was a shift in the air, a shimmer, and something changed. Was it Maria's face, or was it the world itself? For the briefest moment, Maria's features became fluid with expression, and Heloise heard a voice, as clear as a bell, and yet inside her head, answering promptly:

"*I would say, I love you.*"

Heloise froze.

"Oh, Maria, dearest," she whispered, with all her heart. "I love you too."

All at once Heloise realized that her question had been answered.

For this – *this* – was love! This closeness, this affection, this protectiveness, this respect, this cherishing, this friendship, this joy between Maria and herself was not charity but love. And this fear of losing her, and the sadness and loneliness that would come if ever she did – that too was love. Love was joy and love was pain. Love was allowing someone to matter to you. Not for their usefulness to you, or even for your usefulness to them, but for no reason, except that they were they and you were you. Love was everything, all that mattered. And yet, in a strange way, her godmother had been right. For love was a kind of folly, a losing game. *The greatest of all Wastes of Time.*

But then, that depended on what you thought time was for.

At that moment she heard a foot on the stair.

"If you wait just a moment, Mr. Radcliffe, I will ask her …"

Heloise came down to earth with the most disagreeable

thud. For a moment she was too confused to act. She came to her senses just in time, pushed Maria behind the shelf and hid the cloak beneath her orphanage work.

Then she sprang guiltily to her feet.

"Heloise?" her godmother was saying. "The Vicar is here. He finds he must travel unexpectedly to Bell Toll today instead of Friday, and has offered to take the orphans' clothes for us. Have you finished the petticoat? And the stockings?" Then she caught sight of them folded neatly on Heloise's work table. "Ah, but I see you have!" She scooped them up without waiting for an answer. "You have been industrious. That is commendable. Tidy yourself quickly and come down to bid the Vicar good morning." With that she was hurrying back down the stairs.

Her heart thudding, her cheeks flaming, her mind racing, and all her limbs filled with warm relief at not having been caught, Heloise smoothed her hair, straightened her cap, took off her apron, and followed her godmother downstairs.

Mr. Radcliffe was standing in the doorway, having refused the invitation to come in for a cup of tea. He was a slightly shabby, kind-looking man with a receding hairline and rather soulful blue eyes, but he was cannier than he looked.

"Ah," he said, "little Heloise! But you are growing as fast as my own little girls. Soon you will be big Heloise! It is a pleasure to see you looking so well. Why, the child is positively blooming, madam. She must be a great comfort to you, as my children are to me."

"Ahem," said Heloise's godmother, studying her darkly.

"Good morning, sir," said Heloise, with a curtsy.

"I can't thank you enough for the work you do for the orphans, Miss Child – and you too, my dear," he added, nodding at Heloise. "We are trying to raise money for a new dormitory, you know. The current one is overcrowded and dilapidated beyond repair. Sometimes it seems that there are always too many orphans! However, all children are precious. Our orphans at Saint Suffering's will glad be of this warm clothing."

Heloise's pulse was still racing; even so, his words startled her. It had never occurred to her that anyone would consider all children precious. As if feeling her wondering gaze on his face, Mr. Radcliffe's eyes drifted towards hers. Heloise looked hurriedly at the floor, but Mr. Radcliffe said, "That reminds me. I have an invitation. My youngest daughter Lucy is having a birthday party and she would be very pleased if Heloise could attend. Lucy will send an invitation today, but she made me promise to mention it to you. The party will be at two o'clock on Saturday week. I do hope we can expect you. Now I must hurry off." He picked up the box of clothing Heloise's godmother had packed and trudged out to load it on the trap. "Good morning, Miss Child, Heloise!"

Heloise and her godmother stood in the doorway as he drove off. Curiously, Heloise felt sorry for him. She knew the party was out of the question and she did not like to think of him being hurt, even slightly, by the polite refusal she would have to write. For parties, of course, were yet another Waste of Time.

"Heloise, you are idle, and luncheon is almost upon us!" exclaimed her godmother. "I must start you on some new sewing this afternoon. In the meantime, you may copy out the first chapter of the *Book of Numbers* in your very best handwriting. You may start immediately. Make haste, child!"

Heloise went briskly up the stairs.

Anyway, she would rather not go to the party than have to go dressed in dirt brown or black. How all the girls would stare!

It was not until she was writing the last word of the first sentence of the first chapter of the *Book of Numbers* that she realized what had happened. Maria's cloak was gone. It had been scooped up by her godmother with the red flannel petticoat and the knitted stockings. Now it was on its way to Saint Suffering's Institute for Waifs and Strays at Bell Toll.

# Revelations

"*My dear Miss Radcliffe,*" wrote Heloise the following morning, to her godmother's dictation, as soon as the invitation arrived,

> *Thank you for the kind invitation to your*
> *birthday party. I must beg you, however, to*
> *excuse me from attending, as my godmother*
> *does not approve of parties. She considers them*
> *A Waste of Time.*
>
> > *Your humble servant,*
> > *Heloise Child*

Heloise had not slept a wink, and she was having great difficulty concealing her state of mind from her godmother.

She could see no possibility but that the game was up.

"If you cannot finish your meal," said her godmother at luncheon, "you must take a dose of belladonna and go to bed." This was not so very unreasonable, as Heloise had not been able to eat breakfast, either. "There can be no walk for you if you are sickening for something."

Her misery had been interpreted as illness. Heloise could not help but feel fortunate. And she was not averse to going to bed. She rather hoped she might die there.

Upstairs, she undressed and took her medicine. This was administered by Mrs. Moth, who somehow managed to convey the impression that it was the last office she was likely to perform for the child. Then, as Mrs. Moth departed in her usual clomping manner, Heloise got into bed. There she lay, on the cold mattress beneath the cold coverlet in the unaccustomed daylight, staring at the ceiling and wishing for Maria. She dare not retrieve her from her hiding place.

It was all over now, she was sure of it. Somebody at Saint Suffering's would find the cloak, and tell somebody else, who would tell somebody else, who would tell somebody else. The presence of an item of doll's clothing would be so remarkable that the report would come back, in some way or another, to her godmother. Then her godmother would put two and two together.

"What will I do if she takes you away?" whispered Heloise. She knew Maria could hear her, even from underneath the floorboard. After all, she had been listening to Heloise's

60

prayers since before Heloise had known she was there.

Tired and overwrought, Heloise fell into a fitful sleep. And in that sleep she dreamed.

In her dream she was holding Maria so tightly and so protectively that the doll's curved wooden arms were digging into Heloise's chest. Her godmother was standing over her, demanding that she surrender the doll. Heloise felt a terrible anguish, and then a curious swelling against the inside of her skin. Suddenly, big Heloise burst out of her prison, like Samson pushing aside the pillars in the temple. Her voice was so loud that when she opened her mouth and roared, her godmother crumbled into tiny pieces.

Heloise awoke with her nightgown drenched in perspiration.

Her dream frightened her. But now she was frightened of herself.

Despite everything, she had the oddest feeling that somehow, her godmother had more to fear from Heloise than Heloise had to fear from her.

That could not be true. Could it?

When – after a long afternoon spent alternately staring at the ceiling and sleeping, a long evening without supper, and a long night that was sleepless until the early hours of the morning – Heloise finally woke, she felt calmer. It was not that she felt more optimistic. It was just that, like a martyr waiting for her final hour, she felt reconciled to her fate.

When unobserved, she wept. When in company, she pretended to have a cold. And with Maria she did everything, said everything, as if it were being done and said for the last time.

"The Lord giveth, the Lord taketh away. Blessed be the name of the Lord," she kept thinking forlornly. Now she knew what Job was talking about in the Bible.

But as the days passed and nothing out of the ordinary happened, Heloise began to hope.

One morning, four or five days after the Vicar's visit, it occurred to her that a menial job like going through a new package of charitable clothing might be performed by one of the older orphans. If so, might not that older orphan spy the doll's cloak and slip it into the pocket of her pinafore? When nobody was watching, perhaps she would give it to a younger girl with a rag doll. (For surely rag dolls would be allowed?) And maybe no one would notice, or care, that an orphan's rag doll had a new cloak.

Or … what if one of the boy orphans saw it amongst the new clothes and sold it through the gate for extra food? She knew the food was meager in the orphanage and had heard of such transactions. Sometimes items of clothing went missing and, although the governors of the orphanage rarely found out who was responsible, they knew that was why.

Or … perhaps whoever opened the package would not think it all that remarkable that there should be doll's clothing in a donation of clothes.

"Oh, Maria," said Heloise, coming out of her daydream. "Perhaps, despite everything, all will be well."

One morning not long afterwards, Heloise was sitting in her room learning twenty spelling words. Or at least, that was what she was supposed to be doing. What she was really doing was staring into space.

She was to be tested by her godmother at lunchtime. But lunch was still half an hour away, and she had already tested herself on the words three times, and gotten twenty correct on each occasion.

Heloise was habitually diligent, but working any longer on her spelling would have been A Waste of Time. And that, after all, was a sin. So she sighed and glanced around, trying to think of something satisfying and legal to do. Finally her eyes lit upon the Bible. She paused for a moment, then drew it towards her.

Lately, she had begun to have some revolutionary thoughts.

What, she wondered, might be in the parts that had been stuck together?

In the last few days, as her anxiety over the cloak had begun to ebb, she had taken to turning that peculiar, disfigured, much-used volume over and around and upside down in her hands, trying to work out how she might go about undoing her godmother's work – without her godmother being able to tell.

For the censoring must have been her godmother's work. Heloise was now too wise to accept the idea that all books had big clumps stuck together, and other passages blacked out with ink. If these sections were not meant to be read, why print them in the first place?

Heloise glanced nervously at the doorway. Then she looked conspiratorially towards Maria, who was observing her silently and supportively from the gap between her workbasket and the wall. Then, she opened the book.

It had once been a handsome volume, black, leather bound, gilt-edged and sturdy. But the glue had made the book too heavy for its binding and, rendered fragile by constant use, the pages were beginning to come away from the spine. Towards the outer edges of the sealed sections, there were little curling gaps.

Heloise turned to a slim, glued-together clump that fell almost exactly in the middle. It had a particularly promising split in it. Very gently, Heloise eased it apart.

She was frightened of two things: tearing the pages, and damaging the book in such a way that it would be obvious that she had been tampering with it. And if she could not separate the pages without risking either of these things she did not intend to do it.

She did not really think she had any chance of success; if she had thought so she probably would not have been trying.

But when the clump suddenly began to open along the

split, to open further and further and quicker and quicker even though Heloise began to panic and would have stopped it if she could, it was as if she had no choice.

It would have been like trying to stop the blooming of a rose.

Heloise stared at her handiwork, frozen with horror.

What had she done? First the cloak, now this – surely she was born to trouble as the sparks fly upwards. She wanted to shut it again and push it away from her; she even began to think of how she might secretly make some glue – she knew the recipe, one part flour, three parts water – and seal it again.

But somehow, she couldn't take her eyes off this new page, or rather two new pages. It was as if there were two Heloises, the guilty, frightened one, and the one so desperate to read something new, to hear a new voice, to receive some communication from outside, that she would risk anything. The desperate Heloise won. Her trembling hands held the book open, her hungry eyes devoured each word, every sentence, and as she read she grew more and more astounded.

What she was reading was not a story or part of a story, a genealogy, a work of prophecy, or even a list of commandments or exhortations. It was poetry, like the Psalms. But not like the Psalms. For this poem was about one thing only, and that one thing was the last Heloise had expected to find there.

*"As an apple tree among the trees of the wood,"* read Heloise, *so is my beloved among young men.*

*With great delight I sat in his shadow,*
*and his fruit was sweet to my taste.*
*He brought me to the banqueting house*
*and his banner over me was love.*
*Sustain me with raisins,*
*refresh me with apples;*
*for I am sick with love!*
*O that his left hand were under my head,*
*and that his right hand embraced me!*

Heloise's mind was certainly being broadened now.

Love! Love was in the Bible!

What was it doing there?

Until this moment Heloise had known of only two kinds of love: the love between a mother and her child, and the love of a lonely child for her doll. But she recognized this as a third kind – at once different and the same, like another shining tributary running out of the one glorious river.

And she knew something else, too. It was so obvious to her she didn't have to think about it.

This was not the only place in the Bible where love was to be found. Love was the subject of every act of censorship her godmother had perpetrated on it. Hiding amongst every glued-together clump of pages, beneath every impenetrable inking out, was the thing that in all the world Heloise was most interested in. That was what the censorship was about.

Were there only three kinds of love, thought Heloise

wildly as she read and read and read, or were there yet more?

"*There are more,*" said Maria immediately, but Heloise couldn't afford to stop reading and look at her.

"*Set me as a seal upon your heart,*" she was reading breathlessly,

> *as a seal upon your arm;*
> *for love is strong as death,*
> *jealousy is cruel as the grave.*
> *Its flashes are flashes of fire,*
> *a most vehement flame.*
>
> *Many waters cannot quench love,*
> *neither can floods drown it.*
> *If a man offered for love*
> *all the wealth of his house,*
> *he would be laughed to scorn.*

The letters were swimming together, and at first Heloise could not understand why the page had become illegible. Then she realized that her eyes had filled with tears.

"Heloise? What are you doing?"

Heloise's head spun around.

Her godmother was standing in the doorway.

Heloise must have been so taken up in The Song of Solomon that she did not hear her come up the stairs.

It was the very first time she had ever been caught. Strangely, it was almost a relief. But Heloise did not lose her self-possession. She knew instinctively that all was not yet lost. She simply said, "Reading the Bible, Godmother."

"There are tears in your eyes," her godmother observed.

Heloise said nothing.

"Why are there tears in your eyes?"

Heloise cleared her throat.

"Because the passage I was reading is so beautiful," she said.

Heloise's godmother stared at her.

"Lower your voice when you speak," she said after a moment. Then, oddly, she asked, "What did you say?"

Heloise swallowed. Her chin rose slightly, with just the faintest air of defiance.

"The verses I was reading," she explained quietly, "were so beautiful that tears came into my eyes."

"You are raising your voice again," said her godmother. Then she asked, "What passage are you referring to?"

There was no help for it. Heloise slid the Bible along the desk towards her godmother, a finger marking the verses.

"It was the part about the man trying to buy love," she said, "and how, even though he offered everything he had, nobody wanted to sell."

Heloise waited. She had not given up. Instead she watched her godmother like a mouse watching a cat, a mouse who knew she could run pretty fast if she had to.

Heloise's godmother scanned the passage. Then, very

subtly, she flicked her finger along the edge of the page, as if to see what came before it. On either side, however, the pages were sealed, as she quickly noted. Her face was impassive, and yet, there was something in her eyes, a kind of strange, sad, calm acceptance, like one on trial who begins to perceive that the verdict is going against her.

"You are wrong to say those verses are beautiful," she said, in a faintly subdued manner. "Scripture is not beautiful. Beauty is a worldly thing. Scripture is *true*."

"Yes, Godmother," said Heloise immediately.

Then she began to breathe again.

It took a moment for her to realize that she was not in trouble.

It took another moment for her to understand why.

When she did, her mind began to work quickly. Her godmother was in an awkward position. After all, to question the accessibility of the pages Heloise had shown her would be tantamount to admitting that she had censored them. She must surely know that Heloise had been tampering with them, and she must know that Heloise knew she had been the censor, and yet … Suddenly, Heloise realized that she had the advantage over her godmother. The knowledge brought out something reckless, even ruthless, in her. "Who dares wins," thought Heloise, although she knew that didn't come from the Bible.

"Godmother," she said, "love is in the Bible."

Her godmother did not answer.

"Godmother?" Heloise repeated. She sounded like an informant. "*Love* is in the Bible!"

Her godmother turned to leave the room. She seemed to be ignoring Heloise's peculiar announcement. But before she reached the door she said: "Not all of Scripture is intended for the likes of us, Heloise. *Much of it is too merciful.*"

Heloise stared after her.

She stared and stared at the empty doorway, thinking, and yet not thinking.

Long after her godmother had gone, she whispered, as if the conversation had not yet ceased, "The likes of us?"

A few days later, when Heloise and her godmother and Mrs. Moth passed the church on their Sunday afternoon walk, they attracted the notice of the Vicar, who was shaking the hand of the last member of his congregation for Evensong. He waved and hurried towards them down the hillock. He had a pile of books and notes in his arms. His cassock and surplice flew out behind him like wings.

"Afternoon, Miss Child, Mrs. Moth," the Vicar called out on his way down. "Out on your customary constitutional, I see."

Heloise's godmother gazed absently at him through her beautiful eyes. Mrs. Moth grunted. Heloise stared at a beetle climbing a blade of grass at her feet.

Arriving at the roadside, the Vicar smiled at them benignly, then said to Heloise, "I was sorry that you were unable to attend Lucy's party, my dear. Another time, perhaps."

Heloise ducked her head; Mrs. Moth looked suspiciously at him; Heloise's godmother appeared sublimely neutral, almost as if she was thinking about something else.

There was a brief silence.

Heloise's godmother was about to bid him a polite good evening when he slapped his forehead and exclaimed, "Dear me! I almost forgot my purpose in detaining you. I have something here I think you will be very pleased to see …"

He reached into a pocket beneath his surplice and for a moment Heloise wondered what on earth he could be about to produce.

Then he handed her Maria's cloak.

"There!" he said. "I'll warrant you've been wondering where this got to!" With another benign smile and a bright "Good afternoon, ladies!", he hurried back up the hill to the Vicarage.

# Heloise's Sins Catch Up With Her

Seeing what the Vicar had produced, and seeing the unmistakable recognition on Heloise's face, Heloise's godmother had gone so deathly pale that Mrs. Moth – not usually in the habit of swift action – had grabbed her around the waist.

For Heloise, the sunny autumn afternoon had seemed to turn upside down. She could not work out whether she had turned upside down with it, or whether she was the only one in the world who was the right way up.

"I'm all right. I'm all right," her godmother gasped, shaking herself free from Mrs. Moth's grasp. She stared at Heloise as if trying to digest a new reality. Heloise stared back, for all the world like a trapped animal, clutching the cloak against her breast. Then her godmother grabbed her by the hand, turned on her heel and set off marching towards home, leaving various members of the departing congregation staring after them.

Her godmother was moving at such a pace that Heloise had to run and stumble to keep up. Mrs. Moth, puffing and panting, began to drop behind. Finally the older woman stopped and leaned on a fence post to catch her breath. Heloise and her godmother marched on. Heloise could hardly recall her godmother holding her hand before. Now, even in the midst of this turmoil, she found herself distracted by how cold and hard her grip was. Soon she was so close to exhaustion that she could hardly think at all.

When they reached the cottage, Heloise's godmother yanked open the door, letting it bang against the wall. Without slackening her pace, she dragged Heloise down the hall and up the stairs to her room. Then, panting, she wheeled on her.

"*Where is it?*" she asked.

Gasping for breath, Heloise sank to the floor.

"Where is it?" her godmother repeated.

Heloise looked up at her. Her godmother was tall, and her hair had come down. Heloise had never seen her with her hair around her face before. She looked young and fierce and beautiful, like the angel with the flaming sword guarding the gate of paradise. But Heloise was silent.

Heloise's godmother began to pace the floor.

"I might have known," she muttered to herself. "I might

have known. Blood will out!"

Then she stopped and stared at Heloise, her green eyes burning in her flushed face.

"You don't understand, do you? You don't know what's at stake!"

Heloise gazed at her dumbly. Suddenly her godmother reached down and pulled her up sharply by the arm.

"Come!" she said. "I can protect you no longer. It is time you knew."

They clattered back down the stairs, Heloise stumbling and bruising herself, dragged roughly by her godmother. Dimly she was aware of Mrs. Moth limping heavily into the house through the open door and shutting it behind her. But her godmother showed no such awareness. She paused at the hook in the hallway where all the keys were kept and chose one. Then she dragged Heloise back up the hallway, pushing past Mrs. Moth as if she had not seen her. Once outside, she pulled Heloise along the short dirt driveway towards the museum.

Until this moment, Heloise had not fully grasped what was happening. Now she was genuinely terrified.

She tried to sit on the ground.

"No!" she shrieked.

"How else can I make you understand?" asked her godmother, pulling the child up with a vicious yank that almost caused her to overbalance. But she kept herself upright and managed to drag Heloise the short distance to the museum. She unlocked the front door and pushed the sobbing Heloise inside. For one horrified moment Heloise thought she intended to lock her in; but no, her godmother was the guide, and she did not intend to desert her post.

"Be quiet!" she said, and there was such authority in her voice that Heloise could not help but obey. "Look around you! What do you see?"

Still sobbing quietly, in little catches of breath, Heloise took a trembling step forward, then another, and looked around her.

Then she looked again, more slowly.

What she saw could hardly have surprised her more.

"Well?" said her godmother.

Heloise looked back at her in shock and wonder.

"Dolls," she whispered.

# The Museum of Mary Child

They were standing in the entrance hall of a simple, modest, old-fashioned house. The hall opened onto a front room with a fireplace, several armchairs and a chaise lounge, a piano and a harp, a writing desk, and a small table on which stood a delicate china vase. The wall opposite the fireplace was covered with bookshelves. On the boarded floor beneath the furniture lay a large, circular Turkish carpet. The curtains on the windows were drawn back to reveal the dark green shrubbery in the garden outside.

The room would have been pleasant and unexceptional if not for two things: firstly, it had an indefinable air of being frozen in time, as if it had not been tampered with since its last residents had departed many years ago. The other thing was far more dramatic. For it was as Heloise had said. The room was filled with dolls.

There were so many of them. And they were all the same – rag dolls of calico now grey with age, their woolen hair long and faded yellow, stuffed with scraps and clothed in the fashion of another day, with what appeared to be leftovers from family dressmaking. But even stranger than this: each doll was stationed by some kind of hole or opening. Some of these were unsurprising – the fireplace, for example, or an open cupboard – but it was clear that most had been excavated and positioned in such a manner as to make plain what had been one doll or another's hiding place. The room was honeycombed with these cavities – a square hole in the wall here, an incision in the stuffing of the chaise lounge there, four or five leather-bound books pulled out from their place on the shelf over there – and yes, in a dark corner near the library, a pulled-up floorboard like the one in Heloise's room.

Heloise stared at it without breathing.

"Come, come!" said Heloise's godmother. "There is more!"

Through the hallways, in each room, up the stairs, throughout the bedrooms, the dolls sat like sentries beside their hiding places. It was as if the secret police in some long ago reign of terror had raided the house, dragged out its fugitives, killed them, and left their bodies there as a warning to all.

"And let us not forget the garden!" cried Heloise's godmother.

She dragged the child down the stairs, along the hall, and out into the back garden, which proved to be pockmarked with little open graves, the damp earth black against the green grass. And beside each of these holes lay a doll.

"There are scores of them, Heloise," said her godmother, close to her ear, and all at once she sounded almost calm. "And perhaps, even now, not all of them have been found. To be sure of that we would have to destroy the entire house and garden. But still you do not understand. You have not yet looked closely enough. Go and pick one up, if you dare."

Like one in a dream, Heloise approached a doll. She did not want to look, and yet once she had seen what her godmother was talking about, it was hard to drag her eyes away.

But she could not pick it up.

"Come back inside, then," said her godmother. "Look at them all."

Heloise walked slowly through the house, looking at doll after doll. She was still sobbing quietly, as if she had forgotten to stop, and it seemed as if this was the only sound throughout all the halls and rooms and stairways of that long-abandoned house.

It was true. They were all the same.

But not merely because they were all homemade calico dolls. And not just because they all had faded-yellow woolen hair.

It was their faces that made them unique.

From the moment she first caught sight of them Heloise had known that there was something wrong, something even stranger and more disturbing than their number or the fact that they had been concealed, and then dug up. But it was as if something protective in her mind had stopped her from really seeing it.

Now, as her mind began to grasp the truth, she could no longer stop herself from seeing.

The fact was that none of the dolls had a face. Where each doll's face should have been, there was only a frenzy of tiny black stitches, sewn so tight and so close that the dolls appeared to be wearing iron masks.

Heloise's godmother followed her quietly around the house.

"She sat for hour after hour," she said, "as cool as a cucumber, first making the dolls, then sewing over their faces. The only thing that upset her was running out of material. Then, if she wasn't given more calico, more scraps, more wool, she would take to cutting her arms and legs with the embroidery scissors. At first she made the dolls and hid them only when no one was watching. She must have done much of her work in the dead of night, though no one really knew how she'd managed it. Later she abandoned secrecy, as if she had forgotten the need for it. When her mother noticed what she was doing and asked her about it, she seemed unable either to hear the question or to reply. Before long she did not even notice the family watching her as she worked. Finally there

79

came a time when she was incapable of any other activity. She grew thin and ill; and yet, Heloise, she seemed strangely happy, as if her work satisfied her in the deepest possible way …

"They took her away, to an asylum. Do you know what that is? It's a place for mad people. There they took away her calico and her scraps and her embroidery scissors, and there, without them, at the age of thirteen, she died within the year.

"That, Heloise, was Mary Child, and this museum, the museum of her madness, has fed and clothed you all your life."

Suddenly she gripped the child roughly by the shoulders and stared into her frightened eyes.

"Now do you see why you must never, ever play with dolls? Now do you see why you must keep yourself occupied, with useful, charitable work, study your Bible – the parts of it that apply to you – and strive with all your heart to control your imagination?"

"But why should that happen to me?" pleaded Heloise. "There must be thousands of girls with dolls. They can't all be mad! The Vicar's daughters –"

"*Lower your voice!*" hissed her godmother. "Don't you realize that every time you speak with such passion it is the madness in you that speaks? Heloise," she continued steadily, and yet with the utmost bleakness, "thousands of girls, much less the Vicar's daughters, do not have your pedigree. Mary Child is no stranger to you. She was my sister. And – she was your mother."

# No

In her room, Heloise stood limply, head bowed, shoulders drooping, hands dangling by her sides. She looked like a marionette that had been forgotten after a puppet show. The door was shut. And she was staring absently at the narrow line of light under it. As usual, from their secret vantage points, the mice of the house were observing her.

More than half an hour ago, her godmother – the woman she now knew to be her aunt – had dragged her to the cottage, locked her in her room and told her that if she did not surrender the doll (whose existence she took for granted) by morning, the room would be torn apart until it was found.

Heloise glanced at the floorboard under which Maria was lying in darkness, waiting. Then she lay on the floor, curled herself around Maria's strange little grave, and began to weep.

She wept and wept, for there was a lifetime of weeping in her. For once it did not matter if she was heard, as she couldn't be in worse trouble than she was now. There was nothing her godmother could do that was worse than taking Maria away.

And so she did not weep over the horror that was The Museum of Mary Child. She did not weep over the tragedy that had been her mother's life. These were bad enough, it was true, but they were the past, and, as far as Heloise knew, they could not be remedied. It was the present she wept over, for it had not yet been blighted, and thus it was infinitely vulnerable.

In a little while, her friendship with Maria would be no more, for it seemed to Heloise that she had no choice but to surrender the doll.

Every second this terrible event came nearer and nearer and she seemed helpless to prevent it.

When she had no more tears left in her, she whispered, "Oh, Maria, what's to be done?"

For a long moment the room was terribly still. Heloise found herself listening to the sudden, deep silence that followed her weeping.

Then a strange thing happened.

She heard, inside her head, a voice, a beautiful voice, neither too loud, nor too soft, but as clear and translucent as air or water. And the voice said:

"*Is your godmother right?*"

Heloise sat up. As soon as she moved she realized she had

a searing headache. There was still clean water from the pump left in her wash jug; without thinking Heloise crawled over to the washstand, pulled the large china jug towards her, and drank, thirstily and awkwardly, from the rim. Then, the front of her black Sunday dress rather damp, she came back slowly and sat on the floor.

She stared at the loose floorboard. Then she closed her eyes.

*Is my godmother right?*

"No," she answered.

And although her head ached and her eyes burned and she was cold to the bone, she thought it was the most beautiful word that had ever been uttered.

For it was true. Her godmother was not right. Her godmother was wrong.

Heloise stared at the coverlet on the bed, which was as white as snow.

Yes, Mary Child had played with dolls – if what she had done with them could be called playing. And yes, Mary Child had gone mad.

But Mary Child was not Heloise. And Mary Child's dolls were not Maria.

"No," Heloise whispered again.

Maria was good and kind. All of Heloise's heart and mind and soul cried out that this was so. And the love Heloise had learned because of Maria – that was good and kind, too. How could it be otherwise?

Poor Mary Child and her dolls had nothing to do with

goodness and kindness. And they had nothing to do with love.

At that point Heloise understood something.

For so long she had wanted to know what love was. Now, because of Maria, she knew. But since she had seen The Museum of Mary Child she had also learned the meaning of another word.

It was hate.

Heloise rose from the floor to her knees, and pressed her aching head into the coverlet. She was trying to understand something. One could not hate a doll. Could one? What, after all, could a doll do to one to make one hate it? Nothing. So where did all this hatred come from? Who did Mary Child hate?

And immediately, instinctively, Heloise knew.

Mary Child hated herself.

But even that was not the most frightening thing. The most frightening thing was her godmother's hatred of Mary Child. For she did hate and fear Mary Child, even though she was her sister and Heloise's mother, and even though she was dead.

Slowly, Heloise raised her head and gazed through the window.

All her life she had lived next door to, had been fed and clothed by, a Museum of Hate.

It was a museum preserving the hatred of Mary Child for herself, kept up by a woman who hated Mary Child.

Outside, the sun was setting. When it was dark she would have no candle. It was this thought, somehow, which made up her mind.

She sat on the floor and pulled up Maria's board. Maria's calm face seemed to have its own light shining on it, like the moon reflecting the light of the sun. Heloise scooped her out, and replaced the board carefully.

"We must pretend the house is on fire," she whispered, smoothing the doll's beautiful carved hair. "It will be as we planned. I will tie you to my back with my nightgown, and together we will climb down the tree. Then we will travel far, far away, never to return. We will find somewhere safe to live, and she will not destroy you. If she wants to destroy you, she will have to destroy me first."

# Behold the Birds

"Heloise! Heloise!"

Outside Heloise's window grew a beautiful tree, with strong, climbable branches. At the tail end of autumn, its leaves were red and gold, but only during the day. At night, when the moon rose, they were black and silver and pewter grey.

It was into this tree that the members of The Society of the Caged Birds of the City descended at something like midnight. Heloise was asleep.

She had done exactly as she had planned. Fetching her nightgown, she had unbuttoned it and carefully slipped Maria into the open front. Then she had buttoned her in so that her head poked out of the neck, folded up the skirt until it became an envelope under the doll's cage-like base, tied the sleeves around her neck and the folded-up hem under her arms and ended up with an arrangement reminiscent of a Japanese lady with a baby attached to her kimono. She had thought about bringing her pelisse for she knew the night would be cold, but she worried that it would interfere with her climbing. Her long skirt was awkward enough. Besides, she was reluctant to take more from her godmother than the clothes she was standing up in. Then she had waited. She could not safely depart until the women retired to bed.

But the day had been a hard one, and Heloise was hungry and exhausted. Before long she was asleep.

In her dream, she was feeling her way along a passage which seemed to be underground and which would have been completely dark were it not for a dim light way, way ahead, towards which she traveled with a heart full of the keenest longing …

"Heloise!"

She thought it was part of the dream: that shrill, whistly voice so close to her ear, the scratchy feet on her head.

But she was dreaming no longer.

"Wake up, Heloise! Time is short!"

Heloise came to herself with a start. Her room was dark. There was something on her head. And she could hear a faint, murmuring, tweeting, rustling sound from outside her window. Still confused, she walked over to it, passing her hand lightly over her head as she did so, as if to brush away a twig or an insect. She felt her hand meet with something small and warm and feathery, then heard a faint breezy slapping sound in the air immediately above her head.

"Steady on!" the whistly voice said mildly.

"I beg your pardon," Heloise said without thinking.

And, all at once, she understood that the tree outside her window was filled with birds.

"Climb down the tree," said a tiny voice.

"It will hold you," said another.

"But kilt up your skirt first!" said a third.

"When you get to the bottom, we will show you the way," added the first voice.

What time was it? Heloise had no idea. Were the women asleep yet? She had not heard her godmother come up the stairs, but then she had not been awake. A little dazed, she moved back into the room, thinking she would listen by her door for signs of activity. But before she had taken two steps, she heard the voice in her ear again.

"The ladies are asleep," it said. "We looked in their windows."

The bird who had spoken to her first had re-alighted on her shoulder.

Heloise reassured herself that Maria was still fastened securely to her back. Then she moved towards the window, knelt on the window seat and pushed on the casement. It opened outwards. If she stood on the windowsill, the trunk of the tree and a foothold on the nearest branch was one large step away. In between the window and the tree trunk was a sheer drop to the ground. It was perhaps lucky that it was too dark to see the distance.

Heloise began to kilt up her skirt by tucking it into her drawers. Then she leaned out the window and felt the trunk with her hands. She ran her hands downwards to the branch. The damp night air clung to her and filled her nostrils. She began to feel very awake in a strange, dreamlike way. Holding onto the window frame with both hands, she stood on the windowsill and felt out into the darkness for the fork of the tree with her foot. She placed a little of her weight on it. It seemed secure. Then, keeping hold of the windowsill with one hand, she placed the other arm around the tree trunk.

"Now, just one big step! But hold on tight!" said her bird friend, in her ear.

The next moment, Heloise was clinging to the trunk with both feet in the fork of the tree.

She felt strangely, giddily, free, almost as if she were flying.

Now it was a matter of feeling her way, foothold by foothold, down the tree.

"Don't be afraid, Heloise!" said a bird.

"Just be careful!" said another.

"Very careful," said a third.

Holding on tight, Heloise felt her way down the tree. The trunk was rougher than anything she had ever felt before, and yet it seemed friendly. All around her, on every branch or twig, or so it seemed, were the tiny stirrings and tweetings of a hundred birds. The tree was alive with them.

Heloise could see very little, as the tree with its many leaves and branches was filled with shadow. And yet, every so often, as she found a new foothold or slid a little further down, she saw a flash of tiny wings as they caught the light. For the birds, one here, one there, with a series of little jumps or a brief flight, were moving with her.

"Well done, Heloise!"

"You're almost there!"

"Anyone would think you had grown up in a tree!"

Meanwhile the bird who had spoken first stayed perched like a sentinel on her shoulder. Heloise had not exchanged a word with him, and yet she was beginning to feel as if she knew him well.

"It is only a few feet to the ground now," he murmured.

Heloise slid jerkily to the ground. She landed safely, but her palms stung. She shook them and gazed up at the sky. The moon was absolutely full, as lovely as a princess, and the air was fresh and cold.

"Now you must walk," said the bird friend, in her ear.

"Do not be afraid. We will all stay with you."

Heloise made certain once more that Maria was all right. Then she walked down the driveway to the road. And before she could even begin to hesitate –

"This way!"

"This way!"

"This way!" said the voices of many birds. In the moonlight she saw some flying ahead, some alighting on fence posts or in trees, while others perched on her head or hands.

Turning the opposite direction to the one she usually went with her godmother or Mrs. Moth, Heloise set out.

Heloise walked and walked. Fortunately, she was used to long walks, and did not tire easily. It would have helped if she had eaten. It would have been more pleasant if the night had not been so brisk, or if she had been able to wear her pelisse. But if there was anything Heloise understood it was putting up with one thing in order to achieve another. So she swallowed her hunger, ignored the cold, and walked and walked.

And as she walked along the muddy, potholed road which led to the City, past silent moonlit fields and farmhouses and dark spreading trees, past dogs barking forlornly into the night, past the dark masses of sleeping horses and cows, and slinking cats who came out to stare and wonder where she was off to, as she walked and walked, her state of mind became dreamlike and simple. It was as if the many things – both terrible and good – had become one, and as if that one thing was a single desire. And it seemed that following this desire was nothing more complicated than walking this road, no matter how hard it was, no matter how long it went on, no matter how many pairs of shoes, or feet, or how many lives she wore out walking it.

So on she walked, drawn forward by an invisible thread

that had attached itself to her heart.

And the little birds journeyed with her.

Some talked to her. Some sang. (And many a sleeping farmer, or his wife or child, heard passing birdsong in their dreams.) Those who talked avoided the subject of Heloise's recent experiences, although, through their vast network of mice, they were well acquainted with them. Instead, they told her the history of The Society of the Caged Birds of the City.

They told her of the Founding Birds – the first members of the first society, who were long dead, but whose names were scratched inside the hole in their Sacred Tree.

They told her how, although caged birds do not live long, they lived long enough to do more than their share of good, and that when it came time for them to die, they passed their work on to new birds. It was as if the Society were a long relay race. The participants ran for a while, then passed the baton to another. Runner after runner dropped out, having done his or her best; the race went on.

They told her stories of some of their happiest achievements – sometimes little kindnesses, sometimes great missions, like the present one.

Above all, they told her how, although confined to their cages, they had another life in which they had fellowship with other birds and were free. And they told her that, if ever she was in trouble, she need only tell any caged bird, no matter how frail or frivolous it looked,  no matter how trivial or twee, and soon something would be done.

As the darkest hours passed and the dawn grew near, the road began to get busier. Heloise was passed by carts full of cabbages and cheeses and sooty black coal, and farmers driving animals they wished to sell at the market. The birds, aware that they should not draw attention to themselves, made sure to conceal themselves within hedgerows and the dense branches of trees as they traveled.

"Look, Heloise!" said the bird on her shoulder presently, and when Heloise looked up she saw that she was on the crest of a hill. From here she could see the City, with its great Cathedral and Houses of Parliament, pink and grey in the sunrise, while the road between was so obscured in darkness that it almost seemed not to exist.

She gasped with astonishment. She had heard of cities – the City of David, for example – but she had never seen one. This one was –

"Beautiful," she whispered, dazed.

But there was no time to stand gaping.

"Make haste, Heloise," urged her bird companion, "for you have almost reached your goal, and we birds must be back in our cages at dawn!"

So Heloise trudged on. It seemed that in this last stage of the journey she must have slept on her feet, for afterwards she could not remember entering the City. But enter it she did, through an ancient stone gate. The birds guided her down cobbled street after cobbled street, past tall, narrow houses and shops with latticed windows, past markets where the vendors were already setting up their stalls and across one of the many bridges that had been built across the river that ran through the center of the City. And her special friend, the bird on her shoulder, whispered constant encouragement.

"Not long now," came his warm little voice in her ear. "There are but four and twenty steps to go …"

At length they came to a church in a quiet cul-de-sac. The tiny stone building had a wooden stairway and a portico sheltering its entrance; here, abruptly, with a whistling and a breeze and a slapping of many wings, they left her.

"Goodbye, Heloise!" she heard many twittering bird voices calling amongst the faint, feathery sounds of their ascent. "All will be well! All will be well!"

Her bird friend was fluttering around her; automatically, she raised a finger for him to perch on. And it was only then that she saw him for the first time.

"Your feathers," she said dreamily, "are exactly the color of Maria's gown … " For he was a sky-blue budgerigar.

"My name is Merryfeathers," he said to her gravely. "Our leader, Mrs. Schumann, a venerable white canary who is too old and frail to fly long distances, has given you especially into my care. You will be discovered here before long," he added in some haste, although his tenderness was no less apparent. "You will soon be amongst friends. And one day, when it is time, I will come for you again. Until then, God speed, little Heloise!"

He regarded her through his bright black eyes with

his speckled sky-blue head inclined. Then he rubbed his forehead against the underside of her chin, made a chirrup in his throat, took to the air with a shove of his cold feet, and fluttered away. In a moment he was lost amongst the buildings.

Heloise stared after him into the forest of rooftops, so strange, even fantastic, to her country-bred eyes. Then, trying to gather her wits, she looked around her. She was so tired that the bare wood shelter of the church portico looked warm and inviting. She felt she must lie down or die. But she had not forgotten the reason she had run away, and the morning light made her less safe than she had been in the darkness. Her hands clumsy with exhaustion, she pulled Maria carefully from her back, concealed her well within her nightgown, and tied the nightgown into a kind of sack. Then, holding her burden tightly in her arms, she curled up on the top step, at the base of a column.

She did not immediately fall asleep. In her heart, as she lay there longing for peace, some kind of rest – some kind of home – there was an almost unbearable ache. The pain was so bad she found herself writhing with it.

"Oh, Maria," she whispered to the warm, carved wooden creature in her arms. "How can I bear it? How can I bear her suffering? Poor, poor Mary Child. Could nothing have been done to help her?"

Gently, soothingly, sleep settled on her like a mother bird returning to her nest.

When next she opened her eyes, she found herself staring into the face of an old woman.

"Can you sing, child?" the old woman asked.

# Old Mother's Twelve-Voice Choir of Female Orphans, Waifs and Strays

At the very moment Heloise had fallen asleep, some twenty feet below her a door had shut.

The person who had shut it was an old woman. Between her and Heloise there was a small cobbled courtyard and a steep stone staircase. The old woman, having locked the door, crossed the first and, somewhat laboriously, climbed the second. She had a sharp, worn face with a sharp, worn nose, and she wore a sparrow-grey blanket over her head. One of her hands clutched the blanket snugly around her; the other held a large, empty, wicker basket. The old woman was short and plump and bent, and had a curious, rolling gait, seeming almost to limp a little. As she climbed the steps, she scratched herself in a way that recalled a hen scratching in a farmyard.

Reaching the top of the stairs, she passed the church

without looking at it, and so she did not see the vagrant Heloise sleeping inside the porch. She was on her way to the baker's shop and, as always, was listening to a continual stream of music that was playing spontaneously in her head. This morning it was the Glamroch Cantata No 78, a great and perennial favorite.

*Blessed are they that mourn*
*For they shall be comforted*

sang the perfect imaginary soprano and the perfect imaginary mezzo-soprano in the old woman's head as she limped along in waltz time.

"Morning, Old Mother," said the baker, as she entered his shop, just a few doors down from the church. "Brisk, this morning, ain't it? Winter 'round the corner. And how was the wedding? Not a dry eye in the church, I suppose?"

Old Mother – for that was how she was always addressed by those who knew her – peered at the baker in a manner that was at once friendly and irritable, as if, despite her charitable feelings towards him, she found it hard to understand why anyone would talk over such beautiful music. She was generally thought to be a little touched, although harmless, and quite a genius musically.

"The bride was beautiful, Mr. Lahooray," she said rather loudly, talking, of course, over the music in her head. "He's lucky to have her, despite it being such a good match for her, being an orphan, you understand, with no family. And the singing was first-rate, even if I do say so myself."

"What did you sing, Old Mother?" asked Mrs. Lahooray, popping her head around the door. She was flushed from the baking, although her hair was tucked neatly under a clean, white cap.

"We sang, among several old favorites, a new work by the organist, Mr. Callardin-Bowser," said Old Mother. "It is called, 'Many Waters Cannot Quench Love.'"

"Oh," said Mrs. Lahooray, impressed.

"But you're one down now she's gone off and got married, aren't you?"asked Mr. Lahooray, counting out a dozen small loaves. "Where will you find a new chorister?"

"Oh, don't you worry about that, Mr. Lahooray," said Old Mother, with supreme confidence. "She will turn up."

When, on her way back from the baker's shop, Old Mother noticed Heloise sleeping under the portico, the music in her head suddenly stopped.

Truth be told, she did not at first understand what she was seeing. In fact, for a moment she thought someone had left a large china doll lying there. It was rather an eerie thought. When she blinked and realized it was a child, she beamed.

"Well, and look at that," she said. "She has turned up already."

She paused briefly. Then, with the air of a ship at full sail, she changed course from nor' to nor'-east, and headed up the twelve steps to the church door. There she bent down, awkwardly and with some creaking of bones, to examine the sleeping child. After peering into her face, she asked her momentous question.

Heloise opened her eyes.

Old Mother saw a porcelain-skinned, black-haired child with eyes like twin green fires, dressed like an orphan and holding, close to her chest, a small, white bundle as if it was the most precious thing in the world.

Heloise saw Old Mother.

Could she sing?

It was a question Heloise had never considered before. Heloise opened her mouth to answer it and, to her surprise, her answer came out as a whisper:

"I don't know."

For – despite the fact that she was engaged in a full scale rebellion against her – her godmother's words about the madness in her leaking out through her voice had struck home. Somewhere between the caretaker's cottage and the church portico, some part of her had resolved never to speak at full voice again.

Old Mother went on looking at her, as if Heloise had not answered, or as if she herself had never asked the question.

"Are you hungry?" she asked presently.

"Yes," whispered Heloise.

"Then come along," said Old Mother, and she set off purposefully, without looking back to see if Heloise was following.

Heloise was rather afraid of losing her. Though she was stiff with cold, she got up hurriedly and, clutching the white bundle that was Maria, followed.

Down the staircase and into the courtyard sailed Old Mother with Heloise in her wake. Everywhere she looked, Heloise saw arches, stones crumbling with age, and dark-green ivy growing on them. In fact, she was looking at an ancient monastery, but she could not have known that. In a corner of the courtyard was a birdbath with a statue of a saint in the center of it, but no sparrows twittered around it, for the water had acquired a thin sheet of ice overnight. Heloise had never seen a birdbath, a statue, a monastery or even a monk. She thought the sculpture was a doll, and its presence was so odd to her that she was half-convinced she was dreaming.

Old Mother took a large bunch of keys out of her basket, chose one, and opened a door in a wall that was covered with ivy. It was the door she had shut behind her as Heloise had fallen asleep.

"Well, come in," she said.

Heloise stepped inside.

She found herself in a cool, quiet, airy room, large and long and narrow, like a dormitory or a refectory. The room was dominated by a long wooden table, which was bare and scrubbed clean. The wall that contained the door through which they had entered was filled with windows; they were big and arched but so overgrown with ivy on the outside that not much could be seen through them, except leaves. Higher up, in the slanted ceiling many feet above their heads, narrow lancet windows let the grey light in. The wall opposite the door was covered with pictures, which seemed to depict brightly colored scenes from the Bible. Heloise had never seen a picture, let alone a wall covered with them. For a moment she had the bizarre impression that she was looking through another set of windows, into biblical stories that were taking place before her very eyes. Then she realized that the angels running up and down Jacob's ladder were not moving. It must be a special kind of embroidery, she thought wonderingly.

In a far corner stood a squat black cooking stove, and the end wall had wooden shelves with crockery and cooking utensils stacked neatly on them. Heloise could see a small, shadowy pantry through one door, and a much larger, darker room through another. All was silent, and yet at some level Heloise understood that the silence was not really empty, but pregnant with something she could not have named.

"Sit down," said Old Mother. As Heloise sat at one end of the nearest of the two long benches that lay along either side of the table, Old Mother reached inside her basket and produced a small loaf of bread. She handed it to Heloise.

Heloise began to eat immediately, staring at Old Mother with wide, grateful eyes. She knew she was not being what her godmother would consider polite, but something in Old Mother's singular manner seemed to discourage anything that might resemble a pointless nicety. Meanwhile Old Mother disappeared into the pantry. Heloise heard the squeaky hinge of a trapdoor being opened, and cautious steps as the old woman climbed down into the cellar. Presently, having climbed back up the stairs and lowered the door closed again, she reappeared with a large pewter cup full of milk. She placed this on the table before Heloise. Then she busied herself, putting away the shopping.

After a few bustling moments, though not before Heloise had wolfed down the loaf and drained the cup of milk, Old Mother took up a handbell and rang it expertly three times.

Heloise jumped. She stared wide-eyed at Old Mother. But the eccentric lady took no notice, as if she was already so accustomed to Heloise's presence that she found nothing remarkable in it. Anyway, somewhat to Old Mother's relief, the music in her head had resumed. She was now listening to the Kyrie from the Glamroch *Missa Brevis* in C.

Then came a surprise that was not a surprise, for Heloise had already half-guessed it. There was a pause, and then a stirring, and a rustling, and a murmur of sleepy chatter from the shadowy room next door. Then Heloise heard the sound of bare feet padding on boards, the sound of water being poured, and splashed on hands and faces. Then there was the sound of things being moved, drawers being opened, cupboards being closed, of things being taken off, and put on, and taken out, and put away. Finally, in dribs and drabs, buttoning up buttons and braiding hair, one young girl after another came yawning and stretching into the room.

"Good morning, Old Mother!" each of them cried as she entered.

It was just as Heloise had thought. The silence of the room next door was not the silence of emptiness. It was the silence of eleven girls sleeping.

And now they had awakened.

Heloise gazed at them, agog. She had never seen so many girls at the one time.

To her unaccustomed eye there appeared to be every variety of girl available on earth. The oldest ones, Heloise noted with awe, were almost women; the youngest not much older than Heloise – and there were middling ones, too, twelve and thirteen and fourteen-year-olds. Some were tall and willowy, some plump and capable-looking, some dark, some fair, and one with deeply red hair (Heloise was to find out that her name was Nan). The three youngest ones, Heloise noticed with astonishment, were each clutching a kitten. The girls were dressed simply, as was the fashion, and yet becomingly and individually, in colors that suited them. Thus they made a varied picture, like a posy of spring flowers.

The two oldest girls immediately set to work at the stove; oats had been set aside in a cupboard to soak overnight; now they drained them, added milk and set them to cook in an enormous and slightly battered pot. Meanwhile, two of the younger girls had wrapped themselves in shawls and dashed outside to fetch coal to feed the fire. The smallest and thinnest girl, who had freckled skin and sand-colored hair and carried a kitten on her shoulder, was setting the table when she suddenly noticed Heloise, and squealed. Then she recovered and said, "Oh, Old Mother! Who is this?"

They had been so busy – and Heloise so still and quiet – that until that moment they had not seen her. Immediately the rest of the girls began to exclaim and chatter amongst themselves.

But Old Mother just said, "Who is who?"

"Oh, Old Mother!" said the smallest girl, whose name was Melancholy. "The ghostly girl sitting at the table of course! Is she a new one?"

"A new what? A new kitten? Yes, you might as well regard her as a new kitten. I found her on the church steps, just where I found the other kittens."

"Well, she certainly *looks* like a kitten," said a musical voice, and the tallest girl, wiping her hands on her apron, came over from the stove to look smilingly at Heloise. She was perhaps seventeen, and Heloise was overawed. "A witch's kitten, with black fur and green eyes, my favorite kind. What is your name, little kitten?"

Heloise cleared her throat. She was all but dumbfounded by the girls' playful manners. Old Mother's directness she had understood, but what manner of talk, of behavior, was this?

"Heloise," she whispered. "Please, miss," she added.

"You must call me Esther –"

"She's the oldest kitten!" said Melancholy.

"And this is Old Mother –"

"The old cat!" said Melancholy happily.

"And this is Melancholy, the youngest of us –"

"Not any more!" Melancholy put in excitedly. "How old are you, Heloise?"

Again, Heloise felt herself shrinking away. She hesitated, then whispered helplessly, "I don't know."

"You don't know?" Melancholy repeated. "You are an orphan, then," she concluded. "Well, anyway, you're younger than me," she said definitively, doing a little dance. After all, it could not be proved otherwise.

"Ahem!" said Esther, with a slightly reproving glance in Melancholy's direction. "Now where was I? Oh, yes – there is Lizzie stirring the porridge (that's enough, Mellie, if you please), and Nettie and Jenny bringing in the coal (Mellie!), and Nan getting out the plates, and Polly feeding the kittens, and Grace pulling up her stockings, and Daisy bringing in water from the pump, and Rose watering the geraniums and – where is Clementine?"

"I'm here!" said a muffled voice and, after a brief pause, a rather rumpled girl of about fourteen came limping into the room. "I can't reach my other stocking!" she complained, sneezing. "*Hatkashoo!* It's under the bed but my arms are too short. You know how short my arms are. And there's so much dust under there it's started me sneezing. *Ha … ha …*

*Hatkashoo!*"

"Well, sweep it, then!" said Esther, scandalized. "Or better still, mop it. We don't want everyone sneezing. You should never have let it get into such a state!"

Clementine looked thoughtfully at her. "I'm not doing a proper clean-up until the Crown Prince comes home," she stated matter-of-factly. "It is my way of asserting my faith that he is still alive. When the Crown Prince comes home, I shall mop under my bed, not before." Glancing at Heloise as she fished in the pocket of her pinafore for a handkerchief, she added, "She doesn't look like a kitten. She looks like a doll. One of the china ones Mr. Abernathy keeps on the top shelf."

Esther tsk-tsked, muttered something about doing your duty, Crown Prince or no Crown Prince, excused herself and went to see about the stocking. Meanwhile, Melancholy descended on Heloise.

"Can you sew? Do you like singing? Do you want to hold the kitten? Shall I take your bundle for you?"

And now a curious thing happened. Heloise had not been afraid when she had been trudging alone in the middle of the night, with only a hundred tiny birds for protection. But she was afraid now.

Clutching her bundle against her and completely at a loss as to how to respond, she stared blankly at Melancholy. She did not want to hand over Maria. But it wasn't just that. It was that she did not understand friendliness.

Old Mother, who could sum up a person or a situation in

the blink of an eye, said briskly, "Too many questions before breakfast, Mellie, m'dear! Let the child get her breath!"

"The porridge is cooked!" said black-ringleted Lizzie at the stove, and the girls, still chatting, lined up to be served. Melancholy did another little dance, looked quizzically at Heloise, decided she would keep, and joined the line.

"Could you eat a plate of porridge, child?" asked Old Mother. "You've had only a little bread and milk and I'll wager you hadn't eaten for a day or so before that. Line up with the others and let us see how you fare."

When she had served each of the girls, Lizzie brought her own and Old Mother's breakfast to the head of the table, then sat respectfully nearby. Esther, who sat opposite Old Mother at the other end of the table, said grace.

Then – with the exception of Heloise, who was feeling almost completely overwhelmed – they ate a cheerful and rather noisy meal, chairs scraping and voices echoing against the floorboards and walls. Melancholy sat next to Heloise, and looked at her whenever possible, but she was not game to ask more questions.

When the meal was over, the girls washed up with water that had been heating on the stove, and put away the breakfast things. Then they wiped down the wooden table, swept the floor, and set out the day's work things. It was then that Heloise discovered the most surprising thing of all.

The work with which the table was soon covered was sewing. But the girls were not engaged in the making of serviceable clothes for anonymous orphans. And their sewing was not confined to dirt-brown frocks, black stockings and red flannel petticoats.

Instead, as they sat down to their tasks, the room, which was growing lighter by the minute as the sun climbed high enough to light up the arched ivy-covered windows and stream through the narrow lancet ones higher up, the room became positively chaotic with color, with emerald and amethyst and rose-colored velvets, with snow-white and blood-red and sky-blue silks, with laces and feathers and ribbons and even fur-trims. And yet, every scrap of fabric, every half-hemmed garment, every work-in-progress was on a strangely diminutive scale, smaller even than the things Heloise had made for the infants at Saint Suffering's.

And then, all at once, she understood.

*The girls were working on dolls' clothes.*

"You can sew, then, child?" asked Old Mother. "Would you like to join us? Or would you like to lie down for a spell?"

Heloise was so tired that she was suspended between waking and dreaming. But at this moment she could not have closed her eyes for the world.

"They – They are dolls' clothes ... are they not?" she whispered, drawing her bundle unconsciously closer to her.

"Why yes, child. This is how we make our living."

"But – But they are so beautiful!"

"Well, the doll shops would not pay us to dress their dolls badly," said Old Mother practically. "Who would buy them?

Anyway, how else would one dress a doll, but beautifully?"

Melancholy had sat down and was patting the seat beside her vigorously. In a trance, Heloise sat beside her. In front of her was the most beautiful doll's dress she had ever seen. It was of green velvet, with a white lace trim. But it had not yet been hemmed.

"May I finish this?" she asked in a whisper.

"Certainly, child," said Old Mother.

And, as she threaded her needle and took up a doll's dress made of the richest green velvet, Heloise was in a place closer to heaven than she had ever expected to be while still in this world.

Not half an hour later, with the new and yet comforting sound of eleven girls chatting in her ears, and the concealed Maria on her lap, Heloise had fallen asleep over her work.

# The Twelfth Voice

When Heloise awoke, it was to the sound of singing.

At first she had no idea where she was. She was warm, for someone had covered her with a shawl, but she was confused about the time of day, and was sleeping in a most uncomfortable position. Moreover, her ears were filled with a most unaccustomed sound.

All at once Heloise came to with a start. *Where was Maria?*

Safe in her lap.

Heloise went hot and cold with relief. She drew her bundle closer. Then she lifted her head and looked around.

It was a few moments before she understood what she was seeing.

The girls, all eleven of them, were variously standing, leaning and sitting around the other end of the long table.

Sharing yellowed sheets of hand-copied music between them, they were singing with the greatest beauty and discipline.

Old Mother, from whom their eyes never moved, was conducting them.

Unnoticed, Heloise straightened her back, tilted her head, and stared.

Old Mother's whole will and intelligence seemed to be poured into their music-making. She stood, bent and yet taut with energy, her music on a stand in front of her, her hands speaking briskly in signs the girls seemed to read perfectly. She stopped them once or twice and, in a cracked soprano voice that must once have been very fine, demonstrated what she wanted from them. Then they started again, singing even more beautifully than before. They were rehearsing a Christmas carol, but to Heloise the piece was quite unfamiliar. The refrains were sung by all (*tutti*, as it said on the music), in the brightest, richest harmony. The verses were sung as a solo by each of the three oldest girls – all sopranos – in turn.

Heloise had never heard anything like it. Music was almost entirely outside the narrow range of her experience. There had been no instrument in the caretaker's cottage, and neither her godmother nor Mrs. Moth had sung around the house. Heloise had received no music lessons and, having never been to school, had not even heard skipping rhymes or folk songs. Sometimes passersby had whistled, sometimes farmhands had sung. And she had sometimes heard the organ playing, and the congregation singing when they had walked past the church. Heloise had grown up thinking that music was not much more than a peculiar, and always distant, noise.

But this was not a noise. This was a revelation.

Heloise's mouth formed a round O of astonishment.

The whole choir in harmony. Then the voice of black-ringleted Lizzie, as pure and chaste as a choirboy's. Again, the whole choir in harmony. Then Polly's tremulous voice, which seemed to speak of some private, obscure melancholy. The whole choir in harmony. And then …

Esther.

Esther must surely have had the most beautiful voice anyone was likely to hear in a lifetime. She was as thin as a young tree, with mouse-colored hair cut close to her head – the result of a recent fever – and merry blue eyes. Her face was frank and trusting; she looked kind and good; her character was steady and responsible, but her voice, in its plaintive richness, was a lullaby of warmth and solace and compassion, of courage in adversity, and the promise of happy endings. The sound of it was so powerful and resonant that it possessed her frame, as if she were a chiming bell or a songbird.

Afterwards, Heloise found it difficult to remember how, exactly, it happened. At one moment Old Mother was conducting. Then she was swaying and smiling with closed eyes, and all at once, she was dancing.

"*Oh, hail yon hall where none can sin,*" sang Esther.

"*Sing May Queen May sing Mary,*" sang the other girls.

"*For it's gold outside and silver within,*" sang Esther.

*"Sing all good men for the new born baby!"*

Old Mother waltzed as Esther sang. The other girls laughed and Esther tried her best not to. And the smile that spread over Esther's face seemed only to make her voice warmer. Old Mother waltzed right over to Heloise and in sheer joy and abandonment she pulled her to her feet. To Heloise's complete amazement they waltzed around and around as the girls laughed, and Esther only seemed to sing more and more beautifully. Old Mother danced like a hen might dance in a farmyard. Heloise, who was still clutching her bundle, had never danced before. And yet there may never have been a more beautiful dance to watch.

"You see, Heloise? We are a choir!" said Melancholy, as the carol ended and they all collapsed, laughing, around the room. "A Choir of Female Orphans, Waifs and Strays! We live here in the Old Monastery, rehearse every day, sew for our living, and sing on Sundays in the church of St. Mary of the Angels upstairs. We are *monstrous* good, even if I do say so myself."

"And now we are rehearsing for Christmas," said Esther, who was still smiling, "when we go out singing for Unfortunates who need music to cheer them up."

"Will you sing with us, Heloise?" asked Melancholy, as anxious as a puppy. And on seeing Heloise's consternation all the girls joined in coaxing and persuading her.

"Oh, do join us!"

"We will be twelve again, and it will be such fun!"

"Think how surprised Alice will be, the grand old married

thing, when she sees that she has been replaced already!"

"And think of the joy you will help us to bring!"

"Could you sing a little for us, child?" asked Old Mother, who was still catching her breath. Her attitude was gentle and brisk, as if she knew that Heloise would be shy, but also that there was nothing to be shy about. "Perhaps you might sing the tune you just heard?" To encourage her, Old Mother began, in her cracked but perfectly true soprano, "La la, la la, la la la la la …"

Heloise stared at Old Mother. She stood where she had stopped dancing, alone in the middle of the floor, in her orphan-like black dress, clutching her white bundle.

What were they talking about? What was a choir? What was Christmas?

She had no idea what to do, and so she simply obeyed. She took a breath, and – singing at first with Old Mother and then alone – reproduced the tune she had heard.

When she had finished there was a surprised silence. Heloise looked at Old Mother, not really thinking about anything except whether she had done it correctly, this task that was so entirely new to her. Then, in horror, she covered her mouth with her hand.

She had sung in the voice her godmother had warned her about, the voice that was Heloise's madness talking.

"Why, child, what is the matter?" asked Old Mother.

Heloise looked away and shook her head. How could she explain?

"You sing very well indeed," Old Mother continued. "Your pitch is first-rate. Your voice is unschooled, of course, but –" She glanced at the other girls. "Perhaps our surprise alarmed you. We none of us expected a child as quiet as you to be able to call on such depth and resonance."

Heloise looked more troubled.

"Well, that is enough rehearsal for now," said Old Mother, seeing Heloise's discomfort and thinking it best to drop the matter. "You have all done capitally! If we can sing as well for Christmas who knows what miracles we may work!"

When at last Heloise climbed into the spare bed in the dormitory, washed, fed, dressed in a borrowed nightgown, and clutching Maria, she doubted that she would be able to sleep. Everything was so strange and astonishing. On top of that, having slept for hours, she no longer felt tired.

But she did not lie awake in the strangeness of the new bed. She did not even talk, for more than a few minutes, to Maria, whom she had concealed under the bedclothes. Instead, more tired than she realized, she was asleep before the candles were blown out.

But that night, she had a nightmare about Mary Child. "Heloise! Heloise!"

Who was calling? Was it the birds? But she could see no birds, only the faces of dolls disfigured by thousands of tiny stitches.

"Heloise!"

Heloise woke with a start. There were no dolls, and no birds. Instead she saw a candle, a white nightgown, and Esther's flickering face.

"Heloise, my dear, you were dreaming! But you are safe now. Nothing can harm you here. Do you understand?"

Panting and wiping the tears from her eyes, Heloise nodded dubiously.

"There is nothing to be afraid of, Heloise. Old Mother and I have been talking. We know that you have run away from an orphanage – we knew from your clothes. But you need not worry. We will not ask questions. And tomorrow you will have a new dress or at least, a nice old dress that one of us has outgrown. So you will not have to wear black any more, and no one will know where you are from. You know, Nan ran away from an orphanage, too – Saint Suffering's at Bell Toll. And we are all foundlings of one kind or another. Not one of us knows who our parents were!" she said gaily. "Well, none of us except Melancholy. She is the orphaned daughter of two neglected poets, you know, who both expired of sadness when she was one year old. She does not take after them. Anyway, the point is that you are welcome here. You are one of us. We have been expecting you since Alice got engaged. She was the oldest before me, you see. There are always twelve of us. Three in each part when we sing four-part harmony, and four when we sing three. You will be the twelfth voice. Think of that!"

Smiling, she tucked Heloise in, kissed her on the forehead

and went back to bed.

When she had gone, Heloise lay staring at the ceiling. She was not thinking about her dream. She was not thinking about her circumstances. She was feeling something she could not recognize, for she had never felt it before.

It was as if the blood in her veins had turned into something shining and magical.

It was the first time in all her life that anyone had ever kissed her.

# Esther and Old Mother Confer

The next morning, in the strange bed in the strange room in the strange building that was now her home, Heloise woke with a start.

Her first thought was: *Where is Maria?* But Maria lay safe in her arms.

And yet, although she was holding her pressed against her heart, Heloise felt no relief from anxiety.

All at once, she found herself thinking rapidly.

She was in a new place, amongst new people. Indeed it was almost as if her life had begun anew. She knew she had been rescued from imminent danger. She knew she had been delivered into the hands of good people. But she also knew that neither she nor Maria were truly safe. Indeed, they could never hope to be so again.

She was afraid her godmother would come after her. And it seemed to Heloise that her godmother was such a powerful woman that she could polish off Heloise's night-long journey in two, or perhaps three, bigger-than-average steps. Finding her in this obscure cul-de-sac of a great city may have been a challenge for most people, but not for Heloise's godmother. Heloise believed that if all else failed her godmother could probably locate her by sense of smell.

And yet, even while staring these nightmares in the face, Heloise felt a steady, cold determination. Her determination was to survive no matter what. As she lay thinking intensely, she became aware of that strange conviction she had known before: the feeling that no matter how powerful her godmother was, she, Heloise, was somehow more powerful still.

She had been foolish yesterday, she knew that now. She had been tired and overwhelmed, it was true, but she should never have revealed so much, should never have let them know that her bundle was so important.

For Heloise's fear was not only for her godmother. She was afraid of the people she was with now, too.

It was not that she did not realize how good and kind they were. But that did not mean she could afford to trust them. After all, the Vicar, who indeed had imagined he was doing her a service, had betrayed her without thinking. In the end, adults were always in league. She did not imagine that anyone here would steal or destroy Maria. But if they knew Heloise was a runaway from a respectable home, would they not take steps to return her?

And might not Maria serve to identify her amongst all the other female orphans of her age that might be at large in the City?

And how could she have been so foolish as to sing like that? She had not known, of course, that she could sing, but –

And then there was the nightmare about Mary Child.

Heloise bit her lip.

The impossibility of completely controlling her own behavior filled her with despair. Even as she despaired, however, a dissenting voice in her mind distracted her thoughts. She knew it would have been safer not to have had that nightmare and revealed herself to Esther. But if she had not had that nightmare, she would never have gotten the kiss.

For a moment she was lulled, thinking about it. Then she turned her mind away from the memory. She knew she could not stop herself having nightmares. But she thought it possible that she could will herself, somehow, to have silent ones.

Her life here would have to be as watchful and cautious as she could make it, for she felt that her very existence, and Maria's, depended on it.

Under the covers, Heloise clenched her fists. When her fingernails had dug so far into her palms that it hurt, she knew this pact with herself was sealed. She sighed, opened her eyes, and stared at the unfamiliar ceiling.

Esther's kiss was still haunting her.

At the caretaker's cottage it had been easy to live in duplicity, because she had not felt that she owed anyone there anything – let alone her honesty. But duplicity here would be an entirely new game. Everyone was being kind to her. They had welcomed her into their home. They had fed and clothed her. They had given her sanctuary. And that would make her dishonesty a betrayal of their trust.

It might have been supposed that the kindness she had been shown would melt Heloise's neglected heart, and that she would accept it with joy and relief. But it was not like that. Their kindness made her feel empty, poor, as if something was being asked from her which she simply did not have to give.

And so, from the moment she rose on that first morning, Heloise began a new double life.

No longer did she cling to her bundle. Instead, she concealed it under the bed, which was her responsibility to keep clean and tidy.

No longer were there long stretches of solitude for Heloise to share with Maria. Every hour of the day was occupied in community.

At night, after lights out, Heloise held Maria under the covers. She talked to her silently, and reassured her of her love and loyalty. In the morning, before she got up, she carefully concealed Maria within the white nightdress that had carried her all the way into the city and, when she thought no one was looking, slipped her under the bed.

Heloise was good at concealment. But this was not the caretaker's cottage. It was a house full of curious girls, and one sharp-eyed old woman. They were all well aware that Heloise had a secret possession.

One morning during that first week, Esther rose early and went to the market with Old Mother.

"Now, Esther, my dear," said the old lady when they had left the fat little church behind them and were well out of earshot, "you are a wise girl and you know what I'm thinking. I have no wish to think ill of the child, but what are we to make of this concealment?" Old Mother's equilibrium was not sufficiently disturbed for her interior concert to have been silenced but, in keeping with the sensitivity of the discussion and the need for wisdom, she was hearing a particularly calming selection: the second movement from "Glamroch's Cantata No 147," known in English as *Peace that Passeth Understanding*.

"You are afraid that it may be an item of some value, and that it may not be her own?"

"Precisely, my dear. In this strange world, runaway orphans are rarely missed – they are too plentiful. But an item of value, as the world counts value ... My goodness, all thirteen of us could end up in a penal colony in the antipodes, which would be a fine end for a Twelve-Voice Choir of Female Orphans, Waifs and Strays.

"What are we to do? I could send her on an errand and inspect the bundle myself, but that would be underhand, and

123

I despise the underhand, especially when employed against the powerless. On the other hand, if I ask her openly it would be little better than an insult. She is so meek and well-behaved – she must surely know right from wrong." Old Mother paused, listening to a key change in which she found particular solace. "Genius!" she remarked with seeming irrelevance; this did not disturb Esther, who had learned long ago that Old Mother was always thinking about music, no matter what she might happen to be doing in her exterior life. "It could be anything, I suppose," Old Mother resumed, "but it looks like a small statue of some kind. Such a thing could be more valuable than the child realizes."

They walked in silence, the young girl in her eggshell-blue shawl and bonnet, the bent old woman with her customary sparrow-grey blanket thrown over her head and her wicker basket over her arm.

"I think we should be plain with her," said Esther at last. "Ask her privately, on her honor, whether this possession is really her own. If she says it is, no more should be done about it. If she says that it isn't, well –"

"We must cross *that* bridge when we come to it," said Old Mother neatly.

That very morning, before Old Mother rang the bell to wake the rest of the girls, she and Esther roused Heloise and brought her into the main room.

"Now Heloise, you must not be alarmed," said Esther, taking off her shawl and wrapping it around the younger girl.

"There is a little something we must ask you."

"We are all friends here, child," said Old Mother. "And friends worry about each other's welfare. You're a quiet little thing and not given to sharing your troubles with others. But some secrets are dangerous when kept."

"It's that bundle of yours, Heloise," said Esther gently. "Whatever it is you have wrapped up in the nightgown. Is it truly your own? If it is, we'll say no more about it."

Heloise rubbed her eyes in what she hoped was a sleepy manner. She was buying time.

For a second, her mind raced in panic.

Then, suddenly, she understood.

She was being offered an opportunity. It was an opportunity to make herself and Maria a little safer. It was an opportunity to legitimize Maria's presence, at least in the eyes of Old Mother and Esther.

How should she answer?

"*Tell the truth*," said a voice in her head. Instantly she felt calm. She would tell the truth.

But what was the truth?

Was Maria her own?

It seemed a difficult question to answer.

Her first thought was that Maria was nobody's. Maria was Maria, and owned herself.

Then she remembered that she had found Maria in her godmother's home. Did that make Maria her godmother's?

Heloise's third thought passed her lips before she was

125

aware of thinking it. Once she had said it, she knew it to be right.

"She was my mother's," she whispered simply and so honestly that Esther and Old Mother sighed with relief.

"Good girl," said Old Mother. "Go get dressed now. I'm about to ring the bell."

"*She?*" murmured Esther to Old Mother when Heloise had padded obediently back to the dormitory.

"I told you it was a statue," Old Mother murmured. "Her poor dead mother's dearest possession, perhaps. Ah, Esther, my dear, life is sad."

"But happy, too, Old Mother," Esther reminded her.

# In a Glass Darkly

The days at the Old Monastery were as serenely ordered as they had been in the time of the monks.

Every morning, when Old Mother rang the bell, the girls rose, washed, dressed, made their beds and came to breakfast. After breakfast they worked until noon at their sewing. At noon the girls put on their bonnets and shawls and set out to collect their midday meals from a nearby public house – The Rose and Crown – that had a standing arrangement with the church. Thus they always had a hot meal in the middle of the day. They brought the food back, ate it at the long work table, then returned the empty plates. After dinner they sewed until four o'clock. Then they rehearsed.

Rehearsals were divided between two areas: the music for Divine Service the upcoming Sunday, and the music for

Christmas. The girls sang at only one service on Sundays: the Sung Eucharist at eleven o'clock, but it was the grandest and best attended of the week. Old Mother's Twelve-Voice Choir of Female Orphans, Waifs and Strays was so unusual a choir that people came from all over the country to the Church of Saint Mary and the Angels to hear them, and although the novelty was usually considered pleasing, there were those who did not approve. In fact the Rector received letters of complaint almost every week from people who were offended by the very existence of an all-female church choir, sometimes on musical grounds, sometimes on theological ones. On occasion, there were even letters written to the newspapers.

This did not bother Old Mother, or the Rector, one bit. They were both a little on the radical side.

On the occasion of Heloise's first full rehearsal, Old Mother declared her to be an alto. Heloise did not know what an alto was, but she learned soon enough. In this entirely female choir, there were, not sopranos, altos, tenors and basses, but First Sopranos, Second Sopranos, First Altos and Second Altos. Heloise, together with Nan and Clementine, was to sing First Alto, as had the now married and retired Alice before her. The First Sopranos were Esther, Lizzie and Polly. Melancholy referred to herself as a Second Sop.

Old Mother, although excited by Heloise's powerful voice, had thought it would be an exacting task to teach her to blend. But Heloise had learned her lesson, and no such difficulty presented itself. As a new chorister who could not read music, it took her some time to learn the parts. When she did she sang so softly that she was barely audible, even to the girls on either side of her.

With Heloise, Old Mother was learning to expect the unexpected.

And yet Heloise changed the sound of the choir. The change was partly due to Alice's departure; but just as Alice's absence meant that one thing was lost, Heloise's whispered presence meant that something else was gained.

And what was gained was not only musical.

Meanwhile, Heloise was beginning to be apprehensive about what exactly this singing at Divine Service entailed. There was a large cupboard at one end of the dormitory, and when Esther opened it to put away clean linen, Heloise glimpsed a line of twelve purple robes and twelve white surplices, and her stomach tightened with apprehension.

After rehearsal each day they had supper, a simple meal of bread and milk.

Then came the time the girls looked forward to, the few hours before bedtime. The work table was pushed back, and the benches placed upside down on top of it. Then the girls who could play the spinet took turns executing minuets and polonaises and occasionally, when the mood took them, wild Irish jigs or Highland flings for the other girls to dance to, while Old Mother, clapping her hands, coached them in correct deportment, taught them new steps, corrected poorly executed old ones, and sometimes joined in.

After that the little ones went to bed, while the older ones stayed up to work on their individual pastimes and accomplishments: sketching, lace-making, embroidery and so forth. And Esther read aloud.

Esther read as beautifully as she sang. But she did not read from the Bible. She read from *The Arabian Nights* (or "The Book of the Thousand Nights and a Night, all Sixteen Volumes" as it was subtitled.) This collection was apparently on permanent loan from the Rector, and the girls were inordinately fond of it. So the little ones fell asleep listening to a story.

And thus it was that Heloise discovered that there were stories apart from the ones in the Bible, stories of magic lamps, flying carpets and caves full of treasure.

But she was not surprised.

Stories were everywhere, she knew that now.

She was beginning to think that, in all the world, there were really only two things – just two. The stories you knew, and the stories you did not know.

Heloise had been right in thinking that it would be difficult to live a double life in this new place. She had hoped that determination, vigilance and self-discipline would save her. But these things were not enough to stop her having nightmares. And they were not enough to overcome the threat posed by the unexpected, either.

At the far end of the dormitory there was a mirror. Each of the girls was endowed with her own chest of drawers and a china jug and basin to wash her face and hands in, but the mirror was shared. Every morning the girls performed their hurried, shivering ablutions by their beds, got dressed, and then congregated at the mirror to see to their hair. Some girls spent a good deal more time at the mirror than others, and when the space was crowded there was much jumping up and down and peeking over shoulders into unoccupied corners, not to mention the occasional squabble.

However, these arrangements did not much concern Heloise. There had been no mirrors at the caretaker's cottage, and she was accustomed to managing without one. Even if she had wanted the mirror, fighting it out with the other girls (however genially) was completely out of character, and totally against her calculated policy. In any case, as soon as she had realized that there was a mirror in the dormitory, she had begun instinctively to avoid it. Something about it frightened her.

She chose to arrange her hair at her bedside. She did it so quickly and efficiently that it took a few days before anyone noticed. But one morning, coming from the mirror with a fetching red-brown ribbon in her hair, Melancholy pounced on her. Melancholy was a great stickler for her own, and others', rights.

"My dear Heloise!" she exclaimed with an air of

sympathetic solidarity. "The mirror is there for you too! Come!" She took Heloise's arm and hustled her to the end of the room. "Heloise cannot see the mirror, and nobody has noticed!" she said indignantly.

Immediately the girls made space for Heloise, loath to be thought inconsiderate of the new girl.

"Oh, Heloise, you need only have asked!" said Esther, in a tone of kindly reproach.

"Or just shoved," said Clementine, "like some people I know."

"Well, I'd like to see someone manage to shove you out of the way!" scoffed Lizzie.

And so it came to pass that Heloise was forced to look at herself in a mirror.

And thus, for the first time since her pact with herself, Heloise lost her self-possession.

She had never seen herself in a mirror before.

She had had a rough idea of what she looked like, from reflections in dark windows and polished surfaces. But those reflections had been mere shades when compared to this one.

She had not realized how separate a thing one's appearance was from how one felt inside. Her first instinct was to say, "*But that's not me!*" For the face that stared back from the mirror seemed alien indeed.

There was nothing obviously unusual about her; she was not disfigured. She had eyes, a nose, a mouth. She had known that already.

But there was, she realized, something frightening about

her, something chilling, uncanny. She was so pale and waxen, so strangely unruffled. It was almost as if – unlike everyone around her – she was not –

Alive.

But that could not be true. Even if it was it would not in itself have concerned her. What concerned her was that she was not loveable.

Who could love the creature in the mirror? She was not winsome; she was not prepossessing or sweet. She was neither beautiful like her godmother, nor serene like Maria, nor ordinary-looking like all the girls here. She was, simply, *frightening*. She even frightened herself.

I could not be loved, a forlorn little voice said inside her. I *cannot* be loved.

She had not thought of love like that before.

Her shock was such that she could not hide it. They all saw it on her face. She began, visibly, to tremble.

"Why, Heloise, what is wrong?" asked Esther at once.

"I – I –" said Heloise. She had a vague sense that she was supposed to be hiding something. At the same time, she felt that nothing very much mattered any more. Her throat swelled and ached. After a moment she whispered listlessly, "I have never seen myself in a mirror before."

She should not have admitted that, of course. She was falling into the same old trap – clinging to a mysterious bundle, singing, calling out in her sleep. But her misery had temporarily swept away her resolutions.

133

"But – what – ?" began Clementine, wondering what had upset the child so. Then she understood.

For a moment no one knew quite what to say or do.

Then Melancholy threw her arms around Heloise and held her.

"Never mind!" she said stoutly and perhaps not quite tactfully. "Beauty is as beauty does, Old Mother says."

Esther winced. "Mellie is right," she said. "Looks are not important. But truly," she added carefully, struggling to be honest and tactful, "you are not ill-favored. You are singular, it is true – haunting, perhaps, would be the word. But think how romantic that is! I'm sure many girls would give their eyeteeth to be considered haunting! Why, you look like a Gothic heroine …"

"All Gothic heroines have black hair and green eyes and waxen complexions," put in Lizzie helpfully.

"And it is all the rage to be Gothic," said Polly.

"She's like a black kitten with green eyes," said Nan more domestically.

"No, she's like a top-shelf china doll," maintained Clementine, and added quickly, "That's a compliment."

Heloise was not listening.

For in the midst of her pain, something had happened.

What was it, this deep entrancing warmth – this light, this air – as if the blood in her veins had turned into pure sunlight, as if she were drifting on a river of euphoria, as if nothing, no matter how painful, was of lasting importance?

And why was it that it felt like an answer when it seemed to her to have nothing to do with what she had been feeling?

It was as if she had asked a question and received the answer to a different question.

She did not understand, but she knew this elation was happening because Melancholy had embraced her, was embracing her still. What is more, she knew she had felt it before. This was her second glimpse into the beautiful world she had seen when Esther had kissed her.

She could feel Melancholy's heartbeat.

The girl's cheek against her own was the warmest thing to have touched her in all her life.

All Heloise's joints seemed to have turned to honey.

And yet, she did not hug back.

She did not know how.

"Well, don't strangle the poor child," said Lizzie to Melancholy.

Melancholy gave Heloise a squeeze, in token defiance of Lizzie, then let her go. She smiled, but Heloise was afraid to raise her eyes.

"You don't have to look at yourself in the mirror," said Esther, still trying to help. "If you do perhaps you will grow to like your face. I am nobody's idea of a beauty, but I like mine."

Heloise tried to look as if she were listening, but really she was concentrating on pulling herself together.

No matter how cautious she might resolve to be, how could she have prepared herself for this?

On the day after she arrived, Heloise was allocated a morning chore: sweeping the floor of the main room after breakfast. This meant sweeping up, not only crumbs, but also such dressmaking materials as may have fallen during the previous day's work, and which were too scrappy to be of further use. Once a week, on Saturday mornings, the floor was mopped with warm, soapy water. That was to be Heloise's chore, too. The first time Old Mother saw Heloise sweeping she smiled sadly to herself. "So obviously an orphanage child," she murmured to Esther. "Girls from loving homes do not work so hard."

The morning after her third night at Old Mother's, Heloise finished her sweeping before the table was scrubbed and ready for the day's work. Having put the broom away, she felt a little awkward, standing idle while everyone occupied themselves. Melancholy, who was normally never far from Heloise's side, was fussing over the kittens.

Heloise would have liked to pay Maria a visit. But although she may have been able to do that, briefly, without anyone noticing, she resisted the impulse. She wanted to make them forget that the bundle with its secret burden existed.

Heloise stood irresolute. Then she noticed once more the brightly colored pictures on the wall opposite the door.

Heloise felt drawn to them. She always had. But examining them as she would have liked to would have been incautious. She had to keep vigilant; she had to be unnoticeable. And she was realizing, as the days passed, that one of the main things it was necessary to hide was her own ignorance.

Until she had fallen amongst her present company she had not fully appreciated how unusual she was.

Most people, she now knew, had heard music.

Most people had seen pictures.

Most people had looked at themselves in a mirror.

Most people had been kissed; most people had been embraced.

She was learning how important it was not to show surprise – for surprise laid bare what you did not know.

Heloise hesitated.

Then, almost as if drawn against her will, she crept to the wall.

It was like the time she had pulled open the split in her godmother's censored Bible, half of her telling herself not to, the other half disobeying.

Until this moment, the only pictures Heloise had seen were in embroidery. But they were nothing like these ones. The flowers and decorations in them had been constructed from colored yarn; the people in these seemed to be made of flesh and blood.

Heloise was entranced, intoxicated. There was so much to look at. How strange it was to her to actually see these scenes – these stories she had spent so much time acting out, alone, in her room!

So there was Adam, new-made out of the primeval dust, waking up and wondering who had made him.

And *that* was what Pharaoh's daughter looked like!

And those reedy things. Could they be bulrushes?

Jacob's Ladder, David and Goliath, poor blind Samson in the temple, Daniel in the lions' den – all these were familiar to her from reading the Bible.

But there were other pictures that were entirely new.

Heloise moved, lingeringly, from left to right along the wall. Some of the pictures depicted scenes so foreign to her that she could not attempt an interpretation. She had no idea what was happening in them, or why. There was only one thing she understood about them, and as she looked, this thing impressed her more deeply. She knew the pictures were somehow concerned with –

She did not know how to put it into words; then suddenly, a phrase came into her head, a phrase she did not remember hearing before.

The heart of the matter. *The heart of the matter.*

What did that mean?

She did not know. All she knew was that it had something to do with love.

Heloise's resolutions seemed doomed to failure. Nerved as

she was, she had become so caught up in the pictures that she had forgotten to keep watch, and she had not noticed that the room had gone quiet.

The girls had suspended their activities and were nudging each other and looking at her.

She made an odd picture herself, a solitary figure staring ravenously into a painting as if she were a hound who had picked up a scent.

Esther and Old Mother exchanged glances.

"Heloise," said Old Mother, going up to her. "What is it, child?"

Heloise glanced around, blushed deeply, and curtseyed apologetically.

There was no point in lying.

"Where I come from," she explained in a whisper, "they don't have pictures."

That night, Heloise could hardly sleep. Her pact, she felt, was not working. It seemed to her that she was hammering the nails, one by one, into her own coffin.

When at last she drifted off, she dreamed, not of her own worries, but once again of Mary Child: not of the present, but the past.

And, although she did not know it, her understanding of all these matters was about to change completely.

# Heloise Visits a Doll Shop

On Friday morning, Esther and Lizzie disappeared into the dormitory. When they came out they were tying bonnet strings, buttoning pelisses, pulling on gloves, and looking purposeful.

"Where are you going?" asked Melancholy immediately. "Can I come too?"

"My dear Melancholy," said Lizzie, "we are taking the current order to Mr. Abernathy's. We packed it up yesterday, don't you remember?" Her hands busy, she nodded towards a neat, brown-paper package that sat waiting by the door.

"The doll shop!" exclaimed Melancholy. "I might have known!" she added accusingly.

"May she come with us, Old Mother?" asked Esther, ever indulgent.

"Mellie," said Old Mother, "I have already decided who is to go with them. It must be Heloise, for she has never been to Mr. Abernathy's, and ought to be introduced. Besides, I have a most particular errand for you this afternoon."

Melancholy pouted. Then she did a little dance and said casually, "What kind of errand?"

Heloise was dismayed at this turn of events. By the time she had put her borrowed cloak over her borrowed dress, and placed her borrowed bonnet on her head, and Old Mother, having fussed with Heloise's hair and bonnet strings and brushed down her dress, felt satisfied that she looked respectable enough to represent the Choir, Melancholy was reconciled, and waved them off cheerfully.

"Have a *monstrous* good time, Heloise! Remember everything, and tell me all about it when you get home!"

Heloise was uneasy.

She did not want to leave Maria unguarded for so long. She also feared that by going abroad, beyond the excursions to the public house at the end of the street, she would be exposing herself to recognition and danger.

But this time she kept her pact with herself and was silent.

And so, with her gloved hand in Esther's, Heloise set off bravely into the outside world. Lizzie carried the parcel.

Heloise's anxieties were misplaced. Their journey was uneventful, until at length they turned into a neat, tree-lined, cobbled street filled with small shops. The trees were bright with autumn leaves, and each shop front was like a diamond made of dainty, latticed windows whose shining panes caught the morning sunshine. About halfway down they passed a very red-lipped young woman ("Surely that is not *rouge?*" murmured Lizzie to Esther) who was carrying a tiny white poodle in a basket, at which Heloise could not help but stare. While she was still preoccupied with the melting brown eyes of the dog, they reached Mr. Abernathy's.

Heloise had not had time to do more than steal a hurried, astonished glance at the window display before Esther opened the jingling door and, first Lizzie, then Heloise, and then Esther had trooped inside. Heloise was suddenly confronted with one of the most astonishing sights of her life.

The shop was filled with shelves, and those shelves were filled with dolls.

But what dolls!

Spontaneously, Heloise's mouth fell open.

There were scores of them, each different, and each so beautiful in her own way that they brought to mind a room full of princesses exiled from the Land of Imagination. There were dolls as large as little girls, with porcelain faces so real that anyone might have mistaken them for living children. There were dolls with the most luxuriant hair, long and curly and shining, as dark as treacle, as fair as flax, as red as a squirrel's tail. There were baby dolls in creamy white christening gowns, dolls that were clearly children, carrying hoops and sticks, and dolls who were young ladies with gloves and little drawstring purses. There was a doll dressed as a queen with a velvet court gown and a crown. There was a doll dressed as a bride, with a veil and a perfect bouquet of red silk roses. There were large dolls, middle-sized dolls, small dolls and even tiny dolls, not much taller than Heloise's index finger. There were china dolls – the most expensive – that sat, as Clementine had said, on the top shelf, wooden dolls, plaster dolls and yes, even rag dolls.

Rag dolls. They should have reminded her; they should have put the stone weight back on her heart. But so different were Heloise's feelings as she stood in this enchanted place, that The Museum of Mary Child never entered her head.

And yet, even in her astonishment and delight, Heloise found herself searching for something. At first she did not know what it was.

"Heloise! Come along! You have not said hello to Mr. Abernathy."

Esther's grave yet musical voice reminded her where she was. Now she saw that the shop had a counter, and a door beyond it that led into a back room. It was at this door that Esther stood beckoning. Heloise hurried through it.

For, of course, she must not seem surprised.

The back room was a strange sight, although Heloise tried to seem unimpressed. Here, too, were shelves stacked with dolls. Yet these dolls were not clothed, but naked, yet to be dressed and presented for sale. All at once, Heloise understood something. The girls earned their living making dolls' clothes. But other people earned their bread by making the dolls. All of this work was sold to Mr. Abernathy, and Mr. Abernathy made a living selling it to his customers.

She felt rather as if a great mystery had been solved.

And yet, a greater one still tugged at her thoughts.

"Very fine work, as usual, girls," Mr. Abernathy was saying as he looked at the stack of tiny dresses and bonnets that Lizzie had unwrapped. "You must compliment Old Mother for me. No one sews as finely as her choir."

"Thank you, sir," said Esther, with a curtsey. "I will be sure and tell Old Mother. And may I present our new girl, Heloise?"

Heloise curtseyed. Mr. Abernathy was a small, thin, elderly, bespectacled man with a bald head and mottled cheeks. He wore a leather apron over his shirtsleeves, and looked gentle and nervous.

"Well, well, my dear, and do you sew as well as your fellow choristers?" he said, patting her on the head.

In all honesty Heloise suspected that she sewed better than many of them. She had had so much practice, after all. But she whispered meekly, "Oh, no, sir. I am the youngest, you see."

"What's that you say? Child has a soft voice, doesn't she?"

"Well, sometimes," murmured Lizzie.

"She said she was the youngest, sir," said Esther.

"The youngest, eh? Well, never mind, I'm sure one day

144

you'll be the eldest, and the most accomplished, you mark my words. Now if you girls will get busy here I will fetch the fee and your next order." He went briskly into the shop, where he could be heard fussing amongst his account books and cash boxes.

As soon as he had gone Esther and Lizzie set about clothing a stack of chilled-looking dolls in the finished outfits they had brought. The dresses, bonnets and underwear were of different sizes, but it seemed that the older girls could instantly pick what size doll fit a given item of apparel. Esther chose a doll, matched her with a frock, a bonnet, a camisole and pantalettes, and even stockings and slippers, and handed them all to Heloise.

"There you are, my dear. You can learn by doing. Take care not to tear anything!"

Of course Heloise did not tear anything – she was used to dressing dolls. Or one doll, anyway.

And that was when she knew what it was that she had been searching for in the shop.

A doll like Maria.

For amongst all those many dolls, not one of them was anything like Maria.

Not that any doll, however beautiful, could have taken Maria's place or even rivaled her. But that was not what was worrying Heloise.

Before she had discovered Maria under the floor, Heloise had never examined a doll close up. Her knowledge of dolls had come from seeing them from a distance, in other girls' arms. When her godmother had shown her the dolls of Mary Child she had made allowances, knowing that they had been made by a mad creature. Now, having seen a shop full of dolls, she realized what most dolls looked like. At the same time, she realized that Maria was different.

She wondered why Maria did not look like the dolls in the shop.

Then she began to feel afraid.

"Good girl!" exclaimed Esther, admiring the doll Heloise was dressing. "How well you are doing!"

The girls worked quickly, dressing and primping the dolls until they were appealing enough to sit on the shelves outside. Heloise would have found the work easy and pleasant, if she had not been anxious to get back to Old Mother's. She longed to know that Maria was safe.

"My goodness gracious me, what a bevy of beauties!" Mr. Abernathy exclaimed when he came back into the room. The dolls were lying on the table like young girls on a summer's day, napping lazily after a picnic. Lizzie, who was something of a perfectionist, was surveying them critically and putting a finishing touch here and there – straightening a bonnet, adjusting a bow, picking tiny threads off sleeves. Meanwhile Mr. Abernathy counted out the fee into Esther's hand. Esther folded it carefully into her drawstring purse. Then he gave her the next order, and went through it painstakingly to make sure she understood.

"*A dozen bonnets, assorted designs, four large, four medium, four small.*

*A dozen matching frocks, as above.*

*A dozen white linen pantalettes, trimmed with lace, sizes as above ...*"

Heloise was not listening. She was having horrible visions of her godmother arriving at Old Mother's while she was away, banging on the door, demanding to see where Heloise slept, finding Maria and –

"And when would you like it delivered, Mr. Abernathy?" Esther was asking.

"Would the twentieth be a possibility?"

"You may expect to see us with the frocks finished on the twentieth," said Esther, smiling.

"Very well," said Mr. Abernathy, ushering them through the shop. "Oh, and – what was the child's name again? Ellen, Eleanor – ?"

"Heloise," said Esther.

Heloise came back to the present moment with a start.

"Yes, sir?" she squeaked.

Mr. Abernathy went to a shelf behind the counter and picked out a tiny doll. "A little welcome to the business," he said kindly, handing it to her.

"Oh!" whispered Heloise, closing her hand over the doll. "Thank you, sir!"

"You're very welcome, my dear," said Mr. Abernathy, patting her again on the head. "Work hard, and – provided you learn to speak up, when spoken to – who knows what your future will be!"

"Well!" said Esther as they rounded the corner on their way home. "That was kind of him."

"I don't remember him doing that before," said Lizzie thoughtfully. "He must be getting sentimental in his dotage. Perhaps you remind him of his long-lost granddaughter, Heloise, like in a novel."

Heloise could not help thinking how strange life was. If a few months ago someone had unexpectedly given her a doll, no matter how small, it would have changed her life. Now, however – although any doll was still a wonder to her, and although she carried this one with tenderness – she hardly knew what to do with it. All she wanted was to assure herself that her beloved Maria was safe.

When the girls got home Melancholy opened the door.

"What did you see? What was in the shop windows? Was it amusing or dull? What did Old Abernathy say? What has Heloise got in her hand?"

"Mellie! Don't call him Old Abernathy," said Esther, mildly shocked. "He's one of our benefactors. You must not be ungrateful. And he gave Heloise a little present as a welcome, which was kind."

Heloise opened her hand and held it out, so that Melancholy could see the doll. She was wooden, about the size of a clothes peg, and had long, wavy golden hair that reached to her ankles. She was wearing a checked gingham dress and a white apron and mob-cap. Her face, which had been painted with delicacy, consisted of wide blue eyes, red smiling lips and rosy cheeks.

"Oh," said Melancholy, who did not have a doll. "She's beautiful!"

"Then you must have her," said Heloise, pressing the doll into Melancholy's hand. And with that she hurried away into the dormitory.

She did not care who saw her. Once there, she knelt and felt under the bed. But no ... it was obvious, the minute her fingertips touched the nightgown in which Maria was hidden, that she had not been disturbed. Maria was safe.

Heloise sat for a moment on her bed.

All was well. So, again, why did she not feel relieved?

"Dear, kind, good Heloise!" said Melancholy, thumping down on the bed beside her. "How utterly monstrous of you to give me your doll! Are you quite sure? You can change your mind, you know, and I will give her back at once." But Heloise could see that she was not entirely sincere.

"I am certain you should have her," she said, automatically. She was still panting a little with fear. But she had observed the manners of the girls around her closely enough to know the kind of remark that ought to come next. "She has the same color hair as you," she said, in Esther's tone of voice. "It was meant to be."

Melancholy looked at her to make sure she meant it, and failed to notice how preoccupied Heloise's eyes were. "You are *hideous* generous, dear Heloise. I have never had a doll," she said. She paused for a fraction of a second, then admitted, "Well, there was that one that fell into the stew and was never quite the same afterwards, but that was years ago and I try not to think about it." She pulled the doll out of the pocket of her pinafore and gazed at her happily. "I shall call her Antigone, after the noble heroine in the Greek myth who got walled up in a cave. How do you do, Antigone? I am your Mama, and this is your Aunt Heloise."

"How do you do, Antigone?" said Heloise softly.

She was beginning to understand. There was something else she was worried about – something more alarming, more important, even, than the threat posed by her godmother, something of greater consequence.

But what was it?

"Oh, look, the minxes, they're getting ready to go and get lunch!"

"We wouldn't have gone without you," called Lizzie from the front room. "If you're so worried about being left behind, come and put your bonnet on for pity's sake."

"Old Mother has given me a task concerning you," said Melancholy, as she dragged Heloise into the front room. "I have been to the Rector to ask permission. But we have to eat lunch first."

And so the girls set off for The Rose and Crown.

150

But Heloise did not have much of an appetite.

# Heloise Visits a Church

"Are you sure you don't mind the blindfold?" asked Esther anxiously.

"Tolerant child, isn't she?" Old Mother remarked, amused.

"It will be fun!" said Melancholy, taking Heloise by the hand.

Heloise sighed gently.

"Have you ever played Blindman's Buff?" Melancholy asked her.

"Indeed, no," said Heloise, shocked.

"First of all I'm going to spin you around three times … there. And now you must follow me!"

"Perhaps I should go with them," said Esther.

"Where would be the fun in that?" pouted Melancholy.

"I doubt you will come to any harm," said Old Mother.

"But you must guide Heloise very carefully. And behave yourself when you get there. Will you promise?"

"Thereto do I solemnly plight my troth," said Melancholy.

"You're not getting married," said Lizzie. Then she added, after a pause, "Are you?"

But Melancholy was already guiding Heloise through the courtyard to the crumbling stairs.

"Stop!" she said at the bottom of the stairway. "Now you must climb twelve stairs. I'll hold you. Ready?

"One …

"Two …

"Three …"

Carefully, Heloise climbed stair after stair. She looked like she was playing along. But she wasn't really. She did not want to play this game with Melancholy. But what she wanted had nothing to do with it. Still, she did not trust Melancholy to guide her. She had found that by peering out the bottom of her blindfold she could see at least one step in front of her. She was trusting nothing but her own eyes.

"That's the top of the stairs," said Melancholy. "Now we're going to walk straight ahead for a while …"

"Well, well, well," said a hearty male voice rather suddenly.

Heloise was startled. She went to take off the blindfold, but Melancholy stopped her.

"Afternoon Dr. Browne," Melancholy said. "This is Heloise," she explained. "Heloise, this is the Rector of Saint Mary of the Angels. His name is the Reverend Doctor

Bartholomew Browne, but we just call him Dr. Browne.

"Please Dr. Browne, you won't mind if Heloise leaves her blindfold on? Otherwise our game will be quite ruined."

Embarrassed, and not quite sure if she was facing in the right direction, Heloise dropped a blind curtsey.

"How do you do, sir," she murmured.

"How do you do, my dear blindfolded Miss Heloise," Dr. Browne said pleasantly. His voice was so deep it was almost a growl. "No doubt I will have the privilege of seeing your face unimpeded in due course. *For now we see as in a glass darkly*," he muttered. "But then, *face to face*. Hmm. I *could* make reference to Our Lord's image of the blind leading the blind, but that would be uncharitable – and actually the more interesting part was down near the door, Melancholy, my dear, when you were spinning Miss Heloise around … Put me in mind of the whole notion of revolution, turning, conversion … And then of course there is Saint Paul, blinded on the road to Damascus." He gazed absently at them. "Do you know, girls, I believe you've given me Sunday's sermon? Good day."

And he swept away in his flowing black cassock, looking rather as if he'd won a fight. Unfortunately, Heloise could not see him.

Melancholy was preoccupied. "Now there are more stairs," she said, getting back to more important matters. "You don't know where you are, do you?"

Heloise did, but she shook her head solemnly.

"Good," said Melancholy. "There are twelve of these, too.

There must be something about twelve. Well, the disciples, I suppose. And the twelve tribes of Israel. And the twelve dancing princesses. Ready?"

Heloise climbed the steps, pretending to depend on Melancholy's guidance while she looked through the bottom of the blindfold.

No, she did not want to play Melancholy's game.

She wanted to think.

Every night since she had arrived, Heloise had dreamed of Mary Child.

Sometimes she saw Mary Child working at her strange embroidery. Sometimes – and this was worse – she saw her sitting, idle and despairing, in the Madhouse, her work taken from her. One night Heloise had dreamed that she was back in her room at the caretaker's cottage, lifting the floorboard for the first time, about to discover – but it was not Maria who was lying there. It was Mary Child, dead.

Each dream was different. Only the subject was the same. And Heloise always had the same feeling when she woke up. It was a longing to help Mary Child, to save her, to change what had happened to her. *To do something.*

But there was nothing to be done. It had already happened. It was in the past, over and done with.

So why this gnawing anguish? Why this insistent calling, from deep within her?

"Now through here," said Melancholy.

Heloise could see that Melancholy was leaning with all her strength against the door. After a moment she managed to open it wide enough for the both of them to squeeze in. "Shh! We have to be quiet now," she added in a loud whisper, although Heloise had said nothing.

The two of them stood in a sudden deep stillness.

Heloise knew that they were inside the church. She was not greatly interested. But when Melancholy untied the blindfold and Heloise lifted her eyes once more, she was completely unprepared for what she saw.

For a moment Heloise thought she might swoon.

It was as if she were standing in the center of a precious stone – an emerald or a ruby or a sapphire – and as if that stone were on fire.

Heloise put a hand out to steady herself; her hand met a cold grey pillar that stretched like a tree into the ceiling, which was vaulted, midnight blue, and painted with gold stars.

Heloise lowered her eyes.

The church was small and spherical, dim and deeply colorful. Her first confused impressions were of many things at once: candles burning, playing tricks with her eyes in the dimness, pictures, both in stained glass and in relief along the walls, sheaves of lilies in brass vases, polished mahogany, old stonework. In addition to all this, a perfume, a heavy, autumnal perfume like – what? Burnt rose petals, or at least what she imagined rose petals might smell like if you burned them. Heloise had never heard of incense.

She blinked and blinked again.

So this, *this* was a church!

No wonder Heloise's godmother had kept her away from them. There was nothing here that she would approve of.

In all her life, Heloise had never seen so much beauty, and so much Wasted Time, packed in the one place.

She saw, without knowing what they were, mahogany pews, embroidered kneeling cushions, a grand organ – with great brass pipes stretching up to the ceiling – and an altar, covered with white lace. She saw choir stalls, and what seemed to be a golden eagle with its wings outstretched, although she did not know that this was a lectern that held the Bible. And she saw, suspended from the ceiling in front of the altar, the strangest thing: a man, hanging from a kind of tree with only two branches, his arms outstretched as if he were longing to hug the world.

Heloise gazed up at it.

She did not understand. And yet she knew that she was close to the answer.

"So we put on our choir robes downstairs," Melancholy was busy explaining, in a loud whisper. (Antigone was perched in the front pocket of her pinafore with her blonde head poking out, and this rather ruined Melancholy's air of confidence and well-versed efficiency.) "The robes go over our ordinary clothes. First the cassock, which is the purple thing, and then the surplice, which is the floaty white thing. Then we collect our hymn books, and Old Mother reminds us what the Processional Hymn is going to be. We find the right page and then keep a finger there to mark the place."

Melancholy paused. Then she remembered what she was supposed to be doing.

"When the bell starts ringing for church," she resumed hurriedly, "we line up in the right order so that, at the end of the procession, we end up standing near the others in our part, and then we wait for the bell to stop, because that means that the congregation will be inside.

"Then we walk quietly up both the stairways, two by two. Like this." Melancholy demonstrated, walking solemnly around the baptismal font that stood at the back of the church.

"Then Dr. Browne blesses us, and the Verger opens the door for us. We follow the Sacristan into the church and up the aisle with Mr. Callardin-Bowser going at it hammer and tongs and us singing the descant to the hymn like a chorus of angels.

"Mr. Callardin-Bowser is the organist," Melancholy put in. "He is a very fine musician, though quite mad. But then, all organists are mad, in my experience."

Melancholy opened a pretend hymn book and paced up

the aisle in a highly dignified manner, opening and closing her mouth as if she were singing. "Come on!" she hissed, when she noticed Heloise was not following.

Realizing this was to be a rehearsal, Heloise rushed to catch up.

"You have to keep in step with your partner," advised Melancholy. "And as each pair gets to the top of the nave, they bow to the altar – like this – and then proceed into position."

Melancholy stood on one side. Heloise found a seat opposite her. Heloise's eyes were as big as saucers. The church was even more splendid up here. And she could see something that intrigued her: a smaller altar at the side, about halfway down the church, with pews, a bank of burning candles, a vase of lilies and something tall and white standing behind them. She looked up again at the midnight-blue domed ceiling with the gold stars painted on it. She felt like she was floating in space. She felt as if all the world, the sun, the moon and the stars, were somehow inside this little church.

"We keep standing till we've finished singing the hymn. Then Dr. Browne says what he always says and the congregation kneel, but the choir keep standing to sing the Kyrie.

"Heloise? Are you listening?"

Heloise nodded, dazed. There was a good deal to know about singing in a church choir, and Melancholy seemed to know all of it. She went on, in graphic detail, for quite some time.

Her words were wasted on Heloise. She understood hardly

any of them. It had not occurred to Melancholy to talk to Heloise as if she had never been in a church before. When Melancholy set off back down the nave, it took Heloise a moment to collect her wits and catch up.

Halfway down the aisle, Heloise caught sight of the chapel she had noticed from the choir stalls. At first it had been just one of so many dazzling things. But now ...

Heloise looked, then looked again.

Then she stopped dead.

Forgetting Melancholy, she set off urgently, crab-walking through the narrow pew to her left. Reaching the far aisle, she turned and faced the altar with its bank of candles, and few small pews. Then, walking slowly up the short narrow aisle, she came closer.

There was a doll in the church.

Heloise stared.

She was fashioned from white stone, and very old – so old that parts of her were damaged, and parts worn away. She was wearing a long, loose gown and a veil. Her head was inclined, and she was smiling as if in a kind of secret joy. She was holding a doll-baby, who was just at the age to be able to sit up in her arms.

Strangely, she was standing inside a golden cage, the bars of which were as fine as those of a birdcage. On these bars, with a randomness that suggested they had come at different times from different people, were pinned a large number of folded pieces of paper. They looked like brief letters.

Heloise stared. When she came to once more she noticed that Melancholy had come up beside her.

"What – ? Who – ?" Heloise said helplessly.

"It's a statue of Our Lady," Melancholy explained. "Have you never seen one before?"

"Our – ?"

"The Mother of Our Lord," Melancholy explained further.

"Oh," said Heloise.

She had no idea what Melancholy was talking about. But it did not matter what the woman was called. Heloise knew her already, better than she knew anyone else in the world. In fact the statue was so familiar that it was as if Heloise was seeing before her a little piece of her own heart.

Here at last was the doll she had been looking for, the doll that looked like Maria. And she had found her, not in the doll shop, but in the church.

She sat down slowly on one of the pews. Melancholy sat beside her.

"What are the pieces of paper?" Heloise whispered.

"They're prayer intentions. You put a penny in the box, light a candle, write a prayer, and pin it to the cage."

So each burning candle and each letter was a prayer. Heloise swallowed.

"And why is she in a cage?" she asked.

Melancholy seemed taken aback. "I honestly don't know," she said. "You do ask the oddest questions.

"She used to stand in the Monastery Garden," continued

Melancholy. "When it *was* a monastery and when there was still a garden."

Heloise was not listening. Ever since she had seen the statue she had felt herself asking it a question. She was asking it with her whole heart, although she did not know what the question was.

Now there was a kind of shift in the air, a shimmering change that Heloise had experienced once before, although she did not remember when. Then the statue looked at her, very earnestly, her features fluid with expression, and Heloise heard a voice inside her head saying, "Heloise! *Mary Child is still suffering.*"

Heloise sprang to her feet. She stood swaying slightly, then stumbled towards the cage. She peered through the bars, searching the stone face. But she knew that the stone lady would say no more. Heloise went on staring at her, her heart thundering in her chest. She hardly knew what was more world-shaking – that the lady had talked to her, or what she had said.

So it wasn't in the past. It wasn't over and done with. It was still happening.

But how could this be? Mary Child was dead. Her godmother had told her so.

It seemed to make no sense, and yet –

*Mary Child was still suffering.*

She knew it was true. And she knew it changed everything.

Where was Mary Child? How could Heloise find her?

What could she do to help?

Heloise did not know.

All she knew was that, if Mary Child was still suffering, then that was the only thing that really mattered.

She had thought she had come so far. Now she knew that she was still only just at the beginning.

"What are you doing?" said Melancholy impatiently. "Aren't you hungry?"

Heloise slowly turned her eyes on her companion. It was as if she were looking out at her from the mouth of poor Antigone's cave.

"You *are* hungry!" Melancholy accused. "You look like you're about to faint. Come on!"

Heloise allowed herself to be led out of the church and downstairs to the well-meaning questions of Old Mother's Twelve-Voice Choir of Female Orphans, Waifs and Strays. For even after great revelations, life must go on.

That night, as Heloise lay in bed holding Maria, she began to scheme about where and how she could come by a penny, a pencil and a scrap of paper to write her prayer on.

She already knew what it would be.

*Show me how to stop her suffering.*

For if the doll in the church knew that Mary Child was still suffering, surely she would know how to stop it.

She fell asleep wondering whether the stone lady, like the

members of the Society of Caged Birds, secretly knew how to open her cage, and was  accustomed to roaming the city at night doing good.

# A Penny, a Pencil and a Scrap of Paper

The first Sunday Heloise sang with the choir was a bleak, windy day. The girls shivered in their thin choir robes as they paced up the two flights of stairs and waited under the church portico for Dr. Browne to bless them.

Earlier that morning there had been a knock on the door.

"Will you answer that please, Heloise?" Old Mother had said, and Heloise had hastened to obey.

When she was confronted with their guest, she cried out in fright.

Really, one could hardly blame her. Mr. Callardin-Bowser was an alarming-looking man. He was terribly tall, and terribly thin, and wore an ill-fitting, dusty black suit, which left his wrists and ankles poking out like the branches of a dead tree. His feet and hands were large and sinewy – like bunches of twigs – and his face was pale and gaunt, with large, sad eyes. These were quite colorless, or so it seemed, and either stared for an unnaturally long time or darted about like those of some small, hapless animal that was prey to everything and predator to nothing. Perhaps the most alarming thing about him was his hair, which, although he was a young man, had gone prematurely grey, or rather, white. It was long and straight and yet, instead of hanging limply to his shoulders, it stood out from his scalp, as if he was in a permanent state of abject terror. In fact this was not too far from the truth.

Thus it was not surprising that when he saw Heloise, he too yelled out in fright.

Heloise felt very badly over the incident. She had only been frightened for a moment and, as soon as she had finished screaming, had seen her mistake and felt only pity for the poor man.

Mr. Callardin-Bowser was not so apologetic. It was clear that he continued to find Heloise a most alarming creature.

"*Who is that?*" he hissed, pointing at her, as soon as he had recovered himself enough to speak.

Old Mother and Esther came immediately to his aid, guiding him to a nearby chair with soothing words and promises of a nice cup of tea. Melancholy rushed to put the kettle back on the hob.

Heloise stood appalled by the door. She felt she'd been seen through at last.

Lizzie bundled Heloise into the dormitory.

"Stay here till he goes," she whispered. "And don't worry! It wasn't your fault! No one can stop laughing – just look!"

Heloise looked back into the main room. It was as Lizzie had said. While pretending to be busy with this and that, the girls were looking down modestly, trying not to catch each other's eyes. Some were sucking in their cheeks, others were shaking with silent mirth, and she heard a sudden gulp from Nan just as she disappeared into the pantry. Even Old Mother and Esther had strained faces and shining eyes.

They did not take him seriously, that was plain. Because they thought him mad, Heloise was safe. But it was with the gravest sense of flinching recognition that she listened to the rantings that everyone else found so comical. She did not find Mr. Callardin-Bowser funny at all. And she did not think him mad. He had seen something that no one else had been able to see. He had seen that she did not belong.

"Black hair, green eyes, like a wood sprite, a changeling. I grew up with stories like that and who can tell, who can tell, there are more things in heaven and earth Horatio, and how can we be sure she has even been baptized?"

Mr. Callardin-Bowser was muttering.

"Well," said Old Mother sensibly, patting Mr. Callardin-Bowser on his thin shoulder and wishing he could hear the soothing concert that was taking place between her ears. "She's been on consecrated ground since she arrived and I've noticed nothing untoward. The milk has not gone sour. The ivy has not withered. You must not allow these thoughts to upset you,

167

Mr. Callardin-Bowser. You have a service to get through. And think how we depend on you for musical and spiritual solace. The choir would be nothing without your accompaniment, you know."

"Yes, yes, true, true," said Mr. Callardin-Bowser, accepting the cup of tea Melancholy brought for him and sipping it rather erratically. "The music, the music, I must concentrate on the music."

For the next few minutes, they did exactly that, for Mr. Callardin-Bowser and Old Mother were accustomed to having a brief meeting before Sunday service to be certain that all was in order. By the time he left for the church, he was comparatively calm, although Lizzie thought it best that he should not catch sight of Heloise again until he was safely behind the keyboard.

"What if he sees me coming up the aisle?" whispered Heloise, as they waited outside the church.

"He's always at his sanest while he's actually playing," said Lizzie reassuringly.

But whichever way she looked at it, Heloise found that rather cold comfort.

The service passed like a dream, or a nightmare. Heloise's every nerve and sinew was concentrated on copying her fellow choristers. She was determined to walk through this unfamiliar ritual without the smallest false step. And she expected every minute to be denounced. For surely Mr. Callardin-Bowser was not the only member of the congregation who could tell, just by looking at her?

However, it seemed that he was.

And even he took no notice of her during the service.

Heloise stood, and sat, and kneeled, and mimed. She was so caught up that she had no time to spare for the beauty of the church, the splendor of Mr. Callardin-Bowser's performance at the organ, the imposing figure of Dr. Browne, with his growling voice, the solemn eccentricities of the church officials, or even the varied group of people who made up the congregation.

How could she hope to remain unnoticed if she took her mind for a moment off what she was doing?

There were, however, four impressions that penetrated the fog of her self-consciousness.

The first was the occasional disconcerting glimpse of the top of Mr. Callardin-Bowser's dandelion-white shock of mad hair in the space above the organ.

The second was a beautiful, dark-haired lady, not in her first youth, with a pale oval face and dark eyes. She sat in the very front pew and never stopped smiling, apparently from sheer happiness, throughout the entirety of the service.

The third was the spectacle of a very young lady in a rose-pink bonnet, also seated near the front, clinging to the arm of a somewhat morose-looking young man and dabbing frequently at her eyes with a white lace handkerchief.

The fourth was Melancholy, making the most extraordinary faces at her from the other side of the choir stalls (and under cover of a convenient pillar) during Dr. Browne's sermon.

"The effrontery!" she muttered, when at long last they were recessing back down the nave.

Heloise had no idea what she was talking about, and Mr. Callardin-Bowser's improvisations with-all-the-stops-pulled-out made it impossible to think about anything else.

Leaving Dr. Browne at the steps to shake rather fiercely the hands of every member of the congregation, the girls hastened down the second flight of stairs and across the courtyard, and tumbled into the dormitory. Almost before they were out of their choir robes and into fresh Sunday dresses, there was another knock at the door.

Every girl looked at Heloise and laughed.

Heloise looked back at them hauntedly.

Esther only smiled. "Don't worry, Heloise," she said, running to the door. "I'm sure we all know exactly who *this* is!"

She opened the door and fell into the arms of the very young lady in the rose-pink bonnet.

"Esther!" wailed the latter, and promptly burst into tears.

There followed a small stampede as everyone except Heloise – and a smiling Old Mother – rushed to embrace their visitor and shower her with partially audible chatter. Meanwhile the uncomfortable-looking young man Heloise had noticed in the church stood awkwardly in the doorway.

Old Mother greeted him kindly.

"And how do you find married life, Mr. Pettigrew?" she asked.

"Highly recommended," said the young man, rather gloomily.

"Have you met our new chorister?" asked Old Mother, bringing Heloise forward.

Mr. Pettigrew brightened slightly. "Oh, I am glad you've managed to replace her so quickly," he said. "Er, Allie – er – my wi – er – Mrs. Pettigrew, I mean. I was rather worried you might change your mind and want her back. And may I ask your name, miss?" he said kindly, to Heloise.

"Heloise, sir," whispered Heloise.

Mr. Pettigrew then did a marvelous thing.

And it was now that the day, which had started so harrowingly, began to change.

He reached into his top pocket, fished out a penny, and handed it to Heloise.

"A small token of my gratitude," he murmured.

Heloise stared at the penny, then at Mr. Pettigrew, then at the penny again.

Mr. Pettigrew stared back at Heloise; he had noticed that her eyes had filled with tears.

Meanwhile, Alice – for of course the young lady in the rose-pink bonnet was she – had fallen into Old Mother's arms. "Old Mother!" she wailed.

"Now, now, Alice, what's all this?"

"I find, Old Mother, returning here this morning as a married lady, that I am overwhelmed by nostalgia for happy times past!" said Alice, making use of her white lace handkerchief.

"My dear, you always were of a melancholy turn of mind," observed Old Mother. "Perhaps you should go in for poetry."

"Pardon?" said Melancholy, who had been admiring Alice's rose-pink velvet drawstring purse.

"Would it not be more fitting, Alice, dear," said Esther diffidently, "to dwell upon your bright future? After all, the past – delightful as it was – is the past, and you have such happy times to look forward to in your new state of life. And although we miss you, we are all so blessed to have gained – well, a brother, as it were, in Mr. Pettigrew, if he will forgive my presumption."

"I am honored, Miss Esther," said Mr. Pettigrew rather weakly. Heloise was still staring at him, and he was disconcerted to find himself more popular with the choir than he appeared to be with his wife.

"But the future is so uncertain!" Alice sighed tearfully. "That is why the past is so appealing. One already knows how it all turned out."

There was a brief silence as everyone attempted to follow her logic. Suddenly Mr. Pettigrew said, "So you think it turned out well, then? The past, I mean?"

"Why, yes, my dear," said Alice with a wobbly smile. "For my time in the choir ended with my marriage to you."

"And that was a happy ending, was it not?" Mr. Pettigrew pursued a little uncertainly.

Alice laughed, quite as if he had said the drollest thing in the world.

"Well, of course, you silly man," she said, giving him a playful little push. "He is so insecure of my devotion," she explained to the gathering. "I can't imagine why. I never stop reassuring him. I am quite weary of it."

At that point there was another knock on the door, which a considerably relieved, if still slightly confused Mr. Pettigrew answered. In came two females bearing trays. One of them wore a white apron and cap, and appeared to be a maidservant. She was in her mid-teens and kept looking around rather skeptically, as if she did not approve of what she saw. The other was the smiling lady Heloise had noticed in the front pew of the church.

"Good morning, Mrs. Browne!" murmured the girls more or less in unison, and they curtseyed respectfully.

"Good morning, girls, Old Mother, Mr. and Mrs. Pettigrew!" said Mrs. Browne gaily – for this lady, who couldn't stop smiling, was Dr. Browne's wife. "As you see I have brought you refreshments to tide you over until dinner, but I'm afraid I provided only for twelve plus one, not counting on your having guests at this early hour!"

"We were on the point of taking our leave, madam," said Mr. Pettigrew, hoping to leave before the sentimental dimension of not having been brought a cup of hot chocolate struck his wife's all-too-delicate sensibilities. "So lovely to see you all. The singing was capital, by the way."

"My mother-in-law expects us for dinner," said Alice, "and she is a very punctual lady. But we will come again soon. And I shall write once a week, as soon as I have a proper routine in place. Everything is still at sixes and sevens at the moment. The chaise lounge we ordered has not arrived yet. Can you imagine? What is a boudoir without a chaise lounge? At least I have the harpsichord. I think of you every time I play it, Old Mother!"

These last words were faint, as her husband had managed to get her halfway up the stairs before she uttered them.

The girls, having waved and blown kisses energetically, retreated inside to sip their hot chocolate.

"Meanwhile Priscilla and I must get back to our preparations," said Mrs. Browne. "May Dr. Browne and I expect you in half an hour or so, Old Mother?"

"Indeed, Mrs. Browne. The girls are almost ready," said Old Mother, and with another smile Mrs. Browne and her maid hurried away.

A moment later Mrs. Browne returned. "I almost forgot!" she said. "Where is little Heloise?"

Heloise jumped. She was still standing by herself, fingering the magical penny.

"Welcome to the choir, my dear," said Mrs. Browne, and from the pocket of her gown she took a shiny new lead pencil, with Heloise's name carved neatly into the top end, and presented it to her with a kiss. "See you all at dinner!" she said gaily, and hurried out.

Heloise stared after her. A penny and now a pencil.

And the second kiss of her life.

Perhaps all would be well.

Heloise was disconcerted when she entered the dining room of the Rectory, to see Mr. Callardin-Bowser already seated at the table. But he was tapping out an absorbing rhythm with two pieces of silver, and fortunately did not notice her – or indeed anyone else.

In any case, the dining room table was long. When they sat down to dinner, Heloise found herself placed at the opposite end of it. Not only was she sitting as far away as possible from Mr. Callardin-Bowser, she was sitting as close as possible to Dr. Browne, a position that caused her to be the object of some envy.

Dr. Browne was a fine-looking man with graying black hair, a square, dented chin, fierce dark eyebrows and humorous blue eyes that glittered like diamonds. He wore the somber garb of a clergyman and his demeanor was calm and patient, however, there was a certain restless energy about him, as if being peaceful did not come easily to him. In fact he looked as if, should things come to blows, either physically or intellectually, it would be difficult to best him in a fight.

The Rectory was a gloomy house on the other side of the

church. Like the church, it was small, and indeed it seemed too small for what had to be fit into it. Every spare corner was crammed with a dark, shabby piece of furniture, a shelf full of books or a picture, but there was not enough light to see what the pictures depicted, or what the books might have been about. Heloise began to think of Dr. Browne as a man who dwelt in a kind of learned cave, from which he emerged to give sermons and shake peoples' hands. The cavernous ceiling contributed to this impression.

So there Heloise sat, and as the Rector said grace it occurred to her that at this time last week, she had not even seen The Museum of Mary Child yet. She was just getting used to this dizzying thought when, having done the carving and begun his meal, Dr. Browne said to her:

"So, Miss Heloise, we meet again! And this time you are without your blindfold! The scales, it seems, have fallen from your eyes. Or mine perhaps."

"Humph!" said Melancholy loudly from midway down the table.

They all turned and looked at her.

"Mellie!" said Esther, scandalized.

But Dr. Browne's eyes sparkled humorously.

"Why, Miss Melancholy! What could be the matter? Pray assure me I have not offended you."

"You have, sir," said Melancholy fearlessly, "and what's more you know perfectly well how."

"Mellie," said Old Mother.

"Mellie, *really*," said Esther.

"You didn't like the sermon," said Dr. Browne humbly.

"No, sir, I did not!" said Melancholy with her chin tilted towards the ceiling.

"Well!" said Mrs. Browne laughingly. "Didn't I tell you, Mr. Browne, that female choristers may not enjoy having their private games used as metaphors?"

"But it was such a good one, my dear," pleaded Mr. Browne.

Heloise could hardly have been more astonished. Now she understood the faces Melancholy had been making throughout the sermon. She had not been listening to Dr. Browne, but she could only imagine that he had made reference to their prior meeting on the stairs. What was it he had said? Something about the blindfold and being turned around? She did not know which was more surprising – having been the subject of a sermon, or the fact that Melancholy was bold enough to take issue with a clergyman.

"It's no good pleading your case with me, my dear," said Mrs. Browne to her husband. "You must seek restitution with the lady you have offended."

"How can I hope to redeem myself, Miss Melancholy?" asked Dr. Browne theatrically.

Melancholy hesitated for only a second.

"Give Heloise some paper," she commanded. "You have plenty, and she needs some for a very particular purpose."

Heloise stared at her. But Dr. Browne was already hunting

177

through his suit coat. Presently he drew out a trim black leather notebook.

"Your wish, Miss Melancholy, is my command. How many pieces?"

Melancholy raised her eyebrows at Heloise. Heloise shook her head desperately at her. But everybody seemed to be waiting, so she swallowed, looked at Dr. Browne, and whispered: "Just one, sir, would be ample – and much appreciated …"

Dr. Browne tore a sheet and handed it to her.

"I hope, miss, that this small token of my remorse will blot out my offence to both of you." He paused, his face nostalgic. "Mind you, I still think it was a cracking sermon."

Just then a voice said abruptly, "Begging your pardon, sir," and Heloise jumped with shock.

"Yes, Priscilla?" said Dr. Browne, for Priscilla was waiting behind Heloise's chair.

"Old Mrs. Atkins is fading fast, sir, and her son's come to ask if you will visit. He doesn't think she's quite easy in her mind, sir," said Priscilla, whose considerable psychic energy enabled her to convey this important message with appropriate decorum and, simultaneously, to look down at Heloise with the highest degree of unfriendliness.

"Tell him I'll come at once," said Dr. Browne, rising from the table. "Excuse me, Miss Heloise. Excuse me, my dear," he said to his wife. He nodded generally around the table and departed. A moment later they heard him greeting his parishioner and shutting the street door behind him.

Mrs. Browne sighed. "Sometimes I think he will never finish a meal," she said wistfully.

Meanwhile, Priscilla whisked away Heloise's almost full plate. "Not good enough for you, I suppose?" she said maliciously. After a moment of astonishment, it dawned on Heloise that Priscilla had taken offence at how slowly she was progressing with her meal – and indeed everyone else at the table had finished. Heloise was a little upset, but could not help finding it comical as well. In fact she found herself feeling at once tearful and as if she might start to giggle. Fortunately there was (as Melancholy had predicted) dessert, and fortunately Mrs. Browne herself served it.

Not long after that the girls were saying their thank-yous and tumbling back onto the quiet street.

Now Heloise had a penny, a pencil and a piece of paper. Her only concern was how she would get into the church by herself.

"Old Mother," said Melancholy as they passed the church door. "May Heloise visit Our Lady?"

Heloise looked painfully at Melancholy. But Old Mother was unperturbed.

"Very well, Heloise," she said. "But be quick about it, if you please. I will expect you back within five minutes."

The door was open, but the church was empty. Heloise

hastened to the lady chapel. She sat on the end of a pew, retrieved the pencil and the penny and the piece of paper from the pocket of her gown and wrote the prayer she had decided on. Then she folded it inwards, for privacy's sake, attached it to the gold cage, put the penny in the copper box, chose a candle, lit it, placed it carefully amongst the others and knelt for a moment, closing her eyes so tightly in her longing that the imprint of the bank of burning candles seemed like a shimmering galaxy inside her head. Then, with a last lingering look, she departed.

Melancholy was waiting for her as she came down the steps.

"*Will* you shut that door, Mellie!" came Lizzie's voice from inside. "The draft is making my ears ache!"

Melancholy ignored her.

"Come along, Heloise, what have you been doing?" she called impatiently. She ran out, caught Heloise by the hand, and dragged her inside. "Esther has promised to read us *Aladdin* again! And she has said I can be the Genie!"

# The Unfortunates

As the days, and then the weeks passed, winter came on, not gradually, with each day a little colder than the last, but in fits and starts, two steps forward and one step back. There would be two, perhaps three days of mild weather. Then there would be a day when it was suddenly much colder, and if a milder day followed, it would be not as mild as before. The sun, when it shone, was bright, but weak, with little warmth in it, and the girls wrapped themselves up against the cold whenever they went out.

Although Old Mother lit the stove every morning, and the girls fed it at intervals with coal, it was harder to keep warm while they were sewing. They wrapped themselves in shawls and blankets, and kept the stove door open, and sat close to it whenever possible, but their feet were numb more often than not, and their hands so chilled that it was hard to be dexterous with a needle.

If winter was here, Christmas was not far behind, and despite their little sufferings the girls' spirits were high.

Every day they rehearsed for Christmas Eve. They had been engaged, as usual, to sing the Midnight Mass on the night before Christmas, and also the Sung Eucharist on Christmas Day, and there would be singing the day after Christmas, too, because this year Christmas fell on a Saturday. But Old Mother, and the girls themselves, gave special importance to their tradition of out-of-doors carol singing for what they called The Unfortunates. More time and care was spent rehearsing for this than for the church services.

"No, no, no!" Old Mother said vehemently. "It should be like bells, like little silver bells – like this!" and she demonstrated by dancing around on the tips of her toes in what she imagined to be a fairy-like manner. The sight was comical, but it was a testament to the seriousness with which the girls took her direction that not one of them laughed. "Now once more, from the upbeat to bar seventeen …"

As for Heloise, she went along with it all as quietly as she could. She pretended to know what Christmas was. She pretended to be as enthusiastic as the others were about singing for The Unfortunates. She worked hard at her sewing, and walked faultlessly through services she did not understand, without ever singing above a whisper.

Most of all, she waited. There was nothing else she could

do. Except bide her time, keep herself to herself, watch her companions, and listen to everything that was said, believing that one day soon, she would find out something about Mary Child that would tell her what to do.

Melancholy was in the habit of announcing how many more days there were 'til Christmas.

"Only one-and-twenty days 'til Christmas!" she said, one dark, rainy morning.

"Only fourteen days 'til Christmas!" she said on another, when the wind was so high that it rattled the glass in the window panes.

"Only one week left 'til Christmas!" she said, on a brilliantly cold, sunny day.

And on the morning that she told them there was only one day left, they had woken to a world that had turned white overnight.

The girls crowded around the windows. The ivy, being evergreen, was still as green as summer, but the courtyard was no longer grey stone crumbling with age. Now it was as white and as new as if it had just been hewn from the finest marble. And the snow was still falling.

"Girls, you will catch your death of colds!" said Old Mother. She clapped her hands. "Back into the dormitory with you! You must all get dressed at once."

The girls were too excited to eat breakfast. Or at least

those whose tendency it was to eat less when they were excited ate less or nothing, and those who tended to eat more when excited made up for them. Heloise fell into the first of these categories, and Melancholy into the second.

When the washing up and the ordinary chores had been done, the hours until nightfall stretched nervously before them.

In the weeks leading up to Christmas Mr. Abernathy, the doll seller, had kept them especially busy. But the Christmas orders had been completed. Now – strange thought! – there would be no sewing until the New Year.

So they spent the time doing the kinds of jobs for which there was usually not the leisure. Sweeping the cobwebs out of hard-to-reach corners. Cleaning the tops of shelves and cupboards. Tidying the drawers where they kept their sewing tools. Putting their choir robes out to air.

Even so the hours dragged, as hours do when an important event is looming. When at last the clock struck noon, they bundled up and made their way through a biting wind, and the still-falling snow, to collect their midday dinner from The Rose and Crown.

"If this weather doesn't improve," said Old Mother, trudging with them, "we may have to abandon the outdoors section of our program, girls."

Despite their discomfort, the girls looked stricken, and muttered little moans of disappointment.

"Well," said Old Mother a little tetchily – for she was

disappointed, too – "delicate young girls who are not blessed with the resources for furs and furbelows are not intended by Providence to go traipsing around the city after nightfall in freezing weather. You may sing like angels, my dears, but you have not been given their immortality."

The girls' teeth were chattering too hard for them to reply, although Melancholy did try. The trouble was, though she opened her mouth several times, she could think of nothing convincing to say.

Although the girl at The Rose and Crown had wrapped the food up as snugly as she could, it was cold by the time they got it home. But they ate what they could, and returned the plates. Then Old Mother insisted that they all lie down for a nap, as they would be up half the night.

"If you can't sleep," she said, "spend the time praying that the wind drops."

Heloise did not think she would sleep, but she went obediently to bed. There she lay with the covers up over her head and Maria secretly in her arms.

So now, at last, she was about to be initiated into the rites of Christmas. Heloise sighed. She felt bemused. It was not surprising that her godmother had not celebrated this festival. From what she had gathered, it did not sound like the kind of thing her godmother would approve of, any more than she would approve of twelve orphan girls earning their living by dressing dolls. But sometimes she wondered why it was that she had never noticed anyone else celebrating it either.

It seemed odd that all the Christmases of her life so far had passed without a single visible sign.

But then, Heloise's memory was strange. She had often thought so. There was so much she did not remember. Sometimes it almost seemed that her life had started on the day she had lifted the floorboard and found Maria.

When Old Mother rang the bell to rouse them, the evening had grown calm, and it had stopped snowing. Silent with anticipation, the girls rubbed the sleep out of their eyes, dressed, collected their music, and set out into a clear, cold Christmas Eve.

Heloise could not have imagined there were so many Unfortunate places in the city, but Old Mother seemed to know them all. The odd thing was, The Unfortunates seemed to know Old Mother, too.

The girls trudged through the snow to a vantage point of Old Mother's choosing. Then they sang three carols, perhaps four, and moved on to a new place. When it was time to depart, even if they had not seen the audience for whom they were singing (for sometimes they were at work within a building or hiding in the shadows of a makeshift shelter) someone or other called out, "Thank you, Old Mother! Merry Christmas to you!"

And Old Mother called back stoutly, "Merry Christmas to you, my dear!"

And so they walked and sang, and walked and sang. Their feet and hands and faces ached with the cold; they stood as close as possible to one another when singing and, when walking, linked arms. They were a charming sight, twelve bundled-up orphans and their protectoress caroling in the snow, especially if you were looking out at them from a warm room with a good fire.

The hardest part was not the cold. The hardest part was singing in the open air. It was as if, no matter how much effort they summoned, no matter how correct their breathing and posture, the sound of their voices was stolen by the vastness of the night. It was a deflating feeling, so different from singing inside a church, where the friendly architecture served to magnify their every utterance.

But, courageously, they persisted.

They sang in front of a small factory, where tiny children were engaged in pasting together, with foul-smelling and noxious glue, the parts of a contraption whose use they did not understand.

They sang at a hospital, where a community of sisters looked after the desperately ill and desperately poor, almost all of whom would not survive the winter.

They sang at the corners of desolate streets filled with tumbledown, eyeless houses, and for urchins huddled together for warmth, and for policemen and horse-and-cab drivers and doctors – even a midwife – people whose work called them out into the bitter cold of the night.

And they sang at the two most wretched places of all.

"Come girls," said Old Mother at last, "the hardest is still to come, but after that, home."

Heloise wondered what she could mean. She hesitated. As a rule she avoided asking questions, but she could not stop herself.

"Where are we going?" she murmured to Melancholy.

"The Madhouse," said Melancholy matter-of-factly.

"Then the Prison."

Heloise stopped dead in the middle of the street.

"Heloise? What ails you?" said Melancholy.

Heloise opened her mouth, but could find no words.

The Madhouse had been in the city all along.

The shock was almost too much for her.

"Oh, don't be afraid!" said Melancholy, taking her arm. "They're all well-secured."

But that was not what Heloise was worried about. Pulled along by Melancholy, she moved forward like a sleepwalker, her mind racing.

Was it possible that she was about to visit the place where Mary Child still lived?

Was it true that she was so close?

Of course, Heloise had no idea how many madhouses existed. Perhaps there were more than one. Perhaps they were dotted all over the country. Perhaps there were so many mad people that, despite the number of madhouses, there was not enough room for them all, and some of them had been put into boats and sent to a new country altogether, a country that was one big madhouse. She had a feeling she had heard an idea like this before.

Mary Child could have gone to live in a Mad Country.

But she could also be right here.

Heloise's heart knocked against her ribs.

If Mary Child was in this Madhouse, Heloise would be unlikely to see her. Mary Child would be inside, and the girls would be singing in the street.

But even to see the place where she lived – or might live – and to know that, now that she had found it, she could come back …

Heloise had been waiting for a way forward, a next step. And now, perhaps, it had come.

No one who had seen these two terrible buildings could ever have forgotten them, and in all her life afterwards, Heloise never did. Far from the Cathedral and the Houses of Parliament and the Palace, farther still from the better residences and the places of commerce and courts of law, and farther again from the pleasure gardens and parks, they seemed nonetheless to loom over the City as if they were the most important places in it.

It was a taxing walk, all uphill, during which they passed one deserted building or plot of ground after another, and saw no one. Heloise had her own reasons to be somber, but the rest of the girls were in scarcely better spirits. Somehow, the conviction had crept over them that the evening had not been a success. It was disappointing, because they had been practicing for so long, and had wanted to do so much good. But their singing seemed so little, and the misery in the city so large.

Now they had before them the two hardest places of all, and their courage was failing.

When they reached the summit of the hill, and the Madhouse rose before them, they stood huddled, looking palely up at it. The mere sight of the place seemed to suck the very dregs of their courage out of the bottom of their hearts.

Heloise had not looked up since she had been told where they were going. She had been looking at the snowy ground, counting each footstep, then losing count, and counting again. Now that they had stopped, she took a deep breath of cold air, and raised her eyes slowly.

So here it was.

Now she knew.

And the moment she saw it she was convinced.

"*Mary Child lives here*," she thought. "*How could she not?*"

For it seemed to Heloise that the Madhouse looked like nothing so much as one of the faces of Mary Child's crazy dolls.

The simple construction. The thousands of tiny bricks. The many blind windows, through which nothing could be seen from the outside. The sense that people were there and yet not there, at once dead and alive.

Heloise found herself combing the building with her eyes, looking for something or someone, trying to understand – what?

Old Mother could not have known what this place meant to Heloise. She knew her little choir was downcast, but she had music – and doing good – on her mind. And she did not give up easily.

"Come, girls! Your very best!" she urged.

So – with the exception of Heloise – the girls tried to sing like the Choir of Angels they had often been compared to. With all the heart they could muster, they worked through the four carols Old Mother judged to be their most accomplished, although it was hard to sing to a blank wall. It was like singing to the dead. When they finished, they paused uncertainly, for in that deserted street on that desolate rise there was no indication that anyone had heard them.

"It's like the dark side of the moon," said Nan, who was interested in astronomy.

"That's where the word lunatic comes from," remarked Esther, who was uncharacteristically subdued.

"Perhaps they've all gone away on holiday," said Melancholy quite brightly. "Do mad people have holidays?"

"Do you mean do they get a holiday from being mad, or do they go and be mad in another place, just for a change?" asked Lizzie. "Neither, I don't think, my dear."

Old Mother was not listening. She was not unaffected by the surroundings, but she was not unhappy. She felt they had done their best. And who knew what unseen good they might have done? Perhaps, she thought, they had cheered up the rats.

"Good girls," she said. "Come along now. Last one."

And she set off, with most of the girls trudging on behind her.

But Heloise stood staring on the footpath. She had not noticed that the singing had stopped, and –

She did not quite know how to leave.

"*Where are you?*" she thought. "*Are you really in there? Do you know I'm out here?*"

"*You must,*" she thought. "*It cannot be possible for me to be standing out here, and you not know it. Oh, Mary Child, how can I – ? What must I – ?*"

"What are you doing?" hissed Melancholy.

Heloise did not respond. After a moment, Melancholy took her arm and pulled her away. Heloise seemed barely aware of her. She stumbled along, but she kept looking backwards at the Madhouse. Melancholy frowned. "The cold has addled your brain," she muttered. "Perhaps I should tell Old Mother. But we have only one more to go …"

The one more was the Prison.

A dirty, crumbling fortress alongside the Madhouse, it seemed as if it would be impenetrable to the feeble strains of twelve girls singing. Indeed, it mocked the whole silly idea that music could do anyone so wretched any good.

But Old Mother had not given up yet, and she had a friend in the turnkey.

"Cold night, eh, Old Mother?" he said through the grille of the iron door, as he fumbled with what sounded like an extensive bunch of keys. "Now don't go on for too long, mind. The Governor's let you have fifteen minutes. Quite enough of a Christmas treat for the likes of them. They get extra rations tomorrow, too. Let's hope they're grateful."

When he had opened the door he revealed himself to be a tough-looking, stocky little man in a rumpled uniform. The girls did not altogether like him. But he led them protectively through a stone passageway and out into a bare courtyard, on which the bright, cold, starry night looked down with a kind of remote pity. The turnkey stood guarding them as Old Mother got them ready, although there was not a single prisoner to be seen, only four tall walls and what must have been a hundred tiny barred windows.

The girls might have finally succumbed to the cold, and the hopelessness. They could have mewed and squeaked their way through it and gone home defeated. But, somehow, the extreme bleakness of their surroundings roused the asset they did not know they had.

Heloise.

Or at least, the strange power of Heloise's character, which usually slept like a dragon in its lair, but which sometimes awoke.

Heloise had had enough. She was sick of this sadness,

this hopelessness, these blank walls, these incarcerations. She had suddenly become angry, but it was an anger completely harnessed, completely under her control.

When they began to sing, Heloise began to sing too. Not silently, not even softly, but in her full, powerful voice.

Now Heloise was singing First Alto, and choirs are supposed to blend. If the choir had not been capable of matching her, you would have only heard Heloise. And that would have sounded peculiar, as First Alto, by itself, is not usually a particularly interesting tune. But that was not what happened. Instead, Heloise's voice, singing so fearlessly, gave them courage.

It went through them like fire licking up kindling. They all knew it. They all felt it. Now, suddenly, anything was possible. They leaned against each other for encouragement, exchanging steady, brave looks, while Heloise looked at no one, just sang and sang into the night, riding like the most accomplished equestrienne on her own anger. Old Mother had never lost heart. But she had never expected this. It was like the choir had become a force of nature; directing it was like trying to conduct a storm. So she gave up trying, and turned the prow of her ship into the waves.

The girls' hearts filled with defiance – defiance for all things unjust and unkind. They sang for the prisoners they could not see, and who could not see them, and they sang more beautifully, more powerfully, than they had ever sung before. So beautifully and powerfully that soon Old Mother's face was shining with tears. Their voices rang out like silver bells into the emptiness, echoed against the prison walls, and filled the night with music.

Heloise did not know it, could not have put it into words, but in her strange deep anger, with her powerful voice, she was calling to someone, someone whose existence she half-suspected, much as she had called to Maria before she had known that she was lying under the floorboards.

And, in his cell, amongst the dungeons, ten feet below the cobbled yard, the person she was calling to heard.

On their way home they were silent. It was not an experience that could be talked about. Truth be told they were a little afraid of discussing it, especially with Heloise, whose face had an odd, elated glow about it. They ate their supper and got ready for Midnight Mass. And after that magical service, they all went quietly to bed.

They slept like angels. All except Heloise, who, at the darkest hour of the night, was awakened by a tiny voice.

# The Captive

"Heloise!"

That shrill, whistly voice so close to her ear, those little scratchy feet on her head. The last time this had happened, she had thought it was a dream. This time, she did not doubt that it was real. She had not been long asleep, and the events of the evening were still alive in her imagination. Anything could still happen.

"Wake up, Heloise!" the voice said. "The time has come! You must arise and dress at once! Do not be afraid. You will be back before dawn."

It was Merryfeathers.

Heloise had only seen Merryfeathers once. But she trusted him more than any other living thing in the world. So she did not ask questions.

Instead, she got out of bed, kissed Maria, pushed her carefully down under the bedclothes, hunted blindly for her cloak and pulled it over her nightgown. Then, holding her boots, she followed Merryfeathers – whose fluttering path she could just perceive – out of the dormitory and into the main room.

"I came in through the chimney," he said. "But you must go out through the door. You will have to leave it unlocked, for you have no key, but you need not fear; your friends are in no danger."

He was sitting on her shoulder and whispering in her ear. Obediently, Heloise opened the door as quietly as she could. The cold air took her breath away. Her heart quailed, but she braced herself, slipped out the door, closed it and, hopping up and down on the stone slab, made haste to put her boots on her frozen feet.

"We are going back to the gaol," said Merryfeathers.

Heloise was not surprised, although she could not have explained why.

"But," added Merryfeathers, "it will not take as long to get there as it did earlier. I know a short cut. I will guide you. Let us set out."

Heloise crept through the moonlit courtyard and up the twelve icy steps. She was trembling with cold and anticipation. At the top of the stairway she began automatically to walk southwards, towards the middle of the city. Before she had taken three steps Merryfeathers stopped her.

"Ah, but my short cut lies in the opposite direction," he said. "Go north, if you please, Heloise, and into the church."

"Into the church?" murmured Heloise. "But didn't you say that we were going to the gaol?"

"And so we are," said Merryfeathers. "Make haste!"

Heloise was inclined to doubt that the church would be open. She knew that the door was always unlocked during the day, but all night? Surely the Verger would have locked it at the conclusion of Midnight Mass.

But she was wrong. When she got to the top of the steps and pushed the heavy door, it moved inwards. And so – through the small gap she had strength enough to make for herself – she squeezed in.

The church was warm, and dim, and empty, lit only by the candles that burned before the two altars.

"Walk up the nave," said Merryfeathers, "and pause at the steps up to the altar."

Heloise obeyed him. She had that curious feeling, once again, that somehow the whole universe was within this tiny church, and as she walked up the nave, with the candles flickering like stars around her, she felt as if she were walking through space. When she got to the three steps which led up out of the transept, she paused, as instructed.

"Now look down," said Merryfeathers.

Heloise did so.

At first she could see nothing. The light was so muted and wavering. She knew that the floor was tiled, and that the tiles near the altar became a decorative mosaic, but she knew this from memory. In this light she could make out nothing of the design.

Then, in a tiny flicker of candlelight, she caught sight of something that shone like metal. It looked like a large ring or bangle resting on the floor.

"Pick it up," instructed Merryfeathers.

Heloise tried to – and realized she was standing on a trapdoor.

It was one of the strangest moments of her life. At first she thought the door must have been constructed in the hour or so since she had left the church after Midnight Mass. For, of course, although she had walked over this section of the floor many times she had never seen any hint of a door before. Almost immediately, she realized the truth. When the light was stronger, the mosaic camouflaged the trapdoor. Only when the light was dim did the door become visible.

It had never occurred to her that some things could be seen better in less light.

She took a step back, bent down, and pulled the door open by the ring. She had thought it might be heavy, but it was lighter than she expected, made, it seemed, only of wood beneath the tiles. She rested the door against the three stairs behind it. In the flickering light she glimpsed the beginning of an ancient stairway, carved out of stone. Damp air traveled out of the opening.

"Climb down and shut the door behind you," said

Merryfeathers.

Heloise did. There were twelve steps; when she had climbed down six of them she pulled the door closed over her head. She climbed down the second six in complete darkness.

"Don't be afraid," said Merryfeathers once more. "Just follow the passage."

Heloise was not afraid. She was feeling braver than she ever had in her life. The passage was narrow – child-sized – and so cold it might have been a passage through a mountain made of ice. Perhaps she should have been afraid, and yet, she felt that at last she had found the passage she had been looking for, the one that led into the heart of things.

Heloise pushed forward. After a time she began to feel that the darkness was less intense, although she was not at first certain if she was correct. Shortly after that, she was startled by two dim flashes of something grayish-white, to her right and left. She wondered what these things could be and realized that she was seeing her own hands, feeling their way along the passage.

Then, up ahead, she saw something else.

At first she did not know what it was. When she first caught sight of it, it was small, no bigger than the palm of her hand. As she approached, it grew larger. When at last it seemed that she was about ten feet away from it, she realized that what she was seeing was a barred window. Through it streamed criss-crossed patches of grey light; it was these criss-crosses of light that had been so difficult to interpret in the darkness. She stopped, her heart thudding in her ribcage.

"Come closer, and look through the bars," said Merryfeathers.

Heloise was frozen. Her heart was beating so loudly it seemed to be shaking her whole body. She felt Merryfeathers' scratchy feet push against her shoulder as he took to the air. He flew the short distance to the window and perched there, looking downwards with his head inclined.

Forcing herself forward, Heloise walked the last few steps to the window and looked through the bars. There were six of them on the window; the spaces between them were the width of Heloise's face, and the height of the window was twice the length from the top of Heloise's forehead to the tip of her chin. She had to bend her gaze downwards before she saw what she had journeyed to see; when she saw it, or rather him, she knew that she had found what she had been looking for all her life.

She was looking into a prison cell, a dungeon below ground level. To her left, some twenty feet away, there was a small barred window like the one she was standing at, but a cold draft entered through it, and a soft light – perhaps a lantern, perhaps the moon. She knew instinctively that it opened onto the night. In fact it looked out on the courtyard where she had sung a few hours before.

All around was stone – hundreds of tiny bricks of stone. It

seemed damp, if not wet; patches of lichen grew on it, which looked silver; the stone itself looked midnight blue. A steady *drip ... drip ... drip ...* of water fell from the cavernous ceiling into a puddle on the floor. The sound echoed.

The light from the window to her left fell in a shaft into the cell and showed her something she could not possibly have expected, and yet, it seemed to explain everything, all at once. It was a young man in chains. His eyes were closed; his head leaned against the wall behind him; he seemed to be asleep. He was dark-haired and bearded with deep hollows in his cheeks and around his eyes; he wore a ragged shirt that must once have been white, and dark breeches; his feet were bare, and he was very thin, perhaps starving. His face was chalk-white against his black hair and beard; indeed, its sharpness and vividness – the jaw a triangle, the forehead a pale oval – made it look like a sketch in charcoal. Despite the beard, it was the face of a tired child. And yet he was tall, his long limbs cramped in the confined space.

He seemed to have been there for a long, long time. But this man was not one more Unfortunate. He was different.

It was not just his beauty, which shone even in his miserable condition. It was not just his innocence, of which it was impossible not to be convinced. It was not just his robbed youth. It was the gentleness of him, and the intensity of his suffering. He suffered – or so it seemed to Heloise – because he was gentle, and the gentler he was, the more he suffered.

And Heloise knew him. She had never seen him before,

and yet she recognized him at the deepest level of her existence. It was as if she had always known him. And yet, somehow, long ago, she had forgotten it.

Heloise's hands gripped the bars on either side of her face.

Merryfeathers hopped onto her shoulder and rubbed his head against her chin. Heloise closed her eyes; large tears fell down her cheeks; she looked again and could barely see the young man for the tears. And yet she knew that he was no longer asleep.

He had opened his eyes and was looking at her, frowning slightly, as if he did not quite believe what he saw. His mouth was disproportionately small and in repose he held it crookedly; his nose was long in his long face; his eyes were wide-set and very dark and shaped like upside-down smiles. Looking into them was like looking into two wells of alarmingly deep, alarmingly pure water.

After a moment, he smiled crookedly.

And then, so softly that she almost did not catch it, he said a strange thing:

"*Once upon a time … there was a window … and at this window … there stood a girl …*"

"Who are you?" Heloise whispered, in sheer wonder.

That startled him. His face turned comical – the eyes wide, the mouth an "O" of surprise. He leaned forward and peered up at her, causing his chains to scrape against the stone.

"Oh," he whispered. And he smiled, a genuine smile

this time, quick, boyish, and yet at the same time haunted. "Forgive me. You must think me mad. Until you spoke, I did not understand that you were real." His expression altered and he said, "But – you are a child. Surely they would not – Surely you cannot – How is it that you are here?"

Heloise did not know what he was talking about. Then Merryfeathers said, "It is the bars, Heloise. He is concerned for you. From his angle, it is you who seem to be in prison."

"Oh," she said. Somehow the fact that he had imagined her to be in prison intensified her pain. "I'm not in prison. I've come to visit you. I have been here before, or not far from here … I sang, outside, tonight, with my friends. That was hours ago. Then I came back. There is a passage – I followed it, through the dark, from –" Suddenly she could not go on, and what she was explaining did not matter anyway.

The young man looked relieved. And confused. And apologetic. And, somehow, wry.

"Forgive me," he said again. "I heard the singing. Carols. Could it be Christmas again?"

He paused, biting his lip. Then, again, his expression changed.

"If you are real, sweetheart, you should not be here. This is no place for a maid. Where did you come from? Can you find your way back?"

Heloise shook her head. She was trying and trying to grasp something that eluded her. After a moment she asked, "Are you my brother?"

It had never occurred to her that she might have had a brother before, but –

Clearly, he was taken aback. He half-coughed, half-laughed with surprise. Then he smiled again. He looked at once tender and embarrassed. He had a thousand smiles, all different, each with a different shade of meaning; she had never seen anyone with such a vivid play of expression. He had the effect of rendering everyone she had ever known reserved, secretive, pallid by comparison.

"If you like," he said. "One can never have too many little sisters."

He was jesting. But no answer he could have given would have really answered her question, and she was not listening anyway.

"Now I understand," she murmured feverishly. "You are in prison. You are in prison! So many things are in prison. Perhaps everything is in prison. But they all led to you. This must be why. This must be why –"

He stared at her.

"What do you mean, everything is in prison?"

Heloise began to breathe quickly. She pressed her head against the bars.

"You are in prison. I am in prison. *She* is in prison. Her dolls are in prison. Maria was in prison before I found her and got her out. The stone doll is in prison in the church. It is true. It is true. Everything that is important or beautiful is in prison. I – I have to find a way to free us all. But how can I?

And how has this come about?"

She looked at him with all her heart in her eyes. As he looked back at her, his face grew serious, startled, as if he were beginning to recognize something in her.

"Everything is in prison," he repeated in a whisper.

Then he paused.

He closed his eyes. Then he looked at her again. "Still there," he murmured. "How – odd – that you should say that. *Everything is in prison.*"

Heloise stared at him.

"Do you believe in dreams, little one? I mean, do you believe that there is truth in them?"

That was easy.

"Oh, yes," she said. "Oh, yes, indeed I do."

He now paused for so long that it occurred to Heloise that he had forgotten she was there.

"I had a dream – of birds –" he began again. "Small birds – caged birds – birds that talked – like the fellow you have with you. I'm sorry," he broke off, "I don't think we've met?"

"Merryfeathers," said Merryfeathers respectfully.

The young man nodded.

"My name is Sebastian," he said.

"I know," said Merryfeathers.

Sebastian looked at him quizzically. Then, with an air of being past surprise, he resumed, "I thought they told me – the birds, I mean – to tell stories – and so I did. It was a way of keeping sane. That doesn't sound sane, I know, but –"

He attempted to make a gesture with his shoulders, but the chains cut it short.

"No matter. I was speaking of stories. I know hundreds, and I have told myself every one of them.

"*Once upon a time. Once upon a time.* Wise maidens. Wicked witches." He paused then added almost bitterly, "Valiant princes." He sighed. "Then, one day, I understood. I, myself, was in a story. For that is what life is. Do you see what I mean?

"But what story? What story? Or at least, who am I, in this story?"

He began to speak more quickly, and to jig his bent knees with intensity. "Is the story over? Is the moral told? Did I end my days in prison? Is that because I did wrong? I failed, certainly, but does that prove that I did wrong? If I knew what story I was in, or who I was in that story, I would know. It would make all the difference, to know I was here because I did wrong. I may be the villain in my story, and not know it. After all, heroes do not fail. Or do they?"

"You are a hero, so they must," Heloise whispered.

That caught him by surprise. His face softened.

"How kind you are," he said quietly. "And I have not asked your name."

"Heloise."

"You say everything is in prison, Heloise. I believe you. But what if the prison we are trapped in is a story? Our own story?"

Then he looked apologetic.

"Perhaps I have gone mad. It would be fitting." He added, "I do beg your pardon. One should not say such things to a child."

"*You* are not mad," Heloise said quickly.

She paused to collect herself. Her heart was thudding against her ribcage again. She had the agonizing feeling that she was terribly close to something of the greatest value, and yet she could lose it as easily as a hairpin.

"If what you say is true," she said at last. "If we are all of us trapped in a story, then we – you and I – *are in the same one*. And – Sebastian –" It was the first time she had used his name, and it felt strange, serious, almost sacred on her tongue. "I am certain that you can tell me how it ends. Oh, do not send me away," she pleaded suddenly.

The young man looked startled and mystified.

"Why would I send you away?" he asked.

For some reason Heloise was remembering her godmother's face, the first time she had seen it, so winsome and loveable. She was remembering reaching out to touch it, her heart clenching with love, and having her fingers brushed away; and she was remembering how deeply, how definitively, it had hurt.

She felt as if she were in the same place as this memory, standing on the same precipice. She was so afraid it was going to happen again.

"You said I did not belong here," she said. "But I –"

"Oh," he said. "But Heloise, that is not what I meant. Of

course you belong here, because you have offered me your friendship, and friends always belong together. But friends look out for each other's welfare, and I am concerned for yours. I wish only to protect you."

"It is I who must protect you!" she exclaimed, although she did not understand why she felt this so strongly. "You need protecting. I can look after myself."

"None of us can look after ourselves," he said after a moment. "We all have to look after each other."

Heloise was not listening.

"I must tell you the story," she said, thinking out loud. "Will you allow me to tell you the story? The story we are both in?"

"I could not find it in my heart to say no to you, sweetheart. But what makes you think there is this – exceptional – link between us?"

Heloise gripped the bars on either side of her face.

"*I know you*," she said.

"I know you think that," he said gently. "But – could you be mistaken? Who is it that you think I am?"

"The hero of the story," said Heloise.

"You must leave now, Heloise," said Merryfeathers. "You must be back before you are missed. No one must find you here. But you will visit again tomorrow night. Tomorrow I will come for you earlier, and you will have more time."

"I cannot leave," said Heloise. "I will never leave him."

She had said it with such conviction that both the bird

and the young man were startled. There was a short silence.

Merryfeathers looked at Heloise through his bright black eyes. "Heloise," he began carefully, "you are overwrought. It is understandable. But you must listen to me. I am your friend and I guided you here. I am telling you the truth. You must leave. You will be back tomorrow. I swear it."

"Heloise," said Sebastian. He had been watching them attentively, and was half bewildered, and half moved. "You must not distress yourself. This story we are in, sometimes it is a sad story, almost too sad to bear. But it has a happy ending."

"Does it?" said Heloise, truly astonished.

"So I believe," said Sebastian, with a strange smile. "With all my heart. No matter what.

"Anyway," he added more cheerfully. "I will still be here tomorrow."

"I will go now," she said, to Merryfeathers' relief. "But I will be back. And, dear sir, Sebastian, now that I have remembered you, I will never forget again. I know you don't understand me. I don't even understand myself. But you *will* understand – I know it – when I tell you my story. And then you will explain it to me."

She was right. He did not understand, however, he smiled a strangely untroubled smile.

"Sleep now, Heloise-who-may-be-a-dream," he said kindly. "I, who may also be a dream, will await your return."

Heloise nodded and dragged herself away.

She stumbled up the passageway into the darkness. She

heard the flutter of Merryfeathers' wings. Then came a faint, feathery collision against her shoulder. She turned and felt for him in the darkness, but his claws had caught hold of her hair and he had managed to climb onto her head.

"Forgive me," he said. "I can't see to fly."

"I should have waited for you," said Heloise.

"You are overwrought," repeated Merryfeathers. "It is understandable." Then he added, "Go carefully now. You are moving away from the light and at the end of your journey there will be the stairway again. That is the only way you will know where the trapdoor is. And it would be easy to injure yourself finding it."

Heloise looked back towards the window. Already it was small in the surrounding darkness. She wondered what Sebastian was doing, thinking, feeling now. She turned again and stumbled forward, holding her hands out in front of her. Step after step after step in the darkness. She began to long, above all, for sleep.

Merryfeathers too was tired. But he talked to her, all the way back, of the heroic work of canaries in coal mines.

When at last her outstretched hands met the stairway, he stopped in the middle of a sentence and said, "Now push the door up just a little so that I may go before you to make sure there is no danger. You must not be seen emerging."

She reached up and dislodged the door a fraction. Suddenly, the soft, golden light of candles leaked into the passage and the secret stairway was dimly visible once more.

Merryfeathers fluttered into the church. After a moment she heard his whistly voice saying, "You may come up. There is no one here."

She emerged into the church, and closed the trapdoor.

Then, with Merryfeathers on her shoulder, she crept back down the nave, through the heavy door, and out into the night. Down the first twelve steps. Down the second. Across the icy courtyard. Carefully through the door, across the main room, and back into the dormitory.

"Until tomorrow then," said Merryfeathers, when she had undressed and climbed back into bed.

It was almost as if nothing had happened. But she was so utterly spent that, although she tried to thank him, she was asleep before she was able to form the words.

# Christmas

"*D*own in yon forest be a hall*,*" sang a quavering, but still beautiful voice from what seemed like a great distance away,

> *Sing May Queen May sing Mary*
> *'Tis coverleted over with purple and pall*
> *Sing all good men for the new born baby!*

It was like being underwater, and hearing music from the surface. Heloise was so deeply asleep that even though Old Mother's voice was a good deal more shrill and penetrating than the handbell she used to wake them, she couldn't recognize it, or tell what was happening.

> *Oh, in that hall is a pallet-bed*

*Sing May Queen May sing Mary*
*'Tis stained with blood like cardinal-red*
*Sing all good men for the new born baby!*

In fact, Old Mother was traveling steadily along the dormitory singing, pausing at each bed and waking each girl with a kiss on the forehead and a quick, "Merry Christmas!"

*And at that pallet is a stone*
*Sing May Queen May sing Mary*
*On which the virgin did atone*
*Sing all good men for the new born baby!*

Old Mother's progress up the dormitory was punctuated by one new voice after another as each of the girls woke and wished first her, and then anyone else who was awake, a Merry Christmas. So what with one thing or another, there was more and more noise. Yet still Heloise was so exhausted that she did not wake. Instead all of these simply became part of her underwater dream.

*Beside that bed a shrub-tree grows*
*Sing May Queen May sing Mary*
*Since he was born it blooms and blows*
*Sing all good men for the new born baby!*

*Oh, on that bed a young squire sleeps*
*Sing May Queen May sing Mary*
*His wounds are sick and sick, he weeps*
*Sing all good men for the new born baby!*

Then she felt Old Mother's kiss on her forehead, and her perfectly true voice close to her ear. And suddenly, as she awoke at last, she knew where she was, who she was with, and even what was happening, and she was overwhelmed with love. She opened her eyes and threw her arms around Old Mother's neck. Old Mother was so surprised and moved that at last she stopped singing. But only for a moment. She enveloped Heloise in a hug. "Merry Christmas, Heloise!" she said feelingly. Then she resumed, "*Oh, hail yon hall where none can sin* … Come, girls, join me!"

And so they all sang:

*Sing May Queen May sing Mary*
*For it's gold outside and silver within*
*Sing all good men for the new born baby!*

Too happy to notice the cold, the girls ran around hugging each other and chattering in their nightgowns. They were all overtired and overexcited, and their eyes burned like lanterns in their pale faces. Old Mother looked at them, her heart full. But she said quite briskly, "Now hurry and get dressed, all of you. Who knows who may come calling?"

Esther caught her eye, and she and Old Mother exchanged a secret smile.

The next fifteen minutes were taken up with a flurry of hurried Christmas grooming. Then there was the making of the beds, and the tidying of the dormitory. But when Esther and Lizzie came out to the kitchen to make the porridge Old Mother stopped them.

"Just boil the kettle for tea, my dears," she said with a wink. And being old enough to understand such things, Esther and Lizzie smiled under their lashes and did as they were told.

When everyone was dressed and ready and wondering what was to happen next, there was a loud knock on the door.

Melancholy flew to open it; there in the doorway was a familiar visitor. The girls were silent for a moment. Then came a hail of quite heartless laughter.

It was Dr. Browne, but he was not dressed as usual.

"So it is considered appropriate among fashionable young ladies to laugh at Father Christmas nowadays, is it?" he asked with mock severity. He was poorly disguised as a rather fierce St. Nicholas, in a long, red hooded cloak, constructed rather cleverly out of what seemed to be an old blanket, and he was carrying a hessian bag, decorated with mistletoe, slung jauntily over his shoulder. "In an atmosphere of such shameless irreverence I am not sure presents ought to be distributed –" he continued, but then, "*Will* you move inwards my dear!" came Mrs. Browne's exasperated voice from outside, destroying what little illusion there was left. "Poor Priscilla and I are freezing out here! And the mince pies will be stone cold!"

Dr. Browne moved out of their way. Smiling, as always, Mrs. Browne entered carefully. She was carrying a heavy tray with something hot on it, and it was even more bundled up than she was. Esther made haste to take it from her and place it on the table. Priscilla, whose concession to the season was a grimace that may have been an attempt at a smile, followed with her own tray. She placed it on the table next to the first. "Merry Christmas!" she said generally. Considering her difficult temperament, it was rather nice of her really.

"Merry Christmas!" the girls replied politely.

"Well," said Dr. Browne, shutting the door, "presents, and we shall leave you to your feast." He put his sack on the floor, sat on his heels, and reached into it. "Melancholy!" he said, when he had made out his wife's handwriting.

Melancholy squealed and ran to him. Everyone laughed. Her gift was wrapped in brown paper, and when opened, proved to be a little felt book for keeping needles in. "Oh, thank you, Father Christmas!" she said delightedly. "I shall use it all year round!"

Dr. Browne put his hand on Melancholy's shoulder.

"Did you see that, girls?" he asked. "Let Melancholy be your model! Excitement, reverence, proper gratitude, and *the ability to play along.* I cannot commend her example more highly."

"Just so long as you don't put me in another sermon," said Melancholy to the floorboards.

Dr. Browne was busy reaching into the sack again. He started to bring out two or three gifts at a time. "Lizzie, Nan, Clementine …"

Heloise was presented with a wide green ribbon for her hair. "It will bring out the color of your eyes, my dear," explained Mrs. Browne.

Esther was given a piece of sheet music entitled "This Bud of Love."

"I heard it sung at a supper party last summer," said Mrs. Browne, "by someone who really wasn't much accomplished. And ever since I have been longing to hear you sing it."

And there were enough thimbles, combs, pincushions, sachets of lavender and cakes of scented soap to last everyone until next Christmas. The girls were delighted. But the most interesting present was Old Mother's. It was a tuning fork.

"How thoughtful!" said Old Mother, with great pleasure. "It will be in continual use, Mrs. Browne, you may be sure of that."

Then Dr. Browne and his entourage hurried away, for there was work to be done before the Morning Service. When the tea had been poured, the girls fell upon their mince pies with enthusiasm, and without bothering or being made to sit down. Then they washed the cups and plates, put the trays aside for returning to Mrs. Browne later, tidied the main room, and got ready for church.

It was a cold, sunny Christmas morning as they walked through the courtyard, and up the two flights of steps in their choir robes. The sun shone so brightly off the snow that it hurt their eyes.

As they processed, singing, up the nave, Heloise watched carefully for the trapdoor. But she walked across the mosaic in the transept without being able to discern it.

The girls sang almost as well as they had sung in the Prison the night before, although without any unusual behavior from Heloise, who had reverted to singing with her customary caution. But the girls did not need special courage, not in the friendly atmosphere and acoustic of their own church. There was a kind of tremulous joy in their voices. They were all happy.

This was probably the happiest day of Heloise's life.

She felt nervous and dreamy and absent and terribly tired. She was trembling with emptiness as, unlike her fellow choristers, she had not been able to eat breakfast. And yet as she sat in the choir stalls through Dr. Browne's sermon she felt so painfully happy that she hardly knew where to turn, what to do. She had never felt like this before, even at the best times: when she found Maria, when she first saw the stone doll.

She could think of nothing but the wonder of Sebastian's existence and her discovery of him. She could think of nothing but the overwhelming fact that tonight, she would see him again.

And a strange, unaccustomed understanding came along with this. For the first time she had a sense of how precious her own life was, and how immensely sad it would be if she were to lose it. She had never really cared before.

Later, when they were all having Christmas dinner at the rectory, Esther said quietly to Old Mother, "Have you noticed how exceptionally well Heloise is looking? She seems changed somehow."

Heloise was sitting at the other end of the table. She was silent, and only nibbling at her dinner, but her cheeks glowed like summer roses, her hair was as black as Pharaoh's Daughter's, and her eyes were like green fire.

Something like pain crossed Old Mother's worn face.

"When that child put her arms around me this morning," she said meditatively, "I thought my heart was going to break in two."

Esther was moved by her guardian's admission. She laid a hand gently on her arm. "Dear Old Mother!" she said.

"I wonder if we will ever know where she came from?" mused Old Mother, still looking discreetly at Heloise. "Do you know, my dear, when I first saw her, I thought she was no more than eight or so. Now, if I were to guess, I would put her at eleven or twelve."

Esther was a little startled. She searched her memory, and realized that she had thought the same. But how could that be?

"Perhaps she was not well nourished at the orphanage,"

she said uncertainly. "Perhaps it is the hearty meals from The Rose and Crown that have improved her constitution, and made her look her age."

"Perhaps," said Old Mother. But she was frowning. After a moment she turned the conversation back to music, as if into a safe harbor. "Now tell me this, Esther, my dear. How are we going to manage that voice of hers?"

"Well," said Lizzie, who was sitting on the other side of Esther and half-listening, "you might start by convincing her to use it all the time instead of only on the odd occasion when the spirit moves her."

"I'm sure it is only a matter of confidence," said Esther. "She is still very shy."

Old Mother looked thoughtful.

"Is shyness the word for it?" she said.

There was dancing after dinner, although there was precious little room for it in the cluttered Rectory. But the Brownes' three teenage sons were home from boarding school, and there was a harpsichord in the drawing room, and how could Dr. Browne refuse so innocent a pastime? They moved the furniture against the outer walls, Old Mother sat at the instrument, and as many as could fit on the floor at the one time, which was only about three couples, performed cramped country dances with a high degree of hilarity, mainly owing to the boys' talent for amusing remarks. Even Mr. Callardin-Bowser was persuaded to get up, and proved a fine dancer. Although his mood on this special day was comparatively relaxed, he was still unaccountably nervous of Heloise, who had bumped into him on her way out of the dining room.

"Child is wearing a green ribbon!" he had muttered unhappily.

"Why, yes, I gave it to her for Christmas," said Mrs. Browne.

"Madam, can you have forgotten that green is the color of the fairies? There is something not altogether wholesome about that child. I feel it in my bones."

"Mr. Callardin-Bowser, how can you be so superstitious! And you a church organist! This, my dear sir, is an age of good sense and enlightenment, not darkness and superstition."

"Ordinary folk still believe in fairies," said Mr. Callardin-Bowser. "I grew up in the country, ma'am. My nurse was a country woman, as fine a dame as you could ever meet. But the fairies were as real to her as you and I."

Mrs. Browne tsk-tsked and changed the subject. She liked seeing the green ribbon in Heloise's hair, and hoped Heloise had not heard Mr. Callardin-Bowser's unkind remarks.

Heloise had not. She was busy dancing with Dr. Browne, and a rather ill-matched couple they made, as Heloise was not much more than half Dr. Browne's considerable height. But they were very compatible mentally.

That night, Old Mother sent them to bed early. The middling girls made a perfunctory show of protest, but their hearts weren't really in it; the younger girls, and the older girls, were simply grateful.

"Goodnight Esther, Melancholy, Lizzie, Nettie, Jenny, Nan, Polly, Grace, Daisy, Rose, Clementine and Heloise," Old Mother said. "Church again tomorrow, remember."

For the day after Christmas this year was Sunday, and the Feast of St. Stephen.

As the girls breathed deeper and slower in their beds, and one by one dropped off to sleep, two guests arrived at the Rectory in time for a late supper. They were an old friend of Dr. Browne's and his youngest daughter.

Heloise knew nothing of this yet. She fell asleep immediately, in the faith that she would soon be awakened to another night of pain and joy.

# Heloise's Story

That night, just before Heloise stepped up to the window to look into the cell again, she felt a sudden fear that Sebastian would not be there.

But he was.

Heloise breathed out softly.

It was all as it was yesterday: the damp, dark-blue stone, the silvery lichen, the *drip ... drip ... drip* of water, the shaft of light, the young man in chains. But tonight he was awake. As soon as her face came to the window, his eyes met hers.

"Ah," he said, shifting slightly, "you have returned. I did not think it likely that you would be back."

Heloise blinked.

"How could you think I would not come back?" she whispered. She did not want to sound reproachful. But she was hurt that he did not take her seriously.

His expression changed.

"Forgive me," he said at once. "I did not doubt your intention. But things happen, to block the best of our intentions. No one knows that better than I. Sometimes … sometimes I think we are all like tiny, flying things, hurtling alone through space, passing one another, trying to grab hold, but always failing …

"But," he said courteously, "I am talking too much. And you promised me a story."

He looked at her and smiled. It was a sunny smile. For a moment she could imagine him outside on a bright summer's day, careless and free. It struck her that he had momentarily forgotten his situation.

Heloise leaned her forehead against the cold iron. All at once she was overwhelmed with sadness. So many hours of waiting, so little time when she was here! How best to make use of it? What to say? How to begin?

"Beginning is easy," he said, as if she had said it aloud. "Just say, *Once upon a time* … and then say the next thing that comes into your head."

Heloise said, "Once upon a time …" Then she was tongue-tied once more.

Sebastian laughed. It was the first time he had laughed since she had met him. "*Once upon a time* always works for me …" he said.

"It is because you are the hero," said Heloise, "of the story

I want to tell. So I want to start with you. But I don't know how, because I don't know where you fit in …"

"Oh," he said. He smiled ruefully. "In truth, I hoped you might forget that part of it. But I am obviously underestimating you." He sighed, and said gently, "I don't think it can be true that I am the hero of your story. And if I was," he added with a kind of tiredness, "I would not wish to hear it. Heloise, I want to hear your story. Tell me the story whose hero is you." He cast around for encouragement, then said, "Tell me your first memory. That is where everyone's story begins."

"My first memory?" said Heloise. Her face darkened. She hesitated. "What is your first memory?" she asked.

Sebastian looked at her with a kind of mock-suspicion, as if he thought he was being tricked. But then the question interested him. He said – readily, as if he had thought of it often – "Seeing someone, an old man, carving a little statue out of wood. It was a statue of a bird – a dove. I was enchanted. I thought he must have been the cleverest man in the world. I could not have been more than three." He paused and prompted her. "Can you remember being that young?"

"No," said Heloise. And in her heart, as she tried to think back, she felt a vague misgiving, as if she had stumbled upon something sinister. "I remember being taught to read – and to sew. But I don't remember being too young to do those things. The first thing I remember, before learning to read and sew, is opening my eyes … and seeing my godmother."

"Not your mother?" said Sebastian.

"My mother is dead," said Heloise.

"Ah," said Sebastian. "I'm sorry." She saw him looking at something with his mind's eye. He smiled sadly to himself.

"Is your mother dead too?" she asked.

"Hmm? Oh, no. My mother is alive – I hope – but I have not seen her in a long time," he said. "So you live with your godmother?"

"I ran away from my godmother," said Heloise.

Sebastian was looking at her gravely. "Oh," he said. "So she was cruel to you. Then who looks after you, Heloise? You are not alone?"

She knew he was thinking of the street urchins, some of whom she had sung for on Christmas Eve. The city was full of them. She was about to tell him about Old Mother and the choir, when all at once, she had an idea.

She looked at him in sudden desperation. She knew exactly what she wanted to tell him, but she was afraid. She took a breath, opened her mouth, then shut it again. But she knew she had to try, and so she forced her mouth open again, and said in a small voice:

"Once upon a time …"

Sebastian looked up alertly.

"Yes?" he said.

"Once upon a time …" said Heloise, and it was like flying

on the back of some huge night bird, through darkest space; she felt the wind rushing through her hair, across her face, and she knew she was traveling back to the very beginning. "Once upon a time," she said, "there lived a girl who wanted to know what love was."

"Ah," said Sebastian softly.

Something about the tone of that *Ah* filled her with hope.

"She lived," Heloise continued, "with her guardian and an old serving woman, in a mysterious house, next door to an even more mysterious house, in which the girl had never set foot."

Sebastian's face looked like an artist's sketch of deep interest.

"Never?" he asked.

Heloise nodded earnestly.

"Never. The girl was ugly –"

"She was not you, then."

"Oh, but she was!" Heloise protested. Then, a little confused: "Ugly, I mean. If you had met her on a lonely road you would have run for your life. You would, Sebastian, even though you are very brave, I'm sure. But her guardian was beautiful. The girl wanted to love her, but she couldn't, because when she tried, her guardian brushed her fingers away. Like insects."

"Not insects," said Sebastian, looking at Heloise's fingers around the bars of the window. "Birds, little birds."

Heloise was struck by the rightness of this.

"Yes," she said. "Like birds." And suddenly there was a picture in her head, a picture she had never seen before, of her godmother asleep, alone and wretched, and hundreds of little birds alighting on her, trying to comfort her, while she brushed them away in her sleep with her hands. "You see, her guardian didn't believe in love, because she didn't think anyone deserved it. She just believed in doing good to people, whether they liked it or not. She called it charity."

"I see," said Sebastian.

"But the girl," continued Heloise with some difficulty, "had – a kind of – hole in her heart – it felt like a hole, Sebastian, the biggest hole you can imagine, a hole that only love could fill. Was that foolishness?" she asked.

"*No*," said Sebastian.

Heloise was so moved she had to stop for a moment. That simple no meant everything to her. After a moment she continued:

"Well … the girl began to long for a doll. Boys," she added, "– or so I'm told – do not understand about dolls. And you are a boy – a young gentleman, I mean. But you must believe me when I tell you that a doll is something to love. That's why she longed for one. But her guardian didn't believe in those either. I'll tell you why in a moment. So, for a while it seemed that the girl would never have anything to love.

"Then, one day, the girl found a doll hidden under a floorboard in her room." Now Heloise was reliving the moment she had pulled up the floorboard and first seen

Maria. Her eyes softened. "Her name was Maria, and she was the most beautiful doll there ever was. And she was magical, too. Sometimes it seemed to the girl that the doll spoke. The girl had wanted to love, but she didn't know how, because she didn't really know what love was. But, day by day, the doll taught her."

"Magic, indeed," said Sebastian.

Heloise nodded.

"For a while, the girl was happy. She had someone to love, and someone that loved her, and that was really all she needed.

"But then her guardian found out about Maria." Heloise was looking at him as she said this, and she saw a remarkable thing: he seemed to sink slightly, as if with the weight of the story. "*The weight of the world on his shoulders*," she thought. She had heard Esther say that once, and had not understood the expression until now.

"The girl's guardian was very, very angry," she said, as gently as possible, for she did not want to put the weight of the world on his shoulders. "She was so angry that she took the girl to the house next door, the house she had never set foot in, and showed her what was inside." Heloise paused, her face remote. She paused so long that Sebastian prompted her gently:

"What was inside?"

Heloise drifted back to the present.

"Dolls," she said helplessly, and she found herself

beginning to tremble. "H-hundreds of d-dolls. But they were not like Maria. They were not loved. They were hated. They had been made and disfigured, with hundreds of tiny stitches, by a mad girl, who had died – in a lunatic asylum."

And then, all at once, she began to weep. She hid her face in her cold hands and tried to stifle her sobs.

Had she been watching Sebastian's face she would have read another story – a story of such suffering that she would have been frightened to go on.

However, she was not watching Sebastian's face, and so she continued:

"The girl's guardian told her … She told her that … this girl – the mad girl – was her mother."

"Oh," Sebastian said, his voice barely audible.

"The guardian wanted the girl to surrender her doll. She said that if she kept her, she would go mad like her mother. But the girl knew that if she gave Maria to her guardian, she would destroy her. And she loved that doll more than anything in the world.

"So she took Maria and ran away."

Heloise was growing calmer. She took out her handkerchief and mopped herself up. She noticed that Merryfeathers was sitting supportively on her shoulder, peering anxiously into her face. She smiled at him in a watery way, and went on:

"Birds came, hundreds of little birds, to help her. They guided her, through the night, all the way to the City. And there, an old lady, who looked after eleven girl orphans in an ancient monastery, took her in.

"But the girl had to hide Maria, because she was afraid. And, living amongst the orphans, she didn't have time to be friends with her any more. It seemed, at first, that the girl had brought Maria all the way to the City only to lose her in another way. Then I – the girl – began to understand. Maria was still teaching her about love. Now it was time for her to learn how to love people. And so, gradually, she did."

Heloise paused. "Life was very different with the orphans and the old lady. They lived joyously, without thinking it wrong. And they read all of the Bible, not just the stern bits.

"And the orphans kissed and hugged each other. The old lady did it too. It is very – overwhelming – to be kissed and hugged, when you have never been kissed and hugged before. I think this is termed *affection*," she added gravely.

"I believe so," said Sebastian.

"But the girl could not forget about her mother – the mad girl who had made the dolls. Even though she was dead. And even though the house with the dolls was far away, she dreamed of her and it every night.

"Then, one day, she understood why she was still dreaming of her mother.

"She had died when she was thirteen –"

"A mother so young?" Sebastian interrupted.

Heloise gazed at him. She was too ignorant to realize that this was unusual. "She died when she was thirteen," she said softly. "Or so the guardian had said. But the girl knew that she suffered still."

Sebastian was already appalled. It had not been an easy story to listen to. But this new remark startled him so much that he moved forward convulsively. The chain caught him and jerked him back. It must have hurt but he seemed not to notice.

"What did you say?" he whispered.

Just then they heard a sound, the loud, echoing sound of boots on gravel. A prison guard was pacing around the courtyard outside. He walked this way and that, paused near the outside window, then paced slowly away. Sebastian and Heloise had both fallen silent, staring at the window. But Sebastian was so disturbed by Heloise's story that even the guard hardly distracted him. As soon as the footsteps receded he turned to her and repeated in a whisper,

"*What did you – ?*"

"My – the girl's – guardian told her that her mother was dead. But the doll in the church told her that somewhere, somehow, she was still suffering, and the girl knew she must put an end to this. So she asked the doll in the church to tell her how.

"And, one night, a bird came to guide the girl through a long, dark, secret passage. The passage led into … the heart of things. The very heart of things, Sebastian. Do you understand?"

"Yes," whispered Sebastian. "I understand."

"And at the heart of things, there was a prison, and in that prison was a dungeon, and in that dungeon was a cell, and in that cell was a young man, whose only crime was –" She broke off.

"What was his only crime?" asked Sebastian.

"Love."

"Oh," said Sebastian. He sounded matter-of-fact, but all at once the tears had begun to fall steadily from his eyes. "And –" he stopped and cleared his throat. "And how did the girl know that?"

"Do you remember the hole in the girl's heart?"

"Yes."

"The cell was cut from it." They stared at each other, although for Sebastian her image danced through his tears. "How do stories that begin with 'Once upon a time' end?" she asked.

Sebastian looked at her as if she had asked the most penetrating of all questions.

"With *and they all lived happily ever after*," he said huskily.

"I don't know the end of the story," said Heloise. "Or at least, I don't know how to get to 'and they all lived happily ever after.' But you do. I know it. Please. Tell me how."

Heloise was flying again, on the wings of the night bird, through darkest space and back into the present, and she realized that this feeling was like what Sebastian had said, about people being atoms, rushing through emptiness, trying to catch hold but missing one another. But she knew that she had caught hold.

Sebastian leaned against the wall. He swallowed. Then he stared straight ahead into the darkness.

"So this – this is your story?" he asked finally. "It was all true? You are the girl?"

Heloise nodded. "The house," she said, "where the dolls are is a museum. People pay to see it. That is my godmother's living. She was my mother's sister."

"The dead do not suffer," Sebastian whispered. "Are you saying that you think your mother is alive?"

"I don't know," said Heloise.

He stared at her for a moment.

"How old are you, Heloise?"

"I do not know."

"You do not know?"

"I asked my godmother once. But she did not allow questions."

Sebastian tried to collect his thoughts. Almost absently, he bent his head and wiped his eyes on the knees of his breeches. She could tell it was something he had done often.

"You said yesterday," he resumed, "that everything beautiful or important was in gaol …"

"But of all the things in gaol, it is you who matters most."

"Me?" said Sebastian.

"I said that yesterday too," said Heloise earnestly.

Sebastian examined her face, looked away, then looked back.

"I think, after all, that I must tell you my story, although I had wanted to spare you from it. Perhaps our two stories will somehow make sense if we put them together. And I am willing to be guided by your wisdom. You are a wise child, wiser than I. You have said nothing of your father. You never knew him?"

"I do not have one," said Heloise. Then she frowned. "Not everyone has a father, do they?" she asked.

Sebastian smiled faintly. He hesitated and then said:

"We all have the same Father. And we are all brothers and sisters, or so I believe. But –"

"It is time to leave now, Heloise," said Merryfeathers, with some trepidation. He was afraid that she would refuse again. Instead she inclined her head and said to Sebastian, "I must go."

"Yes," said Sebastian. "You must go." But he seemed unwilling to take leave of her. He paused, almost as if he had forgotten that she was leaving, or as if he thought she had already left. "Ah, Heloise," he said at last. "Once, if you had asked my help, I could have put a great deal at your disposal. Now I have nothing – or at least, only what is in this cell. That is, myself. But I will give that to help you."

"You see?" she said. "You are the hero."

# Saint Stephen's Day

The next morning found Heloise in church yet again. As usual, she played her part flawlessly. But she was not really there. Or at least, she was only there in body.

In her heart she was still standing at Sebastian's window, her face between the bars.

She had awakened, picked at breakfast, gotten dressed and ready for church, lined up and processed in with the rest of the choir without really coming into the present. In church, she sang, sat, knelt, prayed and sat again on cue.

But when the sermon began, her spirit seemed to crash like a wounded bird at her feet.

The choir stalls were behind the pulpit and in front of the altar, and, of course, the choristers faced inwards, towards each other. One could easily sit in the choir and never look either at the congregation or the minister. Dr. Browne was present. But, until the moment he began to speak, Heloise had not paid attention to the preacher at all. Without her taking any notice, this gentleman had, at the appointed time, risen from his seat, climbed the steps up to the pulpit, settled himself, his notes and his few learned books, adjusted his spectacles and begun to speak.

But the sound of his voice electrified her.

"Brothers and sisters ..." he began.

Heloise wasn't listening to what he was saying. It was who he was that mattered.

Quick as a bird's, her head snapped around. She stared, aghast, at the pulpit. The man had his back to her, but she knew him well enough to recognize his back. And his voice was unmistakable.

It was the Vicar, her own vicar, from the parish she had run away from just a few months ago. It was Mr. Radcliffe.

Surely, this time, the game was up.

Breathing rapidly, Heloise stared at the floor.

What lamentable chance had brought him here? As her mind raced she remembered a conversation between the girls this morning – a conversation about the guest preacher, with the implication that the same guest preacher came every year at this time. Her vicar happened to be a friend of Dr. Browne's. This was bad luck for Heloise, but perhaps not so terribly surprising. For all she knew, every minister in the country was acquainted with every other. She supposed they would have a lot in common.

She tried hard to compose herself. Perhaps he had not seen her. Perhaps, even if he did see her, he would not recognize her. She knew she had changed, and Mr. Radcliffe had never struck her as a particularly observant man.

But even if he had not seen her so far, and even if she managed not to be seen by him throughout the rest of the service, there would be dinner today at the Rectory. She had no doubt that Mr. Radcliffe would be there. And even an unobservant man could not remain oblivious to the presence of someone he had known all his life, sitting at the same dinner table.

She would have to plead a headache, and ask to be excused. Then she would have to stay out of his way until he went home.

The rest of the service was agony. She tried to bury herself in the ritual, sitting, kneeling, standing and not singing but mouthing to the music, as she had lost her voice with anxiety. The main thing was to do it all as inconspicuously as possible. There was safety in numbers. When it was time to process out, she lowered her eyes and did as she always did, pacing with proper decorum and keeping the correct distance between herself and the choristers in front and to the side.

As she went tremblingly down the three steps and crossed the section of the floor where the trapdoor was, she felt someone's eyes on her. She could not stop herself; her eyes glanced upwards.

Mr. Radcliffe had not seen her. But his daughter Lucy had. She was sitting in the front pew, wearing a bonnet, pelisse and gloves the color of chestnuts, and staring at her in the greatest astonishment.

"A headache, child?" Old Mother placed her hand on Heloise's forehead. "You do seem a little warm. I hope you are not feverish. Lie down and I will brew you some chamomile tea."

"I will stay with her, Old Mother," said Esther. "You are expected at the Rectory."

"We are all expected at the Rectory," said Old Mother. "But bed is the best place for Heloise and I don't want to leave her alone."

"Oh, please, Old Mother," said Heloise meekly. She desperately needed to be alone but did not know how to manipulate the situation to her advantage. "No one need miss their dinner for me. I only need to lie down. With just a little rest I feel sure I will be well again."

Old Mother hesitated.

"It's true we have no food in the house," she said. "And I ought to pay my respects to Mr. Radcliffe. I suppose it is likely that you are just overtired." She thought for a moment and said, "We shall go, but I won't linger. In the meantime, Esther will run down and look in on you. We are only two minutes away, after all, and I dare say it is nothing serious.

You must keep warm. And drink every drop of your tea."

Heloise promised. She undressed and got into bed, and endured many little kindnesses from her fellow choristers before they departed.

When they had closed the door behind them, she lay staring at the ceiling, wondering desperately what she should do.

Her first impulse was to run away. She was convinced that Lucy would tell her father, and that Mr. Radcliffe would tell Dr. Browne and Old Mother, and that, of course, they would send her back to her godmother. And Heloise felt that she would rather die.

She could never give up Maria.

And she could never put herself out of reach of Sebastian.

And she could never give up the hope of ending Mary Child's suffering.

But she did not know where to go.

She needed Merryfeathers – she needed The Society of the Caged Birds of the City. But she had never gone looking for them. They had always found her. And she had so little time. She realized that if she was to go, she should go now, this very minute.

Then suddenly there was a knock on the door.

Heloise froze.

It could not be Esther back so soon. And anyway she wouldn't knock. Dr. Browne would not come without Old Mother and Old Mother's keys.

Heloise hesitated. Cautious as she was, she felt that it was not danger, but help knocking, and, after all, what did she have to lose? All at once she got up, slipped through the dormitory and across the main room, and opened the door in her nightgown.

There on the doorstep, with no bonnet, pelisse or gloves, but a shawl thrown over her head and shoulders, was Lucy.

Heloise stared at her.

"I am pretending to have a headache too," Lucy said.

She came in without waiting to be invited, and shut the door. "Don't be afraid," she said. "I've told no one."

She looked at Heloise seriously. Then she threw her arms around her neck. "Oh, Heloise!" she exclaimed. "I'm so pleased to have found you, so happy that you are safe and well!" Drawing back, she took both Heloise's hands, and searched her face. "You are much changed," she said. "It is – remarkable. Papa would never recognize you. He has trouble enough recognizing me in a new dress. But I would know those green eyes anywhere. They have haunted me since you left. We could have been friends, you know. I always thought so. But your godmother ..." she trailed off.

"I must speak with you, and quickly. No one knows I am here, so you must take me somewhere where you can hide me quickly if anyone comes."

Heloise tried to gather her wits.

"Come to my bed," she said. "If anyone comes, I will be in bed where I should be, and you can hide underneath."

Pulling her by the hand, she drew Lucy into the dormitory and slipped back into bed. Lucy sat beside her on the narrow mattress.

"Heloise," she said, "I was glad when you ran away. I knew you were ill-used. My only fear was that you would stumble into a worse place. But there are good people, as well as bad, everywhere, and I hoped you would find good people. I am so relieved that you did.

"You must not fear me; I will never betray you. I don't know what Papa would say – I know he wouldn't want to take you away from a place where you were happy. But he may conceive it his duty to return you to your rightful guardian. I don't know, and so I shan't risk it. But if I am to act according to my conscience I must tell you what you have a right to know.

"Heloise, your godmother is gravely ill, believed to be dying. She has been in decline since you left. It is very strange, but when you disappeared, she lost the will to live. She is so wasted that perhaps even you would not recognize her. She no longer goes out. She no longer does charitable work. And she has closed the Museum. Papa has talked with her many times, but he has not been able to bring her to reason. He feels – and the physician agrees with him – that the only hope is for her to see you again. Perhaps she needs to know that you are safe, or perhaps she is not easy in her mind, and needs to tell you something. We do not know.

"Dear Heloise, I would understand if you chose never to

go back there. But it may be a matter of life and death. Could you find it in your heart to come back with us and visit her? Do you even think that would be right? I do not know all the circumstances, of course."

Heloise stared at her. She swallowed, then swallowed again. She did not know what to say. Her heart had been sinking as Lucy spoke. She had feared so many things, so many terrible possibilities. But such a thing as this had never occurred to her. She should have been sorry for her godmother, she knew. She should at least have pitied her, if only as someone, once powerful, who had now become a kind of Unfortunate. But all Heloise could feel was – beaten. She had come so far; she had even begun to see some kind of home – a real Home – in the distance. Now it seemed her godmother would win after all.

It seemed to Heloise that her life was over. She would have to go. And yet she could not bring herself to say the words.

"It is your decision," said Lucy. "I will not think the worse of you, no matter what you do. She was a cruel woman, we all thought so. But Papa and I are traveling back tomorrow, by the two o'clock coach. If you want to come with us you must be at the Rectory by half past one. You could perhaps stay with us at the Vicarage. You would not need to bring anything –"

"I have nothing to bring," said Heloise hollowly. She realized that if she were to go back, she would not bring

Maria. She wondered to whom she would entrust her, and suddenly felt as if she were making her will.

"I must go," said Lucy. "I am supposed to be in bed. Until tomorrow, perhaps, Heloise. And if not – farewell. Dr. Browne is my father's best friend from college days. You will be safe under his protection."

Heloise accompanied her to the door. Lucy stole out, but not before kissing Heloise and hugging her once more.

"We could have been friends," she said again. "My mother is dead too."

And, clutching her shawl about her, she ran into the cold afternoon.

## Sebastian's Window

For hour after hour, or so it seemed on that terrible night, Heloise lay sleepless, holding Maria tightly, and waiting for Merryfeathers.

Tomorrow she would have to tell Old Mother the truth, and leave the choir forever. She would have to say goodbye to everyone, present herself at the Rectory, explain matters to Dr. and Mrs. Browne, and put herself in Mr. Radcliffe's hands.

What a strange, awful day it would be, part sheer misery, part humiliation.

This time tomorrow, she would be back where she started.

For the price of her godmother's life seemed to be her own happiness. And yet what could she do but pay it?

Her last night in this bed. The last time she would hold Maria.

The last time she would speak to Sebastian.

She could not cry. It was as if, instead of a heart, there was only a kind of cavern inside her.

She wondered to whom she should entrust Maria. Old Mother? Esther? Melancholy? Dr. Browne? They were all kind and dependable, and she felt sure they would keep Maria safe, perhaps until she was grown-up and could come for her. For one day, surely, she would be grown-up and at liberty?

Ah, but when Heloise thought of what life would be like at the caretaker's cottage without Maria, she despaired.

Feverishly, she fell to thinking of how she might possibly escape her fate. Was there no way she could go on living here? Was there no way she could forget her godmother? Lucy had said that she would not blame her if she were never to go back, and Lucy was good and kind.

But it was not Lucy's decision. It was Heloise who had to decide. And though she could run away from her godmother, she could not let her die.

It was as she had thought. Her godmother had defeated her after all.

Heloise rubbed her cheek against Maria's smooth wooden hair. So little time left until morning! And so much of it spent waiting! She decided to dress herself in readiness for Merryfeathers.

She sat up carefully, kissed Maria, and began to push her gently under the covers. Then she stopped.

She was still sitting there, staring into the darkness, rigid with thought, when Merryfeathers came shooting through the chimney and over to her bed.

"My poor Heloise!" he exclaimed. "I have heard all! Certain mice …"

She said nothing, just stroked him softly and absently where he sat on her shoulder, and then dressed in haste.

This time, she did not leave Maria behind.

If anyone had been in the courtyard that night, and if that person had been watching as Heloise gently opened the door and crept out, they would have wondered what precisely they were seeing. For Heloise's shape, in the moonlit darkness, did not look like that of a young girl.

She was carrying Maria on her back, wrapped in the nightgown in which she had brought her to the City, and over that, like a tent, she had thrown her cloak. On her head, supplying advice and comfort, sat Merryfeathers.

What strange elfish creatures go abroad in the dead of night! All Mr. Callardin-Bowser's instincts would have been confirmed.

Heloise slipped into the church. Then, purposefully, she stole up the nave and located the trapdoor.

He was already looking at the window when she appeared. He had learned to recognize the sound of her approach. But the expression on his face was strange, almost haunted.

"Heloise," he said immediately, without preamble, "those

dolls, with the stitching –"

Heloise was untying the sleeves of her nightgown from around her chest, and pulling Maria out from under her cloak.

"Sebastian," she said urgently, "could you keep something for me?"

Sebastian blinked.

"How do you mean?" he said.

"If I were to give you something, could you keep it by you?"

Sebastian collected his thoughts.

"There is the straw," he said. "And there is a ledge in the stone behind me, although I can barely reach it. There was a time when I was observed more closely, but now I think they have forgotten I'm here … But it depends how big this something is –"

"It is my doll, Maria," said Heloise. "Tomorrow I have to go back to my godmother. I was told today that she is dying. I cannot take Maria with me. I want to leave her with you. I know you are a young gentleman, and that young gentlemen have no interest in dolls. But Maria is special. If you kept her for me, it would make it easier for me to leave."

Sebastian stared at her.

"Please," said Heloise.

Sebastian searched for words.

"How will you get her to me?" he said finally.

"You must catch her," said Heloise. She peeled the nightgown off Maria and looked at her in the dim light. She kissed her reverently on her smooth wooden forehead. Then, holding her carefully by her curving arms, she pushed her through to the other side of the window. "Are you ready?" she asked.

"Wait," said Sebastian.

He edged backwards towards the source of his chains, to give his arms their best chance.

"Throw her here," he said, tapping his ribcage.

Heloise leaned as far as she could through the bars.

"One," she said. "Two. Three!"

And Maria flew in a curve like a bird, up and along, and then gently down, across the cell into Sebastian's arms. The chains scraped across the stone as he caught her.

"Well thrown!" he said.

Then he looked at Maria.

Then he looked at her again.

Heloise was gazing at them dreamily. The sight of Maria in Sebastian's arms was strangely affecting. Perhaps they belonged together, and that was all that mattered.

Sebastian had gone still. The expression on his face was, for once, impenetrable.

"This is not a doll," he said remotely.

"Not a doll?" she repeated.

He looked up at her. "It's a Madonna," he explained. "She – there's something missing. She used to have a baby in her arms. A little wooden baby. You see, the way her arms curve?"

Heloise had no idea what he was talking about. She did

not know what a Madonna was. She just shook her head and said, "I think she is the most beautiful thing I have ever seen."

"Thank you," Sebastian whispered. He was turning Maria this way and that, looking at her with a kind of nostalgia, and even pride. Then he looked at Heloise as if he was beginning to understand something. He gestured helplessly with his shoulders and said, "She's my work. I carved her. I gave her to a girl called Mary Child. How can it be that you have come by her? Where was it you said that you found her?"

"Mary Child?" whispered Heloise. "But Mary Child was my mother," she said stupidly.

Sebastian shook his head.

"I don't know what you have been told," he said, "but that could not be true. In any case, Mary Child did not die at thirteen. She was already seventeen when I knew her. As far as I know, she lives yet."

He glanced up at the outside window, as if wondering how long it was till dawn.

"There is so little time," he said. "And there is so much to tell you."

"Tell her," said Merryfeathers. "There will be time enough."

## PART TWO

# Sebastian's Story

# Once Upon a Time

There was silence in Sebastian's cell, except for that slow *drip ... drip ... drip* of water. Heloise leaned her chin on the iron below her face, and gripped the bars. It seemed like years since the night she had first come here.

She rather wished her life could end tonight. She had forgotten how precious it had seemed, only a day ago.

At last Sebastian said, as if from a great distance:

"Once, long ago ..."

He stopped. His face was calm, and yet she could almost feel the pain in his throat.

"Once, long ago ..." Heloise repeated dreamily.

Sebastian looked at her.

"There lived a boy," he began again. He cleared his throat. "Who had been born in a prison."

Heloise was startled. It had not occurred to her that children could be born in prison.

"Was his mother a prisoner?" she asked.

"Yes," said Sebastian. "And his father. And all his family. The boy was born in prison, and grew up in prison, and was to remain in prison all his life, because the law said he must."

Heloise tried to digest this. "But why?"

"Because of the family he had been born into," said Sebastian. "In that family, being a prisoner was – inherited." He glanced about him absently, and Heloise could tell he was seeing something very different from what was before him. "The prison was not like this one. It was beautiful, luxurious. Everyone in it slept on soft beds, and wore fine clothes. You could say that it was a prison made of gold. But it was a prison nonetheless.

"The boy's father had died before the boy was born, and he missed him, even though he had never known him. That might not seem to make much sense, but it's true. Still, despite that one sorrow, his life was a happy one." He sighed gently. "You see, Heloise, the boy did not, at first, understand that he was in prison. And," he added ruefully, "there was so much to do! In prisons of gold, there always is."

"What?" she asked, for Heloise's prison had been a narrow one. "What was there to do?"

"Art, music, literature, science, philosophy – all the things of the mind. And the things of the outdoors, too – horses, swordplay, archery – for the prison had grounds. You could walk all day before you came to the bars. The boy had gifted tutors to teach him, and he was never idle. He could never bear to be idle, in those days."

Sebastian was seeing something so distant that Heloise felt as if the two of them were not confined in a hole below the earth, but suspended somewhere in space. Just Sebastian and Heloise (and silent, loyal, watchful Merryfeathers), with nothing but darkness around them.

"But of all there was to do, there was one thing he liked more than any other: making things with his hands. People of his ilk don't usually do that, make things with their hands. But, when the boy was very young, he had known an old man, a true artist, who could carve like a master in wood. He taught the boy to carve things –"

"Like doves?" asked Heloise.

"Yes. Like doves. The boy had a talent, and he never stopped practicing. So he grew proficient.

"His mother –" He stopped, looking unhappy.

"What was his mother like?" asked Heloise hungrily.

His face softened.

"Beautiful," he said. "She was the kind of woman who was everyone's mother. If she was here," he said, "in this prison instead of that one, she would be your mother too. Do you know what I mean?"

"Oh, yes," sighed Heloise.

"One Christmas, the boy's seventeenth, he carved a Madonna and Child. It's a kind of statue, Heloise, a doll, you might say, of a mother and baby, and he gave it to his mother." He was stroking Maria's wooden hair with one finger; Heloise knew exactly what its smoothness felt like.

"He did it in the Neapolitan style, because he knew she liked it. They dress their Madonnas, like beautiful dolls. She was pleased; she put it in a niche in her – cell. But I think that was the last joy he gave her. She was unfortunate in her son. You'll understand why in a minute.

"For as his eighteenth birthday drew near, he grew restless. He had begun to understand what he had been born into, and the knowledge oppressed him. He felt – protected, swaddled, distant. He longed to know something of life outside prison walls. He wanted to journey into the heart of things. He wanted to live at the heart of things.

"He wanted – well, in a way, he wanted –"

"What did he want?"

"To be hurt," said Sebastian. "Was that foolishness?"

Heloise stared at him. She was searching for words, but before she could answer he resumed:

"So he began to devise a plan. At first it was nothing more than a daydream. As time passed it became – well, an obsession."

Heloise nodded slowly.

"You see, it seemed to him possible that he could escape – not forever, he knew that was not possible – in the end, he would come back – but just for a while. It seemed to him that he could live amongst ordinary people, unknown. This family

257

he belonged to was well-known. But few people knew his face well, and if he were to go about without fanfare …"

He had begun to jig his bent knees.

"He opened his heart to his mother, talked to her night and day, tried to get her permission. It could be a secret even from the – well, from what you might call the gaolers. He could pretend to go to another prison, but in fact simply dress himself as an ordinary person, and slip out into the world. For the prison he lived in was not particularly well-guarded. It was, after all, made of gold, and it never occurred to the gaolers that anyone would want to escape.

"Oh, Heloise, he wanted to know what it was to be one of the people; he wanted to live out his love for them at close hand – for he did love them, the people outside the prison, he did love them, but he was so – *distant*. He was not without practical skills; he proposed to find work, ordinary work. He thought he could do this for a while, and then return, as was considered his duty.

"For many weeks, his mother said no. Then, one day, when he had almost given up hope, she gave in. He was overjoyed. But he never forgot the look on her face. She was calm, resigned. But it was as if a sword had passed through her heart. It was as if – it was almost as if – *she knew* …"

He paused, his face darkly wondering, then said,

"She took the Madonna he had carved from the niche and gave it back to him as a blessing. But she kept the wooden baby, and made him promise to reunite them one day. The boy did not take this seriously. He intended his adventure to last only a matter of months.

"And so one morning he stole out into the sunshine, as free as – a bird. But you are not free, are you, Merryfeathers?" he said suddenly.

Merryfeathers looked at him so seriously that, for a moment, he resembled a hawk rather than a budgerigar.

"No," he admitted.

Sebastian sighed. "He found work at this and that," he continued, "and lodgings in a hayloft. People thought him an oddity, with his voice and his genteel ways. But they assumed he was just a younger son of good family fallen on hard times, a prodigal, not an uncommon phenomenon. If he had left it at that perhaps all would have been well.

"But his plan worked too well, Heloise."

Heloise noticed she had been holding her breath. She breathed out softly.

"Too well?" she said.

"He had been born in a prison, but it was a golden one. So he had not known about cruelty. He had not known about injustice. He had not understood that, in the world, virtue not only went unrewarded, but was often punished as if it were a crime. And that crimes were often feted like virtues. He had not known there were women and children who lived on the streets, and he had not known that even people who had a home were sometimes mistreated within it. He had not known how many people were trapped in lives of intolerable suffering …"

He smiled wearily.

"He had wanted to know what life was like. He found out."

"Oh," Heloise whispered.

"As time passed," he continued, "he grew more and more preoccupied with these things. He sought them out, tried to understand. And two places drew his unhappy interest more than any other …"

"The Madhouse," Heloise murmured. "And the Prison. This one."

They looked at one another.

"It seems …" said Sebastian, "we understand each other very well." He moved as if to pass a hand over his face but the chains stopped him. "Of course, he had always known such places existed. Prisons that were not golden. But he had believed that the people in them belonged there. It never occurred to him that some people could be put away unjustly, and that others, not without guilt, suffered too much for their crimes. It never occurred to him that guiltier people walked abroad than were, in many cases, in gaol. It never occurred to him that the Madhouse treated its inmates unkindly, or that there were people in the Madhouse who were not mad.

"But he heard rumors. He decided he needed to know these places. He thought he would start with the Madhouse, and he sought employment there, doing odd jobs.

"Nothing could have prepared him for what he found. The mad people – oh, Heloise, they were treated as if they were bad, as if they needed to be punished. Many of them were restrained, day in, day out, in cages. And worst of all, people would pay for the privilege of coming to see them, as if they were wild animals. Some of them were violent, it was true, and needed close supervision, though not cruelty, not punishment. Others, gentle people, did not belong there at all." He paused, and then repeated softly, "Not at all.

"There was a young girl amongst the inmates," he said, gazing into the darkness of his cell as if he saw someone hovering there. "And of all the gentle people who did not belong, she was the gentlest of all."

Heloise's heart had begun to thud in her chest. Her mouth was so dry she had to try several times to get her question out. Finally she managed to ask,

"What did she look like?"

Sebastian glanced at her absently. "I don't know," he said, looking back into the darkness. "Sunlight," he whispered after a moment. "On water."

"The boy never discovered her story," he continued. "No one even seemed to know it. And she never told him. She had been brought to the asylum when she was little more than a child and had grown up there. There seemed no hope of her returning to the outside world, and yet there seemed nothing amiss with her, except that she was deeply, deeply sad. Who would not be, in such circumstances?

"The inmates were never allowed to do anything, to make anything or work at anything. Nothing was allowed. Some of

261

them would not have been capable of any such activity, but others … When he befriended the girl, out in the garden, where she used to wander aimlessly, the boy discovered she was not allowed sewing materials, or tools of any kind. But he knew that what she needed more than anything was some kind of activity. And yet this – this – was against the rules!

"This was when he began to act unwisely … though I have had much time to think about what I – he – did, and if he had his chance again I don't know that he would have acted differently. He was haunted by the girl's sadness – her emptiness – the waste of it – the long days of it … He thought that if she had something to do, she would be – she might be … So he taught her to model in clay. It did not require tools, and no one could hurt anyone with clay, and so he felt the rules had been respected. It had to be a secret, but she was so harmless that they did not watch her closely, and she found opportunities.

"That was when he began to realize how exceptional she was.

"At first he thought her merely talented – extraordinarily so. She learned so quickly, and modeled so convincingly. If she made a mouse you would swear its nose twitched; if she made a bird you would think it could spread its wings and fly.

"Then, one day, she made a lizard."

He paused, staring, wide-eyed, at the wall. After a moment, he looked up at her, taking a sudden breath, as if he had forgotten it was necessary.

"A lizard?" asked Heloise in a small voice.

He nodded faintly.

"A green one, no bigger than my middle finger. Or at least, it was green after it came to life. It started out clay-colored."

It took a while for Heloise to understand what he had said. By the time she had caught up with him, he was talking again, quickly, his face chalk-white.

"She had often shown him things she had made. But this time, she had an odd look on her face. A kind of … challenge. It was as if she wanted to prove something to him, something about herself. But not something good. Something bad. He had the strangest feeling that she wanted to somehow condemn herself in his eyes. As if she was trying to make him – hate her. And he didn't understand why.

"She had the clay lizard lying on her palm. She looked at him very … directly, as if to make sure he was watching. Then she kissed the lizard on its nose. The boy saw green, livid green, licking up along the clay like a flame, from the nose where she'd kissed it to the tip of the tail. Then the lizard twitched, violently, and jumped out of her hand, onto the grass. And ran away, into the bushes …

"I can't – explain to you, Heloise, what it's like to see such a thing. The boy could not eat or sleep for days afterwards. He was afraid, at first, it was true. Then, he thought, she was still – herself – and what had she shown him, but a talent? She could, it seemed, not only make something, but give it life. And who could have endowed her with such an ability but God?

"He began to realize how it might have been that she had been placed in a lunatic asylum. How her family, having seen that she had this gift might first have tried to suppress it, and then, when they could not, decided to put her away.

"And he could not bear it. It was like they had taken something beautiful, something precious, something magical and torn the wings from it. It was like they had buried her alive. But what to do? How to help her?

"He knew she had expected him to abandon her once she had shown him her gift. He wanted to prove to her that he hadn't, that he never would. So he told her he loved her and would never leave her. He told her that he meant to find a way to get her out, or if he could not, that he would stay with her forever. He had forgotten about the other prison, the golden one. The one it was his duty to return to. It didn't seem important. Or perhaps he thought this was his duty. For did not his duty lie where he was most needed?

"He had been afraid that she did not love him. He had been afraid that he was not worthy of her. She had suffered so much, he so little. Who was he to love her? Were it not for the service he could offer her he would have lacked the courage to speak. But her response was …"

Sebastian fell silent. He stared with a kind of haggardness at the wall opposite, as if there was something on it that defeated his understanding, although he longed more than anything to understand it.

"Heloise, you said the other night that your godmother does not believe in love. I did not, at first, put the two together. After all there are many people who do not believe in love, although few of them would be so honest about it. But it was not the first time I had heard such a thing.

"She, the girl in my story, *could not accept love*. Is that not the profoundest of mysteries?

"You see, she believed she had been treated justly. She believed that she belonged in the Madhouse. She *hated* herself, believed she was bad, through and through. And if she was bad, she could not possibly be loveable, or this was her conviction. Furthermore, only the wicked love what is bad. So the boy who had said he loved her, even after she had shown him the truth about herself, must be wicked. His wickedness had been proven by his love for her. And he was lying to her also – or so she believed – lying to her and tempting her in the most evil way, because he was trying to persuade her that she was loveable and good after all.

"She betrayed him to the authorities – told them he had spoken of getting her out. And do you know what they did? They put him in prison, this one – and released her. At the trial, she was so calm and well-spoken that no one could possibly believe her mad. Besides, she had helped to imprison a dangerous criminal. For in the law of this kingdom, there are few crimes more serious than conspiring to free a captive.

"And so she went off into the world, I know not where. And they brought the boy here.

"You were right, Heloise. We are in the same story. Or at least … Your story was about a girl who set out to understand love, and found suffering. Mine is about a boy who set out to understand suffering, and found love. For the boy loves her still. Sometimes he thinks his whole being is nothing but love for her, and he would do anything to help her. And the pain of this makes the pain of imprisonment seem like …" he shook his head. "Nothing."

"Heloise, the girl's name was Mary Child, and I was the boy. I gave her the Madonna, your Maria, while she was in the Madhouse. It seems extraordinary that she kept it, considering what she thought of me. But she must have. I think she must have hidden it under the floorboards, where you found it. It is as I said. Mary Child did not die. She lives still. She was not your godmother's sister. She is your godmother. And you are right. Mary Child is still suffering."

# A Kind of Curse

For what seemed like a very long time, Heloise gazed at Sebastian, trying to comprehend what she had heard.

The water dripped like a metronome. The cell grew faintly lighter. And Heloise's chin, resting against the iron bar, was so cold that the bone suddenly began to ache. She lifted it automatically.

"I don't understand," she said, like someone waking out of a dream. "How can you know that Mary Child is not my mother?"

"You are too old, Heloise," said Sebastian. "She had no child when I knew her, and that was but a year ago."

Heloise blinked. She had thought he had said a year ago. But she must have misheard. She did not realize how important it was, and she was preoccupied with something else. Hatred. For the first time, Heloise simply and purely hated Mary Child.

"So Mary Child, my godmother, put you into gaol," she whispered. "And – I am an orphan after all."

And then, wildly, it occurred to her that perhaps, being an orphan, she need not go back. If in fact she was no blood connection to her godmother – to Mary Child – could it be that she had no obligation to her at all?

If Sebastian had been watching her he might have guessed her thoughts. But he was looking at the window, watching the approaching dawn. The soft light played over the sinews of his neck.

"And now you tell me she's dying," he said remotely. He paused, looking at the dawn as if it were the cruelest thing he had ever seen. Passing from one unhappy thought to another, he said, "It took me so long to understand what you were saying. I have become stupid. Perhaps I always was. I should have known, the moment you spoke of –"

Then he turned his head slowly towards her.

Heloise's heart was still dark with hatred, her head light with the possibility of escape. The combination was intoxicating. But when she saw Sebastian's face she felt a strange kind of sobering chill.

"What is it?" she whispered.

"I see now what she did," he said.

She had never seen his face so clearly before; the greater light showed her not just the vivid charcoal sketch of it – the pallor against the dark hair, and the dark, mysteriously pure eyes – but the honesty of it, the simplicity of it. It struck her suddenly that he did not have a scheming bone in his body. And Heloise felt that she was nothing but schemes. She began to understand why she had always felt that he needed her protection.

"What did she do?" she whispered reluctantly.

"She made dolls. She stitched over their faces. Hundreds of dolls, you said. Thousands of stitches. The dolls were herself. The stitching was – hatred. It was a kind of spell, a kind of curse. But not on anybody else. On herself. Every one of those stitches was an act of self-hatred. She must have started doing it after they stopped her using her gift. It was the frustration. It must have been so intense, it turned inward. She was beside herself. They didn't know what to do with her, and they couldn't let her use her gift again. It frightened them too much. So they took her to the Madhouse. Then, when she was released, she must have gone back. And rather than starting a new life, she made a museum out of the old one. Do you see? The museum is a shrine to self-hatred. She puts her sad self on display, and charges people to see it! She does to herself what she saw done to others in the Madhouse.

"Do you remember what you said to me, the first night you came here, before I even understood that you were real?"

"I'm not sure I want to remember," Heloise muttered.

But he seemed not to have heard her.

"You said that everything was in prison, and that you

had to find a way to free us all. And you thought that, when I heard your story, I would be able to tell you how. I thought it a strange thing for a child to say. Now I see that you were right. There is a way to free her. I see it now. And God knows, it might free us all, though I speak of inner freedom. And yet, inner freedom is all that matters. I ought to know that. You said you were going back, because she is dying?"

Heloise said nothing.

"You would have to reverse her work, Heloise. Do you see? You would have to take the dolls, and unpick the stitches. You would have to – dismantle the museum. And you would have to do it for love."

For a moment it seemed to Heloise as if everything around her was collapsing, as if each of the tiny bricks that made up the prison had worked itself free of its confinement and jumped from its place, leaving nothing but air behind it.

"That would be impossible," she said.

Sebastian looked at her distantly.

"What would be impossible?" he asked. "Dismantling the museum? Or doing it for love?"

Heloise shut her eyes. She remembered now. She remembered the revelation that Mary Child was still suffering, and her prayer, *show me how to stop her suffering.* She had not known who Mary Child was. And yet her prayer had been answered.

Heloise's mind raced. She wanted to say, but now that I know Mary Child is my godmother, I don't want to save her. She put you in prison. And she tried to cut me off from everything beautiful and important. I hate her, and I owe her nothing.

But –

Heloise looked into the cell again. The prison wasn't collapsing. It was still there. How far she had traveled to stand at this window, to talk to this man. Yes, she hated Mary Child. But –

Heloise loved Sebastian. She loved him as much as she had loved Maria. And now that Maria was with him, and she knew he had made her, they had become the same person.

She would have done anything for Maria. Now, she felt, she would do anything for Sebastian. He wanted Mary Child freed. And she herself had prayed that Mary Child would be freed.

They wanted the same thing.

Heloise had thought that her godmother and Mary Child were two separate people. She had feared, even hated one, and greatly pitied the other. Now she knew that they were one and the same person. When she had been pitying Mary Child, she had been pitying her godmother, and when she had been hating and fearing her godmother, she had been hating and fearing Mary Child.

"When you love one person," she said, looking at Sebastian with Maria in his arms, "you love everyone, don't you?"

"Oh, yes," said Sebastian.

"In the end, nothing else makes sense, does it?"

"No," said Sebastian.

"I will do it," she said. "It seems impossible, like David and Goliath, but I will do it, if it can be done. But I don't know if I will ever see you again. If only I could tell you – when it has been done. If only you could know."

"I will know," said Sebastian quickly. And although it did not stop her heart breaking, she believed him.

"There is nothing more to say, then," she said.

"Yes, there is," he said. "Heloise, I was wrong about heroes and failure. Failure is irrelevant. It just doesn't signify. What matters is being true, no matter what the consequences.

"I could have told them who I was. I could have gone back to the Golden Prison. If they'd believed me. But it would have been an offence against honor. I always knew that much. Now I know why.

"I wanted to be treated like everyone else. This is being treated like everyone else. I wanted to live at the heart of things. This is the heart of things. And the heart of things, Heloise, the very heart of things, is love. I just didn't recognize it when I saw it. Do you see what I mean? This –" he said, glancing around him, "this is it. This is what love looks like.

"And that is why I know that all will be well. Even if I die here, all will be well.

"I could not free her. But I think you can. And there's something I have to let go of. I see that now. It's the longing to be the cause of her happiness, to be the one who heals her.

I have to give that job to you. If you are kind enough to take it.

"And – if I do, *that*, at last, will truly be love."

Heloise could not speak. She pushed her arms through the bars and extended them as far as she could towards him, as if to embrace him.

"God speed, Heloise," said Sebastian.

And he lifted up his chained arms towards her as far as they would go, as if to return the embrace.

# Going Back

At two o'clock the following afternoon, Heloise was sitting in a coach with Lucy, Mr. Radcliffe, and three strangers.

Mr. Radcliffe, who was sitting opposite, kept looking at her as if he still found it impossible to believe she was the child he had known back in his own parish. Lucy, who was sitting next to Heloise, was holding her hand. The three strangers, a rather cantankerous-looking old lady and her two morose middle-aged sons, were not friendly and seemed offended by any conversation above the merest whisper. So Mr. Radcliffe, Lucy and Heloise were silent. Which was probably for the best, as they could not have talked in public of what was uppermost in their minds, and coming up with small talk would have been more of a strain than any of them could bear.

"Just two hours, my dear," said Mr. Radcliffe, in an attempt to say something cheery. "Much quicker than it must have taken on foot!"

Heloise smiled wanly.

She had not slept when she had returned to her bed that morning. Instead she lay there for the hour or so before Old Mother rang the bell, knowing that if she behaved normally when she rose, it would still be possible not to go back. It was odd to have so much power over her own destiny, and yet to be using it against herself.

The absence of Maria was terrible. She understood now what it was to make an irreversible decision. She was alone with the consequences of having given her dearest possession away.

When at last it was time to rise, Heloise dressed, made her bed with special care, and sat down to breakfast amongst the chattering girls – although she could eat nothing. Then, when everyone was doing their allocated chores, she approached Old Mother.

No one but Esther was watching Old Mother's face as she listened to Heloise's whispered story. No one but Esther suspected that anything was happening. But when Esther picked up a chair and took it over to where Old Mother was standing, Lizzie saw Old Mother sit down in it blindly, her face pale and distressed. Melancholy stopped polishing the table and simply stared.

"What is Heloise saying to Old Mother?" Nan asked her.

Melancholy shook her head.

One by one the rest of the girls became aware that something was afoot. They went on with their chores, but every few moments one would exchange looks with another, or mime a question, for which there were no answers. Before long the room became strangely silent.

Finally, when Heloise had nothing more to tell, Old Mother conferred quickly with Esther and said to the room at large: "Girls, I am going to call on Dr. Browne, and I am taking Heloise and Esther with me. Lizzie, you are in charge. See that you all find something useful to do while we are away. We should not be gone too long."

The girls did not dare to ask questions. Silent, they watched as Old Mother, Esther and Heloise put on their bonnets and shawls and set out. But when the door shut behind them, nothing Lizzie said could stop their disturbed chatter.

Priscilla, who answered their knock at the Rectory, looked startled to see them. All agog, she ushered them into the drawing room and went to tell her mistress. Then Mrs. Browne hurried in. She was too well-bred to look anything other than serene and welcoming, but Heloise could see that she was wondering what this unusual visit might mean. She led them into the dark, cluttered study where her husband was at work behind his desk and, shutting the door, stayed at their request.

So it was that Dr. Browne and his wife heard the story of

Heloise's running away from her godmother, and of her wish to go back during her time of illness. Lucy and her father had gone out early to run various errands for family members and parishioners who could not get to the City; when they returned they joined those already in Dr. Browne's study, and they too were told. Heloise did not cry easily, and especially not in public, but the ordeal was too much for her, and she began to weep despite herself. Priscilla brought tea, and between Mrs. Browne, Old Mother, Esther, and Lucy, Heloise was almost in danger of being overwhelmed by compassion. Dr. Browne and Mr. Radcliffe looked at each other solemnly, wondering where their duties lay.

Arrangements were made and undertakings set. Old Mother, Esther and Heloise returned to the Old Monastery to prepare Heloise for her journey, and to break the news to the girls.

There was much to be done in the few remaining hours. There was the sympathy and grief of the girls to be borne. This was not easy as, touched and even awed as she was by their kindness, Heloise did not quite know how to respond. There was a dark grey traveling cloak and bonnet to be borrowed and made over as quickly as possible, for Old Mother was concerned that Heloise should look respectable and well cared for. Lizzie, who was the most competent seamstress amongst them, devoted herself to this task; although she had always prided herself on her strength of character, she kept finding that she could not see her work for her tears. And there was Heloise to be fed properly before she left, for everyone knew she had eaten no breakfast.

"What do you think you might be equal to, child?" Old Mother asked her. "Something settling, a plain broth or a junket, perhaps? Minnie at The Rose and Crown will make you a nice milk junket, with nutmeg, if we ask her."

"Yes, Old Mother," said Heloise wanly.

So the junket was ordered, and fetched by Melancholy, and eaten obediently by Heloise before she left. She had vaguely intended to fast for the rest of her life, but it seemed like a long time already since she'd eaten, and anyone could eat a junket. Even a condemned man.

Dressed in her traveling cloak and bonnet, which had been finished just in time, and carrying an old carpetbag filled with borrowed items considered necessary for a young lady in transit, Heloise was embraced by every girl in turn at the door. Everyone was crying, and some hugged her twice. And they gave her a present. Each of them had found time to embroider her name on a plain silk handkerchief. At the bottom, Old Mother had signed herself simply, *Old Mother*, in shaky stitches, and then embroidered, *God Bless You*. Heloise thanked them numbly. Then, as the girls waved and blew kisses and called final messages across the courtyard, Old Mother and Esther accompanied Heloise to the Rectory, where there were further tears and embraces before Mr. Radcliffe and Lucy were due to set out for the coach office.

"You will not be left to fend for yourself, Heloise," Dr.

Browne said. "If indeed you are to live in your old home, which is by no means certain, my friend Mr. Radcliffe will be a frequent visitor, and I will come to see with my own eyes how you are faring. No decisions can be made until your godmother's health is resolved, in one way or another. But you must remember that you have friends. If in need, you must call on them."

He squeezed her hand, and Heloise curtseyed. Then he lifted her easily into the coach. When it finally set out, with a bumping motion that never ceased, but only grew more and more drunkenly erratic as the two hours passed, Heloise discovered that she did not like coach travel.

And yet, exhausted, she slept, with her head on Lucy's affectionate shoulder.

They had become friends after all.

It was five o'clock when they arrived at the Vicarage.

"I think you should stay the night with us," the Vicar said. "I will call on your godmother this evening. I shall make a judgment about the state of her health, and if possible prepare her for your visit. I am certain that she will be glad to see you, but I would not like to answer for the effects of a shock, which might be brought on by your sudden appearance. Unless she is not expected to last the night, it would be best for you to see her in the morning. Tomorrow is another day, and the morning is the time for great undertakings. I shall take you over after breakfast."

So Heloise had dinner with the Vicarage family.

How strange it was to be suddenly close to people she had always observed from a distance! There was Aunt Charlotte with her pale, pinched face and her air of being either just about to get a headache or just getting over one. And there were the five children with their haunting, deep-set brown eyes and their air of wildness. Bede, the eldest, a considerate boy of fifteen, was studiedly matter-of-fact, treating her as he would any other guest, and Lucy, who was the youngest of the three girls, was kindness itself. But the others could not take their eyes off Heloise.

It was clear they too thought it strange to be close to her.

"Is it true she made you sleep in the coal-scuttle?" George, the baby of the family, asked.

"Georgie!" exclaimed Aunt Charlotte. "We do not ask personal questions of our guests. Help yourself to bread and butter, Heloise. Was it a cold journey, Lucy?"

"Yes, Aunt," said Lucy.

"And was your father's sermon well-received?"

"Yes, Aunt."

"And how were Dr. and Mrs. Browne and the boys?"

"Well, Aunt. Though Edward still has that cough."

"I must send Mrs. Browne my linctus recipe." Here it was clear to Heloise that all five of Aunt Charlotte's charges could barely contain their disgust at the mere memory of this preparation, but Aunt Charlotte did not appear to notice the silent sensation her remark had caused. "I have found it most efficacious with you children," she continued. "Mrs. Browne should not send him back to school until the cough is quite cleared up. Schools are careless of boys' health."

Thus Heloise's personal matters were politely avoided.

Mr. Radcliffe came in halfway through dinner. Like Dr. Browne, it seemed he was not in the habit of sitting down to an undisturbed meal. He nodded encouragingly at Heloise. But he did not speak to her until a discreet moment presented itself after dinner. Then, in the hallway between his study and the library, he gave her a brief report on his visit. There had been no change, he said, in her godmother's condition, and the physician did not expect any dramatic turn for the worse overnight.

"I spoke to her about you. I told her that you were safe and well and that you would be visiting tomorrow morning. But she did not respond. I cannot honestly say whether she hears what is said to her or not. You must prepare yourself for a great change in her, Heloise."

That night, Heloise slept in Lucy's bed, for Heloise had not been expected and the guest room had not been prepared. And both Lucy and Heloise were anxious not to cause poor headachy Aunt Charlotte more work.

It seemed a remarkable thing to Heloise that the very night after she had given Maria away, her bedfellow should be a living, breathing girl. She had never slept with another living creature before. There was a very great difference in the experience. Maria, being a doll (or statue, as it turned out) had not been an ideal bedfellow. But influenced overwhelmingly by her love for Maria, Heloise had managed to mold herself to her. The great advantage of sleeping with an inanimate object was that there was no possibility of accidentally waking her or causing her discomfort.

A girl was a very different matter. Heloise could not sleep for fear of disturbing Lucy. And there were, of course, many other things to keep her awake.

Still, Lucy was warm, and her sleepy sighs were calming.

The next morning dawned cold and grey and still, without a breath of wind. After breakfast, bundled up well against the weather, the Vicar and Heloise set out, in the Vicar's trap, for the caretaker's cottage.

# The Face at the Window

"The cold is not too severe for you, I hope?" enquired Mr. Radcliffe.

"No, sir," Heloise replied, though her teeth were chattering.

Mr. Radcliffe, holding the reins in one hand, tucked the blanket firmly around her in a fatherly manner. Then, like Heloise, like the countryside around them, he was silent.

Everything seemed smaller. The snow-covered fields and fences and stone walls, the hedges and the very trees were dwarfs to her memory of them. And yet it was only a matter of months since she had seen them last. Was it that she had become accustomed to the vast scale and height of buildings in the City – the Prison, the Madhouse? Or had Heloise herself become big, like the inner Heloise she had always imagined, chained up inside her? Had big Heloise escaped at last?

It was half a mile's drive from the Vicarage to Heloise's godmother's place. The Vicar's old chestnut pony seemed glad when it was over. She stopped, without being told, in front of the cottage. The Vicar jumped to the ground, tied her up, helped Heloise down, put a careful blanket over the animal and fed her a carrot. Then he sighed and put an encouraging hand on Heloise's shoulder. Together, they walked to the door.

The Vicar pulled the bell.

But as they waited, the Vicar grave, and Heloise in a state of numb resignation, a strange thing happened.

Heloise felt upon her the eyes of an observer.

It seemed to her that someone was watching her from the nearest upstairs window, the window that had once been her own, the window from which she had watched countless visitors to the Museum as they waited at the door.

Slowly, she looked up. And saw, as she had known she would, the face of a young girl. It was slightly out of focus, like a face seen through a sheet of water, but it looked at her with penetration, as if it knew who she was and why she had come. The face was pallid, with a halo of honey-colored shimmering hair, like sunlight on water. It remained long enough for Heloise to meet its eyes, although they were eyes she could not clearly see. Then it disappeared.

Mrs. Moth opened the door.

She had been clomping down the hall as Heloise was

looking at the face in the window. Now she stood staring at Heloise, more startled by her than Heloise had been by the apparition.

Heloise had a sudden memory of Mr. Callardin-Bowser and his peculiar fear of her. She had never been more convinced of her own strange power to frighten people.

And yet, Sebastian had not been afraid.

"Morning, sir," said Mrs. Moth with a bumpy curtsey, remembering her manners. Her face was haggard, and she seemed thinner. She could not quite bring herself to address Heloise, but said to the Vicar, "Child has changed."

"Indeed she has," said Mr. Radcliffe. "And how is the patient?"

"Same, sir. You wish to see her, sir?"

"If you please, Mrs. Moth."

And so Mrs. Moth stood back to let them pass. She closed the door and led them along the hall and up the stairs.

Heloise's heart thumped in her chest, in her ears, in her head. The cottage seemed smaller, but this did not make her feel any more powerful. She felt instead like a creature who had grown too big for its cage, and who dreaded growing larger still, while the cage grew ever smaller. The hall and the stairs seemed as narrow as the hall and the stairs of a dolls' house. The upstairs hall was narrower still, darker than it had been, with the door to her room shut. At the opposite end lay her godmother's room, its door open and the light dim.

Mrs. Moth went first; Mr. Radcliffe followed. Heloise

crept along behind him, her limbs feeling limp, like a rag doll's.

"The Vicar, ma'am," Mrs. Moth announced in the doorway. Mr. Radcliffe went gently to the bedside. Head lowered, hands clasped inside her cloak, Heloise waited outside the door.

"Good morning, Miss Child," she heard the Vicar say. "I hope you had a restful night. I have brought the visitor I was telling you about. Your ward, Heloise, has come to see you. Shall I ask her in?"

There was no answer. After a moment Mr. Radcliffe called softly, "Heloise, my dear?"

And Heloise entered.

Heloise had rarely stepped inside her godmother's room. It had always been austere, like the rest of the house, with nothing in it beyond the necessary furniture, and certainly no decoration of any kind. Now, however, it was the room of an invalid. It was neat and clean, of course – Mrs. Moth had seen to that. But the blinds had been drawn, and the light was oppressively dim. To the original austerity of the room had been added a variety of bottles containing powders and medicines, from which came periodic whiffs of faint, peculiar scent, and contraptions suggesting various treatments that must have been tried by her godmother's physician. The only sound – the only sign of life – was her godmother's clock, which ticked too loudly, like a metronome, or a persistent drip of water.

In the room's large four-poster bed lay her godmother, her face turned towards the ceiling. The bed was so undisturbed, and her godmother so still, and so neatly arranged, that she might have been laid out for burial. In fact she resembled the kind of effigy that might have been found on a tomb in an ancient church. But Heloise had never seen one of those. All she knew was that her godmother was so thin and wasted that the covers seemed to fall in shadows over her very bones, as if what lay beneath them was no more than a skeleton, and that her face, with its halo of honey-colored hair, loosened from the severe coiffure to which Heloise had been accustomed, was like a skull. Her breathing was so quiet she might have been dead. And yet, perhaps most strangely of all, her eyes – green and enormous in her thin face – were open, although she gave no sign of being aware that there was anyone in the room.

Mr. Radcliffe was watching Heloise and looked poised to catch her. He obviously thought she might faint. But she did not faint. Instead she said softly,

"Hello, Godmother."

The clock ticked. Mrs. Moth, who was staring at her mistress, rubbed the tops of her arms with her hands, as if she was cold. Mr. Radcliffe studied Heloise. But Heloise's godmother only stared at the ceiling.

"I'm sorry that you are unwell," Heloise pursued. "I have

come to sit with you, if you like."

Now Mr. Radcliffe and Mrs. Moth were both staring at Heloise. They had not expected such an offer.

Tick. Tick. Tick.

Mrs. Moth kept rubbing the tops of her arms. Her rough palms against the serge of her gown sounded like sandpaper smoothing a distant block of wood. After a moment, she murmured diffidently, as if she was afraid to seem like she were swaying things one way or another: "Would be a godsend, I admit, if the child would stay for an hour or so. Give me a chance to get on top of things."

Mr. Radcliffe looked from Heloise to the immobile face of her godmother, and back to Heloise again. Her godmother had showed no sign that she was aware that Heloise was present.

"Is it your wish that I leave you here for an hour or two, Heloise?" he said. He did not sound entirely happy about the suggestion. "I must continue my rounds, but I could send young Abel to collect you for luncheon ..."

"Thank you," said Heloise, turning to him dazedly. "I will stay with my godmother for good, if she will permit it."

The Vicar was startled again. He noticed that his mouth had gone dry. He swallowed, and looked helplessly at Mrs. Moth, while Mrs. Moth looked unfathomably at Heloise.

Tick. Tick. Tick.

"Child could stay in her old room," Mrs. Moth said presently, a little more loudly than necessary, as if to make sure her mistress heard. "'Twas locked up, but I could unlock it, if the mistress has no objections."

Heloise's godmother gave no indication that she had heard.

Mr. Radcliffe shivered faintly, like a mild old bird, fluffing up its feathers.

"Well, Heloise," he said uncertainly, "if you're sure, and if your godmother and Mrs. Moth are happy to have you, I suppose I could leave you here and call in again tomorrow morning …"

Heloise and Mrs. Moth gazed at him.

"Right-ho, then," said Mr. Radcliffe. Heloise and Mrs. Moth looked at him expectantly. But he did not go. Instead, he paused, irresolute. Finally he said, "Heloise, if you will see me out?"

Downstairs, he said to her, "You are certain about this? Lucy will not be happy that I have left you here. I am not sure I am happy about it myself." He paused, biting his lip. "And yet, I confess, I do not know why I feel this way. You have little to fear from such a sick woman. That, surely, is plain. She can do you no harm. And yet, God willing, you may be able to do her some good …"

Heloise looked at him calmly, though a little strangely.

"It is what I must do, Mr. Radcliffe," she said. "No matter what the consequences."

He frowned. Then, appearing to come to a decision, he lay his hand on her shoulder and left.

She watched as he drove away. Then she shut the door and turned towards her godmother's room.

All that day, as he went about his business, visiting the frail and ill and sitting on charitable committees, Mr. Radcliffe was haunted by what she had said.

"Sheets'll be damp. And dust'll be two inches thick. If you'll watch the mistress, Miss Heloise, I'll change the sheets and dust and sweep. Otherwise things should be exactly what you're used to."

But it was not what she was used to now, not with months at Old Mother's behind her.

That day, Heloise spent hour after hour sitting with her godmother. While Heloise sat, Mrs. Moth clomped around the cottage. First in Heloise's room, and then, more faintly, downstairs, where she evidently had a backlog of housework to attend to. After a while Heloise smelled cooking. It made her feel, not hungry, but odd, as if she had smelled cooking in a graveyard.

She could not help but feel that Mrs. Moth was immensely relieved to have someone else in the house.

At midday Mrs. Moth clomped up the stairs with a tray; on it was a steaming bowl of clear broth.

"I've left you a meal on the table downstairs," she said to Heloise. "Go and eat it, I'll attend to the mistress."

Heloise was surprised that her godmother was taking

nourishment, but as she left she saw Mrs. Moth propping her up with several pillows. She could only imagine that Mrs. Moth somehow managed to spoon broth into her godmother's unprotesting mouth, which explained how it was that she was still alive.

In the kitchen Heloise found a meal of the same broth, augmented generously with vegetables, and laid out invitingly. She ate it automatically, washed up and returned upstairs, upon which Mrs. Moth changed places with her.

Heloise had been sitting in the chair that Mrs. Moth had apparently been using during her own vigils. She had taken off her bonnet, but not her grey traveling cloak, for it had occurred to her that the dress she was wearing underneath, a gay autumn-toned print she had inherited from Nan, would offend her godmother if she were to see it. And yet … it was difficult to imagine this woman – her new, sick godmother – caring about anything at all. Heloise wondered how long her godmother had been lying there. She wondered how many days Mrs. Moth had sat where she was sitting now. She could imagine Mrs. Moth's knitting needles clicking, in counterpoint to the ticking clock, and falling silent on those occasions when, in the dimness and the close atmosphere, she dropped off, only to start awake again and shudder when she saw the nightmare figure of her mistress, not a dream but a waking reality.

Heloise did not drop off. Mostly, she stared at her godmother and tried to love her.

It was not that Heloise was unmoved. No one could have been unaffected by the sight before her. Her godmother had been a beautiful young woman, younger than Heloise had understood, with looks so winsome that they seemed to invite love, despite her stern words and aloof ways. Now, pitiably, all that winsomeness had fled from her. Lying in bed, she looked like a parody of herself, like a sketch made by an artist who hated her, deliberately excising everything that was beautiful. Worse still, she looked empty, like one from whom the life had been sucked out.

No, Heloise was not unmoved, and she was not without pity. But her keenest feeling was fear, and this overwhelmed everything else. She did not so much fear her godmother's death, or even that her death would be Heloise's fault. What she was frightened by was her sense that there was a deep, horrible meaning in her godmother's decline, a meaning she could not decipher, but which was of profound and urgent import.

Heloise wanted to love her godmother. She knew that a great deal depended on it. And yet, try as she might, she could not. For there was something in the way, something that seemed more powerful even than the circumstances in which she found herself.

Once Heloise had wanted her godmother to love her. She had longed for this love, perhaps more than anything else in her life. She had longed for her godmother's love even more than she had longed for a doll.

But her godmother had refused her love, and Heloise had

found love elsewhere. She did not crave her godmother's love any more. That longing had died. And it was as if her capacity to love her godmother had died with it.

Heloise did not want this to be so. She did not even think it fair. She wanted to forgive. She wanted pain and fear and hatred to be over and done with; she wanted to love everyone as she loved Maria and Sebastian, whether anyone loved her back, or not.

But the part of her heart that could achieve this had turned to iron.

Heloise knew this, because every time she tried to open it, the sheer, indomitable strength of it forced her back, bruised and vanquished.

For an hour and a half that afternoon, Mrs. Moth left Heloise alone with her godmother while she hurried into the village and back. That night, she cooked a good dinner, which frankly she looked to be in need of. Then she sent Heloise to bed.

"I'll keep watch overnight," she said. "I don't sit up. Doctor said there was no need. But I wake every few hours and come up to look in on her. It'll be a help to have you sleeping on the same floor. You can call me if she needs anything."

And so it was that, at last, Heloise found herself alone in her old room.

It was true that nothing had changed. Nothing except the most important thing.

Heloise shut the door and, free from observation,

removed her traveling cloak. She thought the room itself was probably shocked by the colors underneath. Mrs. Moth had laid out one of her nightgowns and had filled the china jug with warm water; Heloise took off her dress, washed, and dressed herself quickly for bed. It was cold; automatically she got one of her woolen shawls out of the chest in the corner. Then, wrapping herself in it, she wandered the room, remembering.

She remembered the games she had played with her pillow. She remembered all the work she had done here, the sewing and knitting, both authorized and illicit. She remembered how immensely lonely she had been.

Most of all, she remembered finding Maria.

It was Maria, of course, that was missing. Without her, this room was like a body without a soul. There had, for all Heloise knew, never been a time when Maria had not been present; for secretly, she had been here even before Heloise had found her.

Heloise knelt down and stroked the false board. Scrabbling a little, she removed it with her fingertips. There was nothing beneath it but a black oblong of space, an empty grave. No Maria and no secret passage, leading to Sebastian, either.

Staring into the cavity, Heloise was lost in wonder. What a miracle it seemed that something made by someone who did not even know she existed could find its way into her hands, apparently by chance, and affect her so profoundly.

She began to think about the journey Maria had made, from Sebastian, to the Madhouse, to her room.

She wondered, as Sebastian had, at the fact that Mary Child had kept her.

Then, for the first time, she began to think about how it was that Maria had ended up under the floorboard in her room.

She had always assumed that Mary Child had simply hidden Maria here, just as she had hidden so many other dolls. But now that she knew that Mary Child and her godmother were the same person …

Heloise did not know how long she, Heloise, had lived in the caretaker's cottage, or where she had lived before that. She did not even know what had influenced her godmother to bring a strange child into her home. But if her godmother had put Maria under the floorboards, there were only two possibilities.

Either she had hidden her there because it was a good hiding place, before she knew that such a person as Heloise would live there.

Or she had put her there deliberately, after Heloise came, knowing Heloise might find her.

# Unpicking the Stitches

Heloise waited in bed until Mrs. Moth retired. The old woman sat with her godmother until the clock struck ten. Then she packed up her knitting, tidied the perfectly tidy room, said goodnight and, receiving no reply, snuffed out the light and clomped out of the room. Heloise heard her footsteps approaching, and then receding down the hall, and the squeak of her boots descending the stairs.

Heloise waited until the clomping on the lower floor ceased. Then she got up. She did not dress, or take her boots, for if caught downstairs it would be better if she was not obviously preparing to leave the house. Instead she went to the sewing basket that still stood on her work table and collected a little implement called a seam ripper. She had always used it for the unpicking of stitches. Throwing her shawl around her, she silently opened the door and crept down the hall.

She knew it would be hard to make it down the stairs without causing the boards to squeak, but she was a good deal lighter than Mrs. Moth and, as she kept to the very edges of the stairs, her descent proved virtually silent. Once in the downstairs hall she became conscious of a strange, regular noise, alternating with silences of equal duration; it took her a moment to realize that it was Mrs. Moth, snoring. This was certainly a stroke of luck. She crept to the kitchen, lit the lamp that stood on the table, picked it up, padded back into the hall and carefully collected the bunch of keys from the hook on the wall near the front door. She had to place the lantern, the keys, and her little tool on the hall table in order to have her hands free to open the door. She managed to open it, collect the keys and the lantern and the seam ripper, slip out and close the door without incident. Now she must cross the ground between the caretaker's cottage and the Museum.

The icy ground was torture to her bare feet. Far worse than this was the uncomfortable feeling that she was being observed from one of the windows. But there was nothing she could do about it. The only practicable path between the cottage and the Museum was visible from the windows on that side of the cottage. She would have been less visible without the lantern, but she could not do without it. Biting her lip with the cold, she slipped across the yard and onto the porch of the Museum. Grateful to be standing on wood again, she laid the lantern and the sewing tool at her feet, unlocked the front door and slipped inside. She paused, holding the lantern before her. Then, too late, she realized what she had done.

Until that moment, she had been entirely preoccupied by the fear of being caught. As soon as she shut the door behind her, however, another fear took over; this one made the first seem like a nursery game.

All at once, it was as if Heloise's animal self awoke. Every nerve of her body, every one of her instincts seemed to be screaming at her to escape, at once. She had never experienced anything like it. It had come upon her so suddenly, it was as if there was some kind of charge in the house. Of course it was not the first time she had come through this door. But that other time she had come unwillingly, and had not been planning any action. Now it was as if the house knew she was an enemy.

Heloise stood frozen at the door. The house seemed to be filled with pure evil. All she wanted was to rip the door open, hurtle out again, and run pell-mell back to her room, or better still far, far away, never to return. For a moment she thought the fear would overpower her, would crush her so completely that she was incapable even of escape.

But then –

Then came the anger.

It was not an explosive, anarchic thing, this anger, but a cool, clever thing, a knowledge, a power. She had not stopped being afraid. Indeed, it was the fear that was making her angry – more and more angry – angry at everything that had held her in thrall for so long, everything that had destroyed the joy in her life and the lives around her. Only now did she realize that she was drenched in sweat. She felt herself go hot, and then cold, and then hot all over; suddenly she realized that Big Heloise had indeed broken her chains, that she had escaped, that nothing short of destruction was going to stop her, and that she was prepared to be destroyed if necessary.

She was still trembling as she went recklessly into the main room, dark but for the circle of light provided by her lantern. It was difficult to walk; it was as if the atmosphere had turned viscous. She looked around, and even her eyes felt slowed, as if she were looking around underwater. Nonetheless, she saw the dolls of Mary Child perched about the room, as if they were waiting, their masked faces turned blindly towards her. They seemed both near and remote, as if she and all of them were trapped within a sunken ship.

She must choose one and begin. But even that was hard. There were so many. Each of them seemed to be calling her. Where to begin?

With an effort, she fixed her attention on the doll sitting on the mantelpiece. She placed the lantern on the table, moved with difficulty towards the doll, reached out and clasped it. Then, groping her way back to the light, and seating herself with almost as much difficulty, she set to work.

The task seemed almost impossible. The stitches were

small, tight, and numerous. It was no good ripping them –
she must not destroy the fabric underneath. Each stitch had
to be lifted gently with the sharp end of her tool, and then cut
with the blade. It was dainty work, requiring dainty fingers.
But – whether it was the emotion, or whether the air really
had become as water – Heloise was as clumsy as a puppet. She
seemed to have no precision in her movements, no force.

But still there was the saving anger. And this anger did not
make her impatient. It made her determined, single-minded,
clear-headed.

It was like draining the sea by cupfuls, it was like counting
every grain of sand on the shore. And yet, as she worked,
stitch by stitch, as the little snips of black thread collected at
her feet, as the long moments passed, the atmosphere seemed,
gradually, to thin.

Snip. Snip. Snip.

With every stitch her vision grew clearer. With every
stitch her hands were more dexterous. With every stitch –

With every stitch …

What was this, growing beneath her working fingers?

She could not understand. A creamy white space of calico,
a moonlit cloud in the night sky, a light seen from underwater
– a … what?

The calico beneath the stitching was cleaner, newer-looking
than the calico on the doll's limbs. The doll's arms and legs had
been exposed to the dust and the damp and the air; they spoke,
dully, of death and decay. But its head had been masked by

stitching almost as soon as it had been brought into existence. And so, in this cruel way, it had been protected from time. Though the calico was pockmarked by the tiny holes where the stitches had been, as if the doll had been afflicted by a disfiguring disease.

It was when she began to uncover the first eye that she understood.

She had thought only to unpick the stitches; she had not considered what it would mean to uncover a face.

Now that a face was gazing at her through the grille of depleted stitches, now that she truly understood what she was doing, her task became all the more urgent. Heloise worked feverishly, fearing only that she would be prevented from completing her work. She thought it would probably take a hundred nights to unpick all the stitches on all the dolls, but she would do it, she would finish them all, if it killed her.

The room, the house, the cold night, were silent except for the faint sound of the blade cutting the cotton, and her hand brushing the stitches away from the calico. She was observed only by the blind faces of the other dolls.

Thus, stitch by spiteful stitch, the face was unmasked.

Long before she had finished, Heloise had begun quietly to weep. When at length the last fragment of cotton fell to the floor and she was able to look at the face Mary Child had made and then disfigured, she could hardly see it for tears. But she blinked them away, and held the doll close to the light.

She looked and looked, but found she was barely able to comprehend.

The features had been embroidered with great care onto the plain cream-colored calico head. The doll had, beneath its yellow woolen hair, a red rosebud mouth, pink cheeks, an aristocratic nose, and strongly defined, dark brows. But it was the eyes that were most memorable. They were large and emerald green, with thick black lashes, and they tipped, not up, but downwards at the outer corners. They seemed, in a simple, doll-like manner, to speak of suffering on the part of the doll, and compassion for the suffering of others.

At first she did not know why the face caused her such pain.

Then she realized it was because it was beautiful, and vulnerable, and friendly, and that it looked just like her godmother.

How many years had passed since the doll had been looked at in the face? Surely, in its whole existence, it had never been held with love. Heloise found these ideas heart-rending; she snatched up the doll and held it to her breast and buried her face in its yellow woolen hair.

As she did this, it seemed to her that she had never felt so overwhelmed by love. It was not just the love she was trying to give the poor rag doll as she pressed it to her heart and enveloped it with her arms; it was the curious fact that as she did this, she herself felt loved and held, not by the doll, but by something outside of her, bigger than her. The greater the passion with which she held the doll, the more passionately she was held.

She did not know how many moments passed before she became aware of the sound. It may have begun the moment she threw her arms around the doll. Even when she became aware of it, it did not seem important. It was only as it went on, more and more insistently, that she slowly lifted her head and looked around.

It was a soft, sibilant sound, continuous and graceful, and unfamiliar. She wondered what it could be; then in her imagination there arose an image of a snake sliding away through grass.

But there was no snake. It was the dolls.

Still holding the first doll in her arms, she rose from her seat and went quickly to the doll that was sitting on the bookshelf. She saw an astonishing thing. The stitches on the doll's face were unraveling. A long worm of black thread was pulling itself in and out of the holes into which it had been woven, and dropping to the floor. The doll's face was emerging steadily, gradually, new and clean and shining, like the sun from behind a cloud.

Heloise looked around her. Everywhere, it was the same, the stitches unraveling, the faces gradually appearing. She turned and snatched up the lantern and set off down the hall, looking at every doll she could find; she even ran up the stairs, and out through the back door into the yard. Everywhere she looked the same extraordinary thing was happening.

Acting on some impulse she did not understand she began to snatch up the dolls and bring them – as many as she could hold at once – into the main room; she propped them up on the chaise lounge, feasted her eyes on the emerging faces and kissed them reverently, on their foreheads, on their cheeks, on their hair, on their hands, then flew around the house to collect more. They were all the same, or as similar as something made by hand could be, their large, green, downward-tilting eyes looking back at her in amazement.

She did not hear the door open; she was too busy and excited. She was coming back from one of her joyful trips around the house, her arms filled with dolls, when she saw her godmother standing inside the door.

# The Last Doll

How tall she was, how thin, how pale in her long white nightgown. She was standing just inside the circle of light from the lantern Heloise was holding; one step backwards and she would have been in darkness. In that weak light, she looked spectral.

For what seemed like an age, they stared at each other, Heloise and Mary Child.

Heloise was panting; she had stopped dead in her mad careen around the house and was holding the last six dolls tightly against her, the lantern dangling from two fingers. Despite her godmother's illness she was half-expecting her to fly at the dolls, or her, in a frenzy. But her godmother seemed calm. She was supporting herself against the wall, as if she was too weak to stand.

"So," she said with difficulty. "You have beaten me."

Heloise said nothing. She had no idea what her godmother meant.

"You have spoken to him, haven't you?" her godmother pursued doggedly. "You have been with him and talked to him?"

This time Heloise knew who she was talking about. But again she said nothing. There seemed nothing to say.

Mary Child took a few precarious steps into the room. She was looking at the dolls on the chaise lounge, through eyes that were a mirror image of their own. She was so thin and fragile-looking that Heloise could hardly believe she could move.

"The work of years," murmured Mary Child, "destroyed in a moment. Destroyed – by love."

Heloise was startled. Could love destroy? She supposed, after all, that it could; it had destroyed the stitching on the dolls' faces. But if what it destroyed was cruelty, could destruction be a bad thing?

She felt a strange kind of remorse for having destroyed something that was so precious to Mary Child, even if what was precious was her own self-hatred.

"When I was thrown out of the Madhouse," Mary Child was saying breathlessly, "I walked back here in just the same manner as you walked away. We must have used the same road. But I was not wearing well-made boots.

I was wearing hessian slippers. The only shoes allowed

in the Madhouse. Worn through before I even left the City. By the time I got here my footsteps were filled with blood. It took weeks for my feet to heal."

Suddenly her knees gave way and she sank to the floor. Heloise moved forward to help her, realized she was encumbered by the lantern and the dolls, and placed the lantern quickly on the table and the dolls on the floor, but turned to find her godmother with her hand raised to ward her off.

"There is not much time," she said. "I must explain. If you will just listen ..."

She lowered her head and breathed deeply. She was half lying, half sitting, supporting herself with her hands, which she had placed palms down on the floor. When she began again she spoke rapidly, urgently, as if she had found new strength.

"When the judge ordered my release," she explained, "the governors of the Madhouse put me out on the street, like a cat. I did not want to be released. I had nowhere to go. For three nights, I slept on the street outside the Madhouse. They kept coming out to drive me away, but I crept back. Finally, I realized that I was abandoned again, just as I had been abandoned there in the first place. I did not know what to do. So I went back to the place that had once been my home.

"I walked through the night and arrived as the dawn was breaking. I was afraid they would be angry to see me again. But when I saw the house, I knew that I had been abandoned once more.

"It was not as it had been when I left it …"

Although her voice was soft and she appeared to be saving her strength, she had been speaking with relative ease. Now exhaustion was overcoming her again.

"Every one – of the windows – was broken," she said. "When I put my hand on the front door knob, it fell off. I limped inside. The floor was strewn with dirt, dead leaves, season after season of weather that had come in through the windows. Roof leaking, floorboards rotten, pigeons flying in and out of broken windows, nesting in bookshelves. Everything covered in dust and cobwebs.

"I did not need to call out. I knew there was no one here. Or at least, that the only ones remaining were –"

She lowered her head. Heloise stood frozen in the position she had been in when her godmother raised her hand to keep her away. She was gazing at her godmother with horrified pity.

"I was hungry and exhausted and near-lame," her godmother resumed, "but my mind was strangely clear. I still knew every one of my hiding places. How could I forget? I dragged myself from one to another and found what I had suspected to be true. All of the dolls were still where I had left them.

"I think even then I had the germ of an idea.

"That first morning, I begged food from the farm next door. I offered my services as a seamstress, for I had not forgotten how to sew. I got work immediately, and that work led to more work. I took up residence in the old housekeeper's cottage, fed myself from my sewing, and gradually cleaned and, so far as I was capable, repaired the houses.

"I put it about that, for a small fee, I would open the house to interested parties, and exhibit the traces a dead lunatic had left behind. No one guessed that she and I were the same person. The people round about thought I was a distant relative who had come into her inheritance – an unenviable one, in this case. I explained away my destitute arrival by saying that I had been robbed on the road. People were suspicious. I dare say there were rumors. I did not care. I – did not want – friends."

She lowered her head and breathed deeply. Heloise roused herself with difficulty. It was like trying to wake from a nightmare.

"Godmother," she said. "Can I not – would you not take a glass of water? May I not help you back to bed?"

"There is not time," said Mary Child without raising her head. After a moment she resumed. "My plan was a success. At first it was just the local people who came. But word spread, first to nearby towns and villages, eventually to the whole country. I found I could make a good living out of hating my younger self, and persuading others, if not to hate, than at least to fear her. Soon I could afford to get workmen in to fix the roof and replace the floorboards. I could even pay a housekeeper to assist me.

"But it wasn't enough.

"To hate oneself, Heloise, is to be at war with oneself. It is as if there are two people: the one who hates and the one who is hated. And yet they live within the one mind.

"I wanted to start again. I wanted a new self, who would make no false steps, who would not have to be hated, who would not deserve it as I had.

"There was a deposit of clay on the property. I had been taught – he had taught me – to model in clay. But I had always known how to make something and bring it to life. This was my curse. What set me apart. What had caused them to abandon me.

"I had only ever made little things. Lizards. Butterflies. Now the strength of my hatred made me capable of things that would be believed only by someone who knew the power of hate.

"And so, Heloise, I made another doll. My last."

Mary Child lowered her head once more. Her last sentence echoed in Heloise's mind. For a moment it meant nothing. Then a kind of horror passed over her, a deep shudder that seemed to travel right through her body, before she was even conscious of what had caused it. A moment later, she knew.

"No," she whispered.

Mary Child raised her hand.

"Only listen," she begged. "This doll," she resumed quickly, "was not a rag doll, made from calico and yellow wool. It was infinitely more clever, infinitely more

accomplished, infinitely more precious. It was modeled
from clay, and I breathed into it a part of my own soul, as if
my soul were a tree, and I had taken a cutting from it, and
planted it in new soil. I made it the age I was when things
had begun to go wrong. And I kept it from all the influences I
believed to be dangerous.

"It thrived, or so it seemed to me. It was obedient
and predictable. It showed, at first, no dangerous spark of
imagination. It had no special talents. And its questions were
easily suppressed. I had another me – a me who was not me.
A me with green eyes, like my own, and black hair, unlike
my own. A me who would not transgress. A me who would
not go mad when her transgressions were put a stop to. A me
whom I did not hate.

"But I did not understand myself. One cannot understand
what one hates. And there was another part of me, a part that
had listened to what he said, a part that thought I might be
wrong. It was this part that kept the Madonna."

"No," said Heloise again. She felt dizzy and ill.

"At first I had thought to sell her. I was destitute when I
left the asylum, and although I had no idea what she might
be worth I knew she would feed me for a while. Somehow
I could not part with her. One day, I tried to burn her on a
mound of leaves, but I could not make myself cast her on the
fire. So I buried her in the room that I had set aside for my
Last Doll. I thought, *If he was right, she will find the Madonna.
If I am right, she will not.*

"When you ran away and took her with you, I began to suspect the truth. I had molded a new creature, a creature who would not make my mistakes. But she would achieve this, not by obeying, but by disobeying me.

"Now that you have come back, I know. He was right all along. Love has destroyed The Museum of Mary Child, and it has defeated me. You have grown strong. I have weakened. This very night, the me that loved and accepted love, will live. The me that could not will die. Do you understand, Heloise?"

Heloise felt her knees give way, and for a moment there was oblivion. When she opened her eyes, she found herself on the floor. Her godmother was still a little way from her, but she was dragging herself along the floorboards in Heloise's direction.

"Please," she was saying, "accept from me a parting gift, an act of love. You were a doll, Heloise, but you are no longer. I am giving you your freedom. Live with my blessing. And forgive me – if you can."

She reached out her long, thin arm and touched Heloise's finger. And something of immense power, something so full of light and warmth that it seemed almost to be light and warmth personified, as if all the light and warmth in the world had at that moment concentrated itself in her godmother's body, passed out of her and into Heloise. For a moment Heloise was blinded. When next she could see, she saw something that tore her with grief.

Where her godmother had been lying there was the

most pitiable object Heloise had ever seen. It was a large and intensely beautiful rag doll.

Heloise seized it and held it in her arms, rocking and weeping with it on the floor.

She knew that when she had hated her godmother, she had in fact been hating herself.

But now hatred was over and done with. In Heloise's heart, there was only love.

# The Prison of Gold

Sebastian woke with a start.

It seemed to him that something had happened, something of profound importance. But when he opened his eyes, everything was the same.

He looked around. Blue-black bricks, silver lichen, barred windows. Through one, moonlight and bracingly cold air. Through the other, darkness and silence.

"No miracles," he whispered.

Then he moved slightly and noticed that he was unchained.

The first thing he felt was fear.

He sat staring at his bare wrists as if they were something uncanny. His heart thundered in his chest. He found it terrifying to look at them; he found it terrifying to look away.

Nevertheless he raised his eyes slowly and looked towards the door.

He gasped, moved back, hit his head against the bricks behind him but barely noticed.

In the semi-darkness, the door was usually suspended in a thin frame of light, a regular oblong somewhat above his sight-line, as the entrance to the cell was on a steep slant.

Now, however, the oblong leaned towards the right, and a wide band of light framed it on one side. In other words, the door was ajar.

Sebastian looked from the door, to his wrists, and back to the door again. He hesitated. Then he moved experimentally out of the chains.

The moment he did so, pain shot through him. He understood, suddenly, what was before him. His heart still thundered in his chest, but now his mind began to race. He was trying to think strategically, but he could not. All he could think of was how terrifying it was to hope.

He turned, reached towards the ledge behind him, almost cried out with the pain, but managed to retrieve the Madonna from her hiding place. Staring abstractedly into space, thinking about everything and about nothing, he managed to tie her into the front of his ragged shirt, though this operation, which would once have been simple, was more difficult than the most delicate feat of carving.

Every movement was a stab of pain. When he had secured the statue, he pulled himself forward onto his hands and knees, and began to crawl up the steep incline towards the door. He could not yet stand.

His progress was slow and swaying, like that of a praying mantis. At every moment he expected to be stopped and driven back to where he belonged.

But he was not stopped.

When he reached the ledge before the door he paused, his long limbs taut, his pale face set in a kind of shock. He peered incredulously around the door into the corridor. Torches burned in sockets in the walls on either side, but the hallway seemed deserted. He hesitated, then squeezed through the opening and out of the cell.

On his hands and knees in the dim corridor, he pulled the door shut behind him. It was heavy and cost him precious strength, but he knew it should not look open from the outside. Crouched in the doorway, he looked to the left and right, momentarily uncertain. He knew this corridor was parallel with the street, and that the Madhouse was to the right of the gaol. So he chose the right.

Sebastian crawled up the hall. The icy stones hurt his knees, every movement was a stab of pain, but the most painful thing of all was the hope.

Surely he would not be allowed to succeed; surely he was not crawling to liberty?

On his right, the wall was punctuated every ten feet or so by a slab of iron – a cell door, signifying another soul imprisoned. He had not gone far before a new wild hope crossed his mind. Could it be that they all had been unchained, that they all were to walk free on this transfigured night? Panting with emotion as much as effort, he began, not so much to crawl up the hall, as to crawl from door to door, pausing at each, pushing his shoulder against it.

None were open.

What little strength he had was all but drained by the disappointment. A black sickness of sympathy overcame him.

He thought that he simply could not desert them. What would freedom be worth, knowing they were still in prison?

But then, how else could he hope to help them?

If I live, he thought, I will come back for them. And if I cannot free them, I will improve, I will comfort. But the tears stung his eyes.

They were blinding him. He wiped them with the backs of his hands. When he looked up, he saw something he had not noticed before.

A door, on the left, ajar.

This one, he knew, did not lead into another cell.

As soon as he saw it, some distance along the hall in front of him, all he wanted was to increase his pace. He had a chance and he must take it. But he could go no faster. It was all he could do to keep going at all.

Step by crawling step, Sebastian approached the door. He leaned against it before he had the strength to peer through the gap. When he raised his eyes, he saw a narrow passage, with a dim light at the end. He pulled the door open, and slipped through. Then he shut the door behind him. Now he was in almost total darkness.

He knew that the light ahead came through a barred window set high in a door. And he knew that, beyond the door, lay the street.

He crawled forward, his eyes turned to the light.

It was so silent that the sound of his hands and knees passing along the floor, the sound of his ragged clothes brushing against the wall, the sound of his breathing, filled his ears as if they had been so many gunshots. The beating of his heart seemed as if it would shake the very prison down.

He could not crawl any more. His knees hurt too much. When he reached the door, he used the enormous lock on it, and then the bars on the window, to pull himself to his feet. For a moment, he thought he was going to collapse. It was partly his head, which was spinning, and partly his knees, which seemed unable to take his weight. He leaned against the door, his head bent like one praying. And although this door, unlike the others, was not ajar, he felt it move inwards with his weight.

When he pulled, it opened. Swinging slowly backwards, it pinned him against the wall.

For the second time that night, he gasped. He was not sure if he would have the strength to push it off him. Instead of pushing, he squeezed himself out gradually from behind it. More than ever he felt like an insect.

When he emerged, he was standing at an open door.

Dark, empty street, falling snow. Then he staggered out, pulling the door closed behind him.

When it shut, he fell down. But he dragged himself across the snow to the next building. When he reached the corner, he pulled himself again to his feet.

Sebastian walked up the street. If anyone had seen him it would have made a strange sight: an exceptionally tall, exceptionally young man, moving like an exceptionally old one. But no one saw him.

He passed the Madhouse. He paused briefly and gazed up at the blind windows, the snow collecting in his hair. Then he moved on.

He turned, and began to creep down the hill towards the heart of the City.

It was the dead of night, but the farther he moved from the Prison and the Madhouse, the more people he saw, however, not one of them glanced twice at him. They were hurrying, for no one was out at that time for their own amusement. And after all, misery, destitution, even madness on the street in wintertime was nothing to wonder at.

He passed dark, tumbledown buildings and toppling rubbish heaps.

He passed public houses and newspaper offices.

He passed stuffy workshops where, during the long day, seamstresses and cobblers and milliners and wigmakers plied their trade.

He passed the shabby, mean-looking buildings

honeycombed with rooms to let, where workers slept, hungry and exhausted, through the too-short night.

He passed empty markets where stray cats foraged and fought. He passed physicians' consulting rooms and apothecary shops; he passed theatres and churches and squares. He passed the grand houses of the rich and the tumbledown houses of the poor. He passed the great Cathedral, and the Houses of Parliament.

Then he came to another prison.

Its gates were made of pure gold.

He walked across the snow towards them. As he approached he could not understand why they seemed to be getting bigger. He was moving as if suspended by strings; something was telling him to go forward, and he suspected it was his own will, but his will seemed immeasurably distant from his body; and he could not remember what he was doing any more.

The bars stopped his progress. He could not pass through them, so he leaned against them and waited.

It took a while for the guards to notice him. They were used to giving alms to beggars; their orders were to turn away no one. That was said to come straight from the top. So they kept bread from the kitchens, and coins from the treasury, in the guardhouse.

But this one was different. Destitute, certainly, but he

wanted nothing, only gazed at them kindly through dark, hauntingly pure eyes. He pulled something out of his ragged shirt, pushed it through the bars, and said something they could not understand.

"What's that, son?" asked the sergeant, a kindly bachelor who rather enjoyed working nights. These odd little things always happened at two o'clock in the morning; if you worked during the day you missed all the fun.

"For the Queen," the beggar whispered, then collapsed.

The Queen was not the kind of person you hesitated to disturb. She always wanted to know, and it could never wait. Consequently, no one in the chain of command hesitated, or hesitated long, in handing the wooden statue from outside guard, to inside guard, from downstairs servants, to upstairs servants, from third lady of the Queen's bedchamber, to second lady of the Queen's bedchamber, to first lady of the Queen's bedchamber. Anyway, it was well known that the Queen did not sleep well. She might as well have a novelty.

But no one could have expected what happened next.

Who was this unkempt, wild-eyed creature in white, flowing night robes, billowing out behind her as she ran barefoot down the palatial staircase, long hair loose and flowing to her waist, her hands clutching a small Madonna?

The footmen standing at the door recognized her, but hardly knew what to do. It was clear she wanted to get out, though she had lost the power of speech. But at such an hour, and in such a state of undress? However, the night butler, a wise man, strode to the door himself and simply opened it for her, without a word being spoken, as if letting out a bird.

And so the Queen ran barefoot, weeping, into the snow and across to the golden-barred gate.

There she threw herself to the ground and, without waiting for the gate to be opened, held her son through the bars, though he knew nothing of it.

# Epilogue

In the transept of the little round church of Saint Mary and the Angels, a very young woman stood alone, staring at the mosaic at her feet.

It was a Saturday in summertime, and there was no one else in the church. But if someone had come in they might not have noticed her. She was dressed in black, for she was in mourning, and, as her hair was also black, and her pale face turned away from the entrance, she was well camouflaged in the dim light.

If someone *had* come in, she probably would have fled, for she was still averse to drawing undue attention to herself.

But today she had good reason to believe she would not be disturbed.

The City had thrown itself into a great celebration – a

Coronation, no less. Even now, she could hear the great Cathedral bells tolling, faintly. Everyone she knew, every man and his dog, every woman and her cat, had gone to watch. Old Mother and the choir had gone. Dr. and Mrs. Browne and Priscilla had gone. Mr. Radcliffe and Lucy, who had traveled with her from the country, had gone.

Mr. Callardin-Bowser and the entire congregation of the church, poor and not-so-poor, had gone. Even the staff and patrons of The Rose and Crown had gone, and the publican had shut his doors for the day and left a sign.

Heloise could not go, for people in mourning did not attend celebrations of any kind, and anyway, someone had to stay home to keep Esther company. Esther was in bed in the Old Monastery with a nasty summer cold and fever. Old Mother had left them in charge of each other, saying they would be back early. But Esther was asleep, and Heloise had stolen up the stairs to the church.

She had arrived in the City the day before, and she wanted to see if the trapdoor was still there. But it was something of a miracle that she was there at all.

It was Mrs. Moth who had saved Heloise from the fire. On the night Heloise had unpicked the stitches, The Museum of Mary Child had burnt to the ground. Heloise would have been lost with it if Mrs. Moth had not burst in with a soaking blanket over her head and pulled her off the floor, ripping a large rag doll out of her fingers, and hurling it into the house before she hauled Heloise out.

Heloise knew that one of Mary Child's dolls had upset the lantern and set the house alight, but she was equally certain that they had meant her no harm. She knew she was meant to escape.

"You must forget all this, child," Mrs. Moth had said with an odd, dead grimness as they stood under the black night sky, watching the Museum burn down.

In the village, the church bells were ringing the alarm, and people from neighboring farms had panted up the hill with buckets. By the time they began to fill them at the pump it was too late. Now they stood around like mourners at a funeral, watching the flames licking up into the night, murmuring amongst themselves.

"Thank God there is no wind," said one of the men.

"Otherwise the cottage'd go up too."

"'Let the dead bury the dead,'" Mrs. Moth urged Heloise in an undertone. "That's from Scripture. One of the parts you weren't allowed to read. You must go away, and never come back, and above all, forget."

In some ways, Heloise had followed her advice, for although she had not exactly forgotten, she had been numb at heart ever since. She had not cried, but neither had she felt glad, or even at peace, as perhaps she should have.

For the curse, it was true, was expiated.

But she felt so alone.

In the months since then, she had grown to womanhood. Her godmother's physician had been so alarmed by her unnatural growth spurt that he had insisted she stay in the country for as long as possible, drinking new milk and breathing fresh country air. He feared she would outgrow her strength and fall into a consumption.

Heloise had submitted, and put off her departure until the summer. But really, no one could tell her what to do any more.

She had Old Mother and the orphans, and now, if she wished, she could be truly one of them. And there were Dr. and Mrs. Browne and Lucy Radcliffe.

But there was no Mary Child, no Maria and no Sebastian.

Heloise knelt and scrabbled at the tiles. Stare as she might, she could see no door, and she knew in her heart that the way was barred to her forever.

What had happened to him?

Had he been freed?

Sadly, she stood up, then took a few steps backward, staring up at that strange carving, the one of the man hanging from the tree with two branches, looking as if he wanted to hug all the world. She could still make no sense of it. Perhaps, she thought idly, I should ask Dr. Browne to explain.

Then she heard something.

What she heard was in fact two noises, both of them

confusing, and yet familiar. One was the sound of the heel of a riding boot meeting the tiles near the fount. The other was the sound of wings.

Heloise turned to see Merryfeathers coming in to land on her head.

"Rejoice, Heloise," he was saying, as he hopped from one wiry foot to the other, and then fluttered to her shoulder. "Rejoice! For you have been accorded a great honor. Last night, at the Annual General Meeting of the Society of the Caged Birds of the City, it was decided, by unanimous vote, to accord you the greatest honor we are capable of conferring. My master and mistress are at the Coronation, and so I am at unusual daytime liberty to come and tell you the great news, knowing, as I did, from certain mice, that you were back in the City." He fluttered into the air and, in a complicated maneuver worthy of his days of freedom under Antipodean skies, kissed her with his beak first on one cheek, then on the other, then on the first again. She put up her finger so that he could perch on it in comfortable proximity to her face, and was taken aback to hear him announce: "For your services to Love, you, Heloise, are henceforth to be regarded an Honorary Caged Bird!"

Heloise blinked. Then, slowly, like one whose sleeping heart was beginning to wake, she smiled one of her rare smiles.

"For services to Love," she repeated dreamily.

"But do not think about that now," said Merryfeathers. "I

wanted to tell you before you were taken up by other matters. Look behind me, Heloise. You have a guest."

Heloise obeyed him, and was so startled her heart skipped a beat.

At the opposite end of the nave, in front of the baptismal fount, stood a very tall young man, splendidly dressed.

In the dim light she could not see him well, but she knew he was looking at her. She had no idea who he was, or what he was doing there. And yet, at the same time, her mind was teased by a faint sense of familiarity, as if she were looking at someone she had known a very long time ago.

"Don't you recognize me, Heloise?" he said at last. Then, tentatively, he came forward a few steps. "The wonder of it is that I should know you, changed as you are. But then, I have changed too." He tried to smile, but could not. His mouth was crooked beneath his long nose. "My name is Sebastian," he said.

Heloise saw a pale face – shaven now, and clean – black hair, clipped short, and very dark, wide-set, earnest eyes. For a strange moment she thought she saw bars in front of her eyes.

"Sebastian is in prison," she said.

"Not any more," he said.

And then suddenly, almost as if he did not know what else to do, he held out his arms.

She did not understand the gesture. Then she remembered the last time she had seen Sebastian – the Sebastian on the other side of the barred window. She remembered how she had pushed her arms through the bars and extended them as far as she could towards him, as if to embrace him. And she remembered how he had lifted his chained arms up towards her as far as they would go, as if to return the embrace.

Merryfeathers pushed off from her fingers and flew down the nave.

And Heloise ran into Sebastian's arms.

He had leaned over to catch her; he straightened and twirled her around. "You are as light as a feather," he said. "As befits an Honorary Caged Bird." Then he set her down. "But why are you not at the Coronation?"

"I am in mourning," said Heloise, and it was true that she was crying. But they were tears of pure happiness.

Sebastian took the splendid cloak from his shoulders, and set it on hers. "Not any more," he said again. Then he took her hand. "Come, we have work to do. You and I are going to change the world. But first, you must meet my mother."